AN INTERRUPTED FRIENDSHIP

AN

INTERRUPTED FRIENDSHIP

BY

E. L. VOYNICH

AUTHOR OF "THE GADFLY," ETC.

> "Thou hast brought me to that dull calamity,
> To that strange misbelief of all the world
> And all things that are in it, that I fear
> I shall fall like a tree, and find my grave,
> Only remembering that I grieve."

Fredonia Books
Amsterdam, The Netherlands

An Interrupted Friendship

by
Ethel Lilian Voynich

ISBN: 1-58963-752-6

Reprinted from the 1910 edition

Fredonia Books
Amsterdam, the Netherlands
http://www.fredoniabooks.com

AN INTERRUPTED FRIENDSHIP

AN INTERRUPTED FRIENDSHIP

CHAPTER I

THE funeral procession trudged down the wet, brown, village street, and up the muddy lane to the cemetery on the hill, and the people uncovered their heads and crossed themselves with more than conventional respect as it passed. Several old women in white coifs brought up the rear, some weeping. Madame la marquise had been good to the poor, and they would miss her.

Not that anyone in Marteurelles-le-Château was really very poor. Poverty in the old sense, poverty the ogre, the grinding, hideous poverty those same women had known in their youth, had passed with the passing of the life before the deluge. It had vanished three-and-thirty years ago, with corvée and gabelle, with taxes and tolls, with all the pride and privileges of the old de Marteurelles. The smoke of the burning château had carried away with it so many things that even those who could remember their world as it was before 1789 remembered it only as a monstrous dream.

B　　　　　　1

But to be poorer than one's neighbours is to be poor; and in Marteurelles, so utterly had one generation changed the face of rural Burgundy, a poor person, nowadays, was a person who did not own a cow.

To such unfortunates, and to anyone that was sick or sorrowful, the dead woman had been a kind friend. Her charity had not expressed itself in bountiful gifts, for the Revolution, which had made the village prosperous, had made the château poor. But she had always been both neighbourly and motherly; and, though she could not afford to give a cow, would give a jug of milk with so kind a smile and so affectionate an interest in the baby's health that, as old Pierrotte remarked to Mother Papillon: "No one would ever guess she was one of the accursed aristocrats."

In point of fact, she had been one of them only by marriage. A physician's daughter from Dijon, she had brought to her husband merely a modest bourgeois dowry, and no other nobility than that of character. But he had quarterings enough for two, as the broken monuments and brasses in the parish church could testify; for the rest, she had been, like Cordelia, herself a dowry, and the void she had left was proportionately great.

He looked curiously forlorn as he stood by the

graveside with his two sons; so forlorn that one might have fancied it was a widow who had died and left not two but three orphan boys, one of whom was going rather grey on the temples.

Indeed, it was hard on a middle-aged and tranquil Egyptologist to be thus lifted up by the hair and flung into the depths of black tragedy. This was the third coffin which he had seen lowered into that same grave within a fortnight. The death of the children had grieved him, though, living so much with his books, he had known them but slightly; that of their mother shook the foundations of his life.

He turned slowly away. It seemed difficult to realize that it was his wife who was buried there; that he and the boys, when they reached home, cold and wet, would not find her waiting for them with warm slippers and a smile of welcome. For fourteen years she had been always ready to come forward when anything was wanted, just as she had been always ready to efface herself when he was busy. She had been part of the indispensable furniture of existence; comforting, useful, quite unobtrusive.

It had not, in the beginning, been a love match. The marquis had married because his friends considered he ought to have a wife; being indifferent in the matter, he had left the choice of the bride to them; yet neither he nor she had ever, for a moment, regretted the marriage. During all the years that it had lasted he had been invariably courteous to her, because he was incapable of being otherwise to any woman; and invariably faithful, because intellectual pleasures were the only ones which had any charms for him. But though she had borne him five children; though she had been a mother to him as well as a wife, had kept the strain of poverty off him, and sheltered him from all the jars and frets of domesticity, he had never known anything about her, or suspected that there was anything to know; she had been just Françoise. Now she seemed to him strangely august and rather terrible; less because she was dead than because she had died with an aureole around her, a halo of glorified maternity.

Could she have known that the manner of her death would awake in him this new timidity towards her, she would have been sorely puzzled. In her eyes her desperate and unaided fight against the typhus fever that had seized on three of her children would have seemed, had she thought about it at all, a natural consequence of the fact that she was their mother. But, being a simple soul and having much to do, she had not troubled her head with abstract questions of the difference between motherhood and fatherhood, but had risked her own life and protected that of her husband, as a matter of course. Distinguished scholars were too precious to be allowed to run risks. He, for his part, had refrained from interference, not out of cowardice, but simply because he never interfered. He had every confidence in Françoise, and would no more have thought of questioning her authority in practical matters than she of disputing his judgment on a papyrus. Now, having saved one child, she had followed two others out of the world with no more exalted dying sentiments than a gentle anxiety as to whether the servants would keep the children neat and make the coffee properly when she was no longer there to attend to things herself.

Henri, the elder boy, walked by his father's side, sobbing bitterly. He was thirteen, old enough to understand that his mother was really dead. Also he was only just up after the fever, and was suffering from the physical depression of convalescence as well as from grief. The marquis patted his shoulder kindly, and Henri looked up to smile through tears. His love for his father was a reflection of the mother's single-hearted and adoring devotion. There was no one so clever as father, or so learned, or so wonderful; the honour of a caress from father was consolation in any trouble. He left off crying with a convulsive gulp and sniff; and rubbed a wet cheek gratefully against the kind hand.

The marquis was glad that René did not sniff too. He was very sorry for his motherless boys; but he had always found children rather trying when they cried; they seemed to have such difficulty in managing their handkerchiefs properly. René had not cried at all; he was barely ten, and possibly, like the baby girl at home, might be still too young to feel his loss. He had been quite passive the whole way and looked pinched with cold.

The château, huge and damp and ruinous, was a desolate-looking place at the best of times; but now, as the draggled and shivering mourners drove in drizzling rain up the lime-avenue and through the great stone arch of the gateway between the broken pigeon-towers, its aspect struck a chill to the heart of its owner. Never had he felt more strongly the barren austerity, the still and grave aloofness of the place; yet never had he loved it more. It was, as it had always been, the core of his heart; dearer than his children, dearer even than his books.

The books were personal possessions; he had loved them for thirty years; but the chain which bound him to the house stretched back through four centuries. Generation after generation of de Marteurelles had lived and died here; never very rich or powerful or distinguished; but serenely convinced of their own right to existence, and well satisfied with themselves, and, on the whole, with their Maker. In Paris, on the rare occasions when business or pleasure drew them there, they might be snubbed for country bumpkins; here no doubts could chill, no problems assail them; the Lord's anointed on his throne was not more securely hedged away from truth than they in their moated manor-house. Then, in one hour, was their judgment come.

He shivered as he entered the great hall. Surely to-day had sorrow enough of its own; why, just to-day, must that dreadful memory of his childhood come back to haunt him?

The battered old linen-press had escaped fire and loot. It still stood by the recess in front of which his foster-mother and her big son Jacques had dragged it to hide him before the gates were forced. There he' had crouched in the dark, a small, huddled thing, not so big as Henri now, stopping his ears with frantic hands to shut out the roar of shouting and cursing and trampling of feet, and the shrieks on the stairs that broke off and were still so suddenly.

Oh, those cries on the stairs! The fear of them had echoed through all his youth, had taken the music out of the world and made the dear house, when he came back to it after a boyhood spent in England, a terror instead of a joy. Only the coming of Françoise had laid the spectres; no

bugbear of the imagination could live in so whole-
some, so cheerful, so utterly prosaic a presence.
Would they come back now that she was gone?

They seemed horribly close. Even the high-
pitched screaming of the child in the nursery
brought them back. So uneventful had been
his career that nothing had effaced that one
tremendous impression; and now, when he was
shaken and weary, it came back upon him with
the vividness of a nightmare. He could almost
smell the thick, stifling smoke; almost hear the
anxious voice of Jacques: "Étienne! M. Étienne!
Are you there? Are you safe? They're all gone,
my little one!"

The same Jacques, grey-haired now and still
protecting, came up to him at the study door with
red eyes.

"M. le marquis will not forget to change his wet
things? It's a chilly day. And Marthe has some
hot soup ready."

"Thank you, Jacques," the marquis answered
gratefully. "You are always thoughtful. See
that the children are attended to, will you? And
don't let anyone disturb me; I wish to be alone."

Once safe in the study, with a locked door between him and the outer world, and the friends
of his youth waiting on the bookshelves with
dumb offers of noble consolation, he breathed
more freely. He opened a bookcase and took

out the Republic of Plato; then put it back, sighing; the Greeks could not help him to-day. For a while he hesitated, doubtfully passing a caressing hand along his favourite volumes: Voltaire, Diderot, Hobbes, Gibbon; then he took down Montaigne, and, drawing his chair close to the blazing logs, opened the book at the essay on experience.

The tapping of walnut boughs against the window roused him. The trees, huge and old, were planted too close to the house; in summer their thick foliage shut out air and sunshine; and on winter nights the soughing of their branches was like a perpetual moan. Françoise had often wished these sombre giants further away for the children's sake; but she had never suggested cutting them down; she knew too well how dear they were to her husband. They were bound up with the earliest memories of his babyhood, and every twig of them was sacred.

Now the tapping on the glass seemed to him the greeting of a friendly hand. He rose and opened the window, pulled off a few great yellow leaves and crushed them against his face. Though it was late autumn, their scent still lingered; to him the dearest scent on earth.

Somehow the touch and smell of these fading leaves softened the hard grief that pressed upon him. Smooth and clean, cool and aromatic, they were dying with a dignity as sweet, as tranquil, as that of Montaigne himself. The patient words came back soothingly: "Que les bastimens de mon aage ont naturellement à souffrir quelque gouttière. Il est temps qu'ils commencent à se lascher et desmentir: C'est une commune nécessité: Et n'eust on pas faict pour moi un nouveau miracle."

Yes; but Françoise had died young.

He leaned on the window-sill and looked out across the rolling wooded country to where the distant towers of Vézelay crowned the hill, grey under grey skies. Indeed, his life was as grey as the sky. It had always been somewhat colourless, since its blood-red opening; now that Françoise was gone it would have few gleams of sunshine. But, joyless as it might be, it would still be worth having if he could keep his peace of mind and go on with his work.

But even peace of mind was impossible with Marguerite screaming like that. Her crying had been the first sound that had struck on his ears when he entered the house an hour ago, and it was still going on, discordant and continuous. The nurse must be very careless or incompetent; Françoise had never let the children cry that way. Not only was the noise insufferable, but it must be bad for a child of three years old to exhaust itself with such prolonged and violent effort.

He could not let it go on any longer; but the thought of interfering, for the first time, in domestic affairs appalled him, and he opened the nursery door with a timid and miserable reluctance.

"Berthe," he said gently, "Marguerite has been screaming for a very long time.   Do you think she is hungry, or . . ."

The woman turned a scared and tearful face.

"It's that careless hussy, Suzanne, M. le marquis. I only went to the church for a moment, just to say good-bye to my sainted lady; and she . . . and she . . ."

"Yes?" said the marquis, trying to understand, but wincing slightly under the noise. "She has not hurt the child, has she?"

The nurse began to cry again.

"It was not my fault; indeed, indeed, it was not. How could I know she would be so careless with the precious little one?"

"Berthe," said the marquis, coming forward with a stern face; "has anything happened?"

She threw her apron over her head. A few sharp questions brought a confession; she had stolen out to see the funeral, leaving her charge to a kitchenmaid of fifteen, who, looking out of the window in her turn, had let the baby girl toddle in new shoes to the head of the stone stairs, and fall. There were several bruises, and a cut on the head.

The nearest doctor lived at some distance; so, as the screaming continued, old Mother Connêtable, who was considered skilful in sick-nursing, was called in. She administered a decoction of poppy-heads, which soon put the child to sleep; then pronounced the damage unimportant, as no bones were broken.

The marquis still felt vaguely anxious; but a few hours later a more pressing emergency drove the subject out of his mind. Henri had taken cold at the funeral; and, being still in a weak state, became dangerously ill during the night. For ten days the dread of a fourth bereavement was the only thought in the father's mind; by the time Henri was out of danger Marguerite's bruises were nearly healed.

The long succession of shocks and anxieties seemed to be over at last; but it had left the nerves of the marquis badly shaken. He was unable to sleep, and at night wandered from room to room, possessed by fantastic terrors lest some new disaster should have happened to one or other of the children.

Day by day it became increasingly clear to him that the servants, though well-meaning, were not to be trusted. Apart from physical matters, such as Marguerite being allowed to fall downstairs, and Henri to go to the funeral in thin shoes and stand about afterwards with wet feet, there were other reasons, no less serious, why the children should not be left under the influence of these ignorant and superstitious peasant folk. He had discovered that stories of ogres and were-wolves were current in the house; also, though so short a time had elapsed since the mother's death, an amount of familiarity which seemed to him highly objectionable was developing between the nursery and the kitchen. René, especially, being the favourite of the servants, was insufferably spoiled and petted by them. He was always about with Jacques; riding pick-a-back, listening to long tales of saints and miracles, dodging behind the old cook to untie her apron-strings, grinding coffee for her and receiving hot cakes in return, picking up slovenly ways of eating and a slow Burgundian drawl. Doubtless all the servants meant kindly, and Jacques' attachment to the family was beyond all question; but his effect on René might be none the less pernicious. And, apart from the miserable discomfort, for children, of a house with no mistress, how was Marguerite to grow up as a lady without a lady's influence in childhood?

Something must be done; but what? The idea of taking a second wife was repugnant to the widower, partly because she would have seemed a rival to the dear memory of the dead, and partly because a woman's presence would disturb his

academic tranquillity. Françoise had possessed
a genius for self-effacement which had been in his
eyes the most precious of her many beauties of
character; but one could not expect to meet with
that rare quality twice.

The most obvious solution of the practical
difficulty would have been to offer a home to some
female relative who would make herself responsible
for the welfare of the family. But that would
be scarcely less intolerable than a second marriage; perhaps even worse, since in marriage it is
possible to have some choice, whereas the only
female relative available was his sister-in-law,
Mlle. Angélique Laumonnier, a maiden lady of
narrow means and many virtues. Without doubt
she would be delighted to leave her dull home
in Avallon and feel herself really of use in the
world; would show her sympathy by invading
his study to offer him religious consolation, and
filling the house with underbred priests and
chattering nuns.

The only other alternative was to send the
children away to places where their bodily and
mental needs would be properly cared for, and
where they would be trained in accordance with
their station. The cost of separate board and
education for them would be difficult to meet with
so small an income; but his own wants were few
and simple, and he was prepared to make any

sacrifice of material comfort which would preserve
the peace and dignity of his intellectual life.
Unfortunately, however rigorously he might pinch
and deny himself even the few small luxuries to
which he had been accustomed, it would still not
be possible to board the children out in a suitable
manner without selling part of the already im-
poverished and heavily mortgaged estate. But
a good education would be more useful to the
boys than much land, and there would always
be something left for Marguerite's dowry.

The money raised, the little girl was placed
under the care of her aunt, with so generous a
provision for her expenses that Angélique, knowing her brother-in-law to be hard pressed, hesitated
to accept the amount he offered her.

"It is too much, Étienne, indeed. What does
such a baby cost to feed and clothe! As for the
trouble, you don't think I want to be paid for
that? She will be only a treasure to me, a keep-
sake from my dear Françoise."

The ready tears came into her eyes. The marquis frowned, involuntarily, and caught himself
wondering where Françoise had got her breeding;
she never used to cry. Jacques and the old cook
could have told him differently; but it was true
that he had never seen her cry.

"My dear Angélique," he said, in his gentle
voice, "leave me the one luxury of a poor man —

the right to pay my debts honestly. Of course I can never pay you for the love and care you will give to my daughter; but the least I can do is to save you from worries about ways and means. I do not wish Marguerite ever to feel the lack of money; it is hard enough for a girl to be mother-less, without that. For me, a crust and my books are all I need."

The next step was to put the boys to school. For Henri the Cistercian College in Avallon seemed an admirable choice; the child was outgrowing his strength after the two severe illnesses through which he had passed, and, being of an affectionate and clinging disposition, would probably mope and suffer from home-sickness if sent far away. At Avallon he would have his aunt and baby sister, and would be within easy reach of his father.

As for the teaching . . . the marquis shrugged his shoulders resignedly. He was himself, by conviction, an atheist; but Françoise had been, in her unobtrusive way, deeply religious, and would have been glad to know that her eldest boy would be brought up a good Catholic. Also the school was cheap and convenient; and the whole of the local gentry was of uncompromis-ingly clerical sympathies. If Henri should after-wards choose to be a country gentleman, he would find it socially an advantage to share the opinions of his neighbours. There was really no reason why he should not grow up devout; he was a good boy, an excellent boy; but perhaps rather dull.

René was a more complex problem. The good Cistercians would probably not make much headway with him; whatever else he might be, he was scarcely dull. Meanwhile the marquis received a letter from his brother, the only other member of the family who had not perished in the sack of the château. A distant relative had adopted the two orphaned boys, and during the terror had fled with them to England, where the younger had settled, becoming a British subject and modifying his name into plain Henry Martel. He was now a successful professional man, with an English wife and a home in Gloucestershire. He wrote offering to take Henri for a few years and put him to school with his own boys.

As Henri was old enough to be consulted, his father showed him the letter; but he only burst out crying for all answer. Much as the marquis disliked tears, he consoled the boy in his kindest manner, assuring him that he should not be sent to England against his will. At this moment René's clear treble rang out from the garden:

"Oh, Jacques; you are an old silly! I can make it work without all that bother. Look here, that's how it goes; see? Now turn it round — no, the other way. There you are!"

c

"Think of that now!" cried the admiring voice of the cook. "Did you ever see such a clever child? Knows what to do the very first minute!"

"Yes," added Jacques; "and I might have gone on for years and never found out. You'll do something with that head of yours one of these days, M. René!"

That was enough for the marquis. If he allowed the servants to have their way they would utterly ruin the child with their indiscriminate flattery. There was nothing like English schools for taking the conceit out of boys. He sat down at once and answered his brother's letter, saying that he had already made arrangements for Henri, but would gratefully accept the offer on behalf of the younger boy.

René was so white and silent when he left home that for a moment his father's resolution wavered. The shock which the marquis had received in childhood had left a morbid sensitiveness of the nerves which made him shrink from the sight of any suffering. He was on the verge of saying to the child, as he had said to Henri: "Well, then, you need not go." But he reflected that such pampering is no real kindness to a high-spirited boy, and that René would doubtless be very happy in England when he got over the first strangeness. Certainly he would have a kind

home. And, after all, what else was there to do
with him?

The marquis went back into his study and shut
the door. Of late he had thought of nothing but
the children; now that he had done all he could
for them, to go on worrying over things already
settled was mere criminal waste. He put the
subject out of his mind with a resolute effort,
and settled to his interrupted translation of the
hieroglyphics on a sarcophagus in the Louvre.

*   *   *   *   *   *

Henri left the Cistercian College at nineteen.
He had grown tall and strong in body, and in
character had retained the modest and unselfish
docility of his childhood. After learning something of practical fruit-culture and dairy-farm-
ing, he settled at home, taking over the manage-
ment of the estate, dismissed the incompetent
and dishonest steward, and devoted himself,
like his mother before him, to freeing the father,
whose intellect he adored, from the petty worries
and interruptions of poverty.

René, meanwhile, had remained in England,
spending all his holidays at his uncle's house in
Gloucestershire. He seemed to have become
more English than French; his letters home,
awkwardly worded and consisting chiefly of
reports of cricket matches, were signed: "R.
Martel." He left school at the age of eighteen,

having won for himself the goodwill of boys and masters and an enviable reputation for proficiency in swimming, mischief, and geography.

To Henri the return of the brother whom he had not seen for eight years was an event of the first magnitude. He went some miles up the dusty Paris road to meet the post-chaise, and hugged and kissed the traveller so earnestly that René, fresh from his English school, flushed a fiery red and muttered: "Oh, I say . . . !"

The marquis, coming out of his study at the clang of the great iron gates, stood on the terrace, watching the tall brothers as they walked up the drive together. In height, build, and colouring they were much alike; yet the contrast between them was striking. Henri looked, his father thought with a smile, like a careful copy of which René was the original. He met the boy with an English handshake and a laconic: "Well, my lad?" and observed him attentively during lunch. The slim, excitable René of eight years ago had grown into a big shy creature, athletic and sunburnt, afflicted by an obvious difficulty in finding anything to say. He carried his head finely, with a pose that suggested the startled watchfulness of a stag; one could almost fancy him flinging it up at a too friendly touch, and disappearing through the verandah door into the garden in a shower of broken glass.

After lunch he made a hasty escape from the room, dragged open his bag to get out sundry parcels, then ran to the kitchen door and knocked, asking gaily:

"Marthe, can I come in?"

The old woman began with a deferential curtsey and ended by flinging her arms round his neck.

"Ah, my own dear boy come back at last. . . . And so big and strong . . . and just the same as ever. . . ."

She was almost in tears. René slipped his hands round the fat old waist.

"Just the same as ever, am I? Look out then."

Her apron tumbled on to the floor. As she stooped, shaking with laughter, to pick it up, he pinned an agate brooch into her cap, and was gone before she had time to speak.

"Isn't it fun to be back here?" he cried, bursting like a joyous whirlwind into the courtyard where Henri was waiting to show him round the place. "It's like being a kid all over again!"

"You are not more glad to be home than we to have you," Henri murmured affectionately. "But you were not unhappy at the English school, were you?"

René stared.

"Unhappy? How could any fellow be unhappy at a jolly school like that?"

"And the masters? Were they kind?"

"Oh, they were all right, I suppose. Old Briggs was the best cricketer we had. The Head used to get a bit fussy sometimes, but that was his gout; he was a brick whenever anything went wrong with anybody. And the sports were firstrate. Did you know we beat Rugby last match?"

"And you were not lonely or homesick ever, so far away from us all?"

"But I had Gilbert and Frank. And one could always have got at Uncle Harry or Aunt Nelly if there'd been any trouble. It's just like having two homes of one's own. I say, this is a splendid place! One could swim in that fountain. . . . Oh, by Jove!"

He had caught sight of the great walnut trees. He stood for a long time looking at them silently; then turned to his brother with shining eyes.

"I didn't remember they were so big."

They went round the buildings. René at once made friends with the seven large rough dogs, and was deeply interested in pigeon-house, rabbit-hutches, and poultry-yard. He looked over-critically at the horses, and unconsciously wounded his brother's feelings by failing to appreciate the sleek, broad-flanked, ivory-coloured cattle and fat black sows. Presently Jacques clattered into the courtyard with packages from the market, and dismounted hastily to salute the newcomer.

The old man's eyes filled with tears when he opened the present brought from England.

"To think that M. René has remembered all these years which sort of pipe I like!"

René had turned to pat the old brown mare.

"Yes, M. René, it's the same Diane. You had your first riding-lesson on her back. There's good in her yet; she has trotted all the way from Avallon, and see, her coat is not even damp. You may judge if I was in a hurry to see you again after all these years. Ah, but you are grown! When I saw you last you were a little thing with a white face, sitting in the Paris coach, all eyes. I wanted to cry when you said: 'Good-bye, Jacques'; so pitiful and quiet you were, and so small to go among those English all alone. And now! A fine young man, and as tall as M. Henri!"

Then he became dimly conscious that René was looking uncomfortable; and, stopping in his stream of reminiscence, took a letter out of his pocket.

"From Mlle. Marguerite."

When the brothers walked on, Henri began in a hesitating way:

"I hope Jacques didn't annoy you just now. He is a faithful old servant and he saved my father's life, so we get into the way of allowing him a good deal of license. We are very simple here in the country; but I forgot that perhaps in England you have been used to more deference from inferiors. Jacques is talkative, but he doesn't mean to be disrespectful."

René looked more ill at ease than before.

"Oh, inferiors! It's nothing to do with all that stuff! He's welcome to talk as much as he likes — only I hate sentimental jaw."

Henri puzzled over this for a moment; he had not the faintest notion what his brother could mean. When he looked up, René was frowning over the letter. It was a stiff, conventional message of welcome, obviously dictated as a caligraphy lesson by some grown-up person, and written on ruled paper in a large, round, careful hand. The signature occupied three lines:

"Marguerite Alo-
ïse de Marteu-
relles."

René shook his head as he folded up the letter. "I can't think what a scrap that size wants with a name three times as long as herself," he said wistfully. "I should have thought 'Maggie Martel' was name enough for any child. I say, Henri, when do her holidays begin? She asks me to come and see her as often as I can. Won't she be home soon?"

Henri looked at him in surprise. "But . . .

of course she never leaves Avallon. How should
she?"

"Never leaves Avallon? What, no holidays?
You don't mean to tell me that poor mite is shut
up there alone with an old dragon of a spinster
aunt, all the year round?"

"My aunt is very kind and good," said Henri
with mild reproof. "And I am sure Marguerite
is as happy with her as anyone so sadly afflicted
can be."

René stopped short.

"Sadly aff . . . Look here, is there anything
. . . wrong with her?"

"Surely you know that she is bedridden?"

"Bedridden! Since when?"

"But . . . for more than three years now;
ever since she had that bad illness."

"I never heard of any illness. Do you mean
she's always in bed? Always?"

"No, no! She has a couch, an invalid's mov-
able couch that runs on wheels. She can be
moved from room to room; and in fine weather
they carry her out into the garden. But it is
extraordinary — your not knowing!"

René was silent for a moment.

"Did you ever tell me, in any of your letters?"

"No; I suppose I . . . thought you knew."

"I suppose that's what everybody thought.
What's the matter with her?"

"She fell downstairs the day our mother was buried. Don't you remember?"

"And she's been like this ever since?"

"Oh, no; she seemed to be all right, only she was rather awkward and not very firm on her feet, and used to go lame sometimes and complain of her leg. Then, three years ago last winter, she slipped in the snow, and hip-joint disease set in. The doctors said there must have been some slight injury there ever since she fell downstairs. It has been a dreadful grief to my father. Indeed, we never mention it."

"And never bring her here?"

"My dear René, when you see her you will realize why that is. She could not stand the journey."

"Does the leg hurt her?"

"Mercifully there is hardly any pain unless she moves; but it is pitiful to see her try to lift herself up. The jolting of a carriage would be intolerable. Then, it would distress my father so to see her."

René cast a sidelong glance at his brother.

"Doesn't he ever see her?"

"Oh, yes; he goes in to Avallon on purpose almost every month. You cannot think how good and kind he is. But my aunt and I are careful not to let him see any painful sights. My dear father is so terribly sensitive; you will understand when you know him better."

"Oh, I think I understand all right," René murmured. Presently he began to talk about fishing, and made no further reference to Marguerite.

In the evening the marquis asked Henri whether he had shown his brother over the farm.

"Not yet; I thought he would be tired after the journey. Perhaps to-morrow . . ."

René looked up.

"Another day, please. I should like to go to Avallon to-morrow, if you don't mind, sir."

He was looking at his father, and saw a shadow of melancholy cross the delicate, high-bred face. But it passed instantly, and the marquis answered with a friendly nod and smile:

"Certainly, my lad; go and see your sister. Henri, aren't there some ripe strawberries we could send her?"

Early next morning René started for Avallon. Henri had offered to come too; it was incomprehensible to him that anyone should prefer solitude when company was obtainable. But René answered lamely that he "always rode alone," which, though not quite true, was the best reply he knew how to give; and the elder brother, puzzled and vaguely disappointed at the queer stiff ways which he mentally put down as "English," tied the basket of strawberries to the saddle and went off to his day's work on the farm.

René found Aunt Angélique's house as tidy,
clean, and close as his childish recollections of it.
Aunt Angélique herself came out to him with a
white apron over her plain dark dress, and the
old big black rosary at her girdle. She was in
the middle of making jam, and found this sudden
invasion by a gawky, tongue-tied schoolboy in
the busiest part of the day somewhat ill-timed;
but she received him very kindly, asked about
his progress at school and whether he had attended
confession regularly while in England; then,
not knowing what else to do with him, brought
out wine and aniseed biscuits.

"You must pardon me a moment, my dear,"
she said, after struggling for a while to get anything but monosyllables out of the boy. "I
must attend to the jam."

René found his tongue with an effort.

"But, aunt, mayn't I see Marguerite?"

"Certainly, my dear, later. She is engaged just
now; Sister Louise is preparing her for confession.
Father Joseph always comes on the first Saturday
of the month. Perhaps you would like to walk
round the garden?"

The garden, like everything else in Avallon, was
narrow, steep, and surrounded by high walls;
but it was charmingly pretty. Fruit trees were
trained on every wall; lilies of the valley, pansies,
and violets ran riot all over the ground, the

arbour was a blaze of roses, and from the grass-grown steps by the sundial one could see thirty miles of rolling hills and woods.

After what seemed to him a very long time he was called in, and at the door encountered Father Joseph and Sister Louise. The priest, thin-lipped and cold-eyed, passed him with a murmured greeting, bowed to Aunt Angélique, and went down the sunny, hilly street with a face as joyless as the black cassock flapping round his legs. René stood for a moment looking after him; then, turning to enter the house, found himself caught by the fat white hands of the old nun.

"So this is my little René come home at last! And tall; I'm scarcely up to your chin! Don't you remember me? Why, it was I that nursed you through the measles, when your sainted mother was so ill, after the poor darling Marguerite was born. Dear, dear, how the time goes, to be sure! You will have to be finding a bride for this young gentleman before you are many years older, Angélique, that is evident. And so you have come over to bring your sister these fine strawberries, your very first day at home? Quite right; I see you take after your dear mother, both Henri and you; she was always thinking of others. And really our poor little martyr deserves it; she is a model of Christian patience. Indeed, you will find her an example. Father

Joseph was saying just now, it tends to edification to see her; only eleven years old, and yet as wise as if she had worn the veil for years. Well, well, my dear Angélique, I will just taste the jam, since you press me. But I must not stay long; my poor are waiting for me."

Aunt Angélique conducted the boy through two big, meagre, cheerless rooms, and stopped at the door of a third one.

"I am sure I can trust you, my dear, to be very gentle with your sister."

René's nostrils dilated. Confound her cheek! Did she think he was going to knock the kid about? His expression for a moment was not pleasant; but, as he was looking away from her, she failed to see, and went on in placid ignorance:

"I know you would wish to be kind to a poor little afflicted girl; but, of course, boys are not used to invalids. Try not to frighten her by talking of anything rough or . . . Well, you understand, don't you? — My dear, this is your brother. I will leave you alone to make friends."

When she had shut the door and gone off to gossip with Sister Louise, René crossed the room, treading carefully that his boots might not creak, and put the basket of strawberries down on the table. He both felt and looked awkward; and could scarcely raise his eyes. In this first moment of miserable shyness the small figure on the couch seemed to him unapproachably formidable.

"Thank you very much for coming so soon," she said in a thin, clear voice. "It was kind of you to think of me. Won't you take a chair?"

He obeyed feebly. Her prim and grown-up politeness had completed the rout of his self-possession. He looked cautiously at her, wondering whether it was really possible that any live creature could be so like the good child in a Miss Edgeworth tale. Then he looked at her again, with a startled sense of finding himself close to something uncanny.

"As wise as if she had worn the veil for years. . . ." Sister Louise and her foolish chatter came back into his mind. In feature, this was the face of a child, even of a child who might have been pretty but for her colourless and waxen fragility. In expression it was the face of a nun; old and secret, stamped with the mark of long silence.

Seeing that he was unable to begin talking, Marguerite began for him and entertained him with carefully learned samples of polite conversation. She inquired after the health of her father and Henri, and, with just the same degree of courteous interest, after that of the English aunt and cousins whom she had never seen. She asked whether he had liked living in England, whether the climate was very foggy, whether he was glad to be at home again; and while she talked her thin fingers worked busily at a braiding pattern as mechanical as her smile.

As for René, he grew more tongue-tied and uncomfortable with every moment. The thing was like a nightmare; he wanted to pinch himself and wake up. Presently Aunt Angélique came in to call him to lunch.

"I have persuaded Sister Louise to stay," she said. "Marguerite, shall we wheel you into the dining-room, or would you rather lunch here by yourself?"

Marguerite leaned back against her cushions. She had the weak voice of the tired invalid as she answered patiently: "Just as you think best, aunt."

"I think, perhaps, it is better for you to be quiet now, after so much excitement. You can rest for half an hour after lunch, and then your brother can wheel you into the garden and have a chat with you there, while I get the jam-pots ready. I suppose you can stay, René?"

"Oh, yes," he answered hastily, "if . . ." He stopped and turned to Marguerite. "If I don't bore you?"

"My dear, how could you think such a thing!" Aunt Angélique protested. "Of course she is delighted to have your company."

But René was looking at Marguerite, and saw

her lashes lift for an instant's furtive glance at him, and drop again. He had never seen such lashes; they lay on the white cheeks like silken fringes. It was no easy matter to get to know eyes so curtained.

"I shall be very glad if you will stay," she answered in her small demure voice.

He sat down to a dreary lunch with Aunt Angélique and Sister Louise, resentfully conscious that four eyes were watching to see whether he remembered to cross himself. The atheistic proclivities of the marquis had been at one time much discussed in Avallon; and René had spent eight years in a notoriously heretic and heathen land. During the meal the two women regaled each other with clerical and philanthropic gossip, and commented on the failings of their neighbours, and the details of a dispute between Father Joseph and another priest, till the boy wanted to stop his ears and run from the table.

He wondered whether the white-faced little thing in the next room had to listen to such talk every day of her life. True, she was a girl, and girls, of course, don't mind that sort of thing as much as boys; but when your leg is hurting you it must be difficult to care which priest told the bishop stories against the other. Then he wondered whether her leg hurt her often, and how much it hurt. One couldn't go by anything

D

Henri said; even his letters were always in super-
latives. Anyhow, if it didn't hurt at all, it was
hard enough luck to be born a girl, and then to
have to lie always on your back and never be
able to walk, let alone playing cricket or swimming or anything sensible. . . .

"My dear," said Aunt Angélique, "will you not
render thanks after food?"

Renè crossed himself hastily, and went out
into the garden, feeling as if he must gasp for
breath.

Sitting in the arbour, while the women sipped
their coffee and talked their pious scandal in the
shaded room that still smelt of yesterday's fish-
dinner, he fell to wondering again. First he wondered whether the fish had come from the tiny
river far below his feet, and whether there was good
fishing to be had in the district; then whether the
fishes in the old stew-pond at Marteurelles were
any stupider than Sister Louise or any more cold-
blooded than Father Joseph; then whether Marguerite liked being a show-child, tending to edification; then whether she would like to have a
rough-haired Irish terrier to romp about the
garden, instead of a canary moping in a cage in a
stuffy room with all the blinds down.

"René," said his aunt's voice outside the arbour; "where are you? Come and help with
Marguerite's couch."

In the inner room he found Sister Louise bending over the child and kissing her tenderly.

"Good-bye, my quiet little mouse. I will tell the Mother Superior how pleased you were with her pretty book."

"I hope the Reverend Mother will be as pleased with her present," said Aunt Angélique, taking up the braiding and examining it critically. "This is a toilet bag for her name-day; but you mustn't tell, Sister Louise, it's a secret."

"Quite so, quite so. Dear me, very pretty indeed! And what is going in the middle? A flower?"

"A monogram, I think. Marguerite wanted St. Catherine's wheel; but I thought it scarcely suitable to put holy emblems on a toilet bag. Now, René; will you take the head? Very carefully down the steps, please."

When the couch had been set down on the grass-plot, Aunt Angélique hurried back to the jam, and Sister Louise kissed her pupil again and went away. René shut the gate after her; then, still tingling with annoyance at her affectionate and greasy farewell pressure on his hand, returned to the garden. The couch was so placed that Marguerite could not see him till he was quite close to her; and, coming up noiselessly on the soft turf, he saw her get out her handkerchief and rub off the nun's kiss. She scrubbed the place so viciously that when he sat down beside her there was an angry red mark on her cheek. But she at once took up her braiding again and worked with demurely downcast eyes. Both were silent for a long time.

René began at last with a desperate spurt: "Would you like a dog?"

The small hand paused for a moment with the blue braid curled round one finger. Then she went on working again.

"Thank you very much; it is kind of you to think of me. . . ."

"By Jove!" the boy said to himself; "that's just what she said before. Why, they've taught her like a parrot."

The careful voice went on: "But my aunt does not like dogs."

"I wasn't offering it to her, you know," said René. "Well, a kitten, then? It's not as much fun as a good terrier pup; but it's better than a rubbishing canary, anyway."

Marguerite put down her work.

"Aunt Angélique doesn't approve of any pets. Henri wanted to give me a tortoise last year; but she objects to animals about a house."

"Well, but you've got a canary."

"It's not ours. We are only taking care of it for a time. It belongs to Father Joseph's niece. Father Joseph says it doesn't matter having pets if one doesn't allow oneself to get too fond of them. . . ."

"Oh, Father Joseph be hanged!"

He pulled himself up in dismay; had he utterly horrified her? Then he saw that she was looking at him, for the first time, with wide-open eyes; and realized what amazing eyes they were.

There was silence till her lashes dropped again. René mumbled a hasty apology and relapsed into paralysing shyness. After floundering for another half-hour through successive attempts at conversation, each of which left him more disconcerted than its predecessor, he trumped up a lame excuse about the pony needing a shoe, and, escaping hurriedly from her presence, rode back to Marteurelles, wretched and ashamed.

All the way home he pondered over the incidents of the day; and the more he thought, the more stupid and abominable did his own behaviour seem to him. Whatever he might feel about Aunt Angélique's friends, Marguerite was probably satisfied with them; and if she was, so much the better, seeing that she had to live among them. After all, these people petted her, and were kind in their way, even though it might be a greasy way. At least they hadn't shoved her aside and forgotten her existence as . . .

He checked himself, scared at the thing he had come so near to thinking. Of course father was

only doing the best he could for her; and as for
all the pious talk, perhaps she liked it. Girls
never minded jaw; and they mostly enjoyed being
coddled and fussed over. Anyway, it was no
business of a stranger like himself to come blundering into the middle of things that had been
settled for years, and upset the kid by slanging
her friends. He had been furious with Aunt
Angélique for doubting that he would know how
to behave; but he had more than justified her.
And, after all, mother was dead and father was . . .
busy; and most likely Marguerite was fond of
Sister Louise and Father Joseph, and it was a
caddish thing to let her see one didn't like them.
But . . . why had she rubbed off the kiss?

By the time he reached home he had convinced
himself that it would be better for him to keep
away from Avallon in future, since he only made
an ass of himself there. At supper he had not
much to say, and was so snappish under Henri's
innocent cross-questioning as to what impression
his sister had made upon him, that, looking up
a moment later from his plate, he found his
father's serious eyes watching him attentively.
Henri sighed unconsciously as he pushed his chair
back from the table.

"I shall be going in to Avallon on Tuesday, to
the pig market. Perhaps you would like to come
with me and take the opportunity to get to know

her better," he said with a wistful glance at his
brother's frowning face.

"What's the use? I don't want to be always
hanging about there."

A gentle reproach crept into Henri's voice.
"She can't come to us, remember. And she has
so few pleasures."

"Oh, shut up!" René muttered in English.

On Sunday evening he asked his father to let
him have the use of one of the horses, as he was
accustomed to riding before breakfast. The
next morning he was up at dawn, and before ten
o'clock presented himself at Aunt Angélique's
door, embarrassed, ungracious, and dusty with
the long ride. This time the poor lady could
hardly conceal her regret that he had chosen so
inconvenient an hour; but her ideas of hospitality
were strict, so she assured him that his visit was
"a delightful surprise," and "for once" allowed
Marguerite's lessons to be interrupted.

The child was struggling with the parsing of a
passage from Télémaque. She laid her book
aside without any sign of either pleasure or annoyance; and for nearly an hour aunt and niece
between them entertained the visitor with admirable politeness. The talk, as before, was of
parish affairs and church embroidery, of charity
to the poor, and the reprehensible tendency of
servants to imitate ladies in their dress, of Father

Joseph and his niece, of Sister Louise and the
Mother Superior. Then, with an effort, the boy
stumbled through an awkward leave-taking and
went away.

He now definitely made up his mind that he
didn't like Marguerite. She was a little prig if
she did enjoy being fussed over by all those people,
and a little sneak if she didn't; and in either case
she was detestable. All the same, he wished she
would get fatter, and not look at him with such big
eyes. On Saturday she had kept her lashes down;
but to-day she had been looking at him nearly
all the time, and it made him feel hateful. Why
should she have to be always on her back in that
beastly room? It wasn't fair. He didn't like
her, but he did wish she hadn't tumbled downstairs. Anyhow, he couldn't do anything for her,
and he had better keep out of it.

Nevertheless, Thursday afternoon found him
again in Avallon. It seemed quite impossible to
ring Aunt Angélique's bell without some excuse,
so he bought cherries in the market-place, and a
cheap basket for them. If he should be driven
into a corner, he could say that he had been
asked to bring them from home. Being a habit-
ually truthful boy, he had no desire to tell a
lie about it; but the thought that he had one
ready to tell if necessary afforded him much
comfort.

His aunt had gone out, he was told, to visit the sick poor; Mlle. Marguerite was alone, and would certainly be pleased to have company. He followed the maid into the garden, struggling with a panic-stricken desire to run away. Last time he had wished Aunt Angélique at the other end of the world; but now he longed for her to come back; the prospect of an afternoon alone with his sister dismayed him.

The couch was in the same place as before, and Marguerite was still working at the toilet bag for the Mother Superior's name-day. Apparently she was in a hurry to finish it, for after giving him one thin hand for a moment she went on sewing. He made no attempt to kiss her, nor did she offer her cheek as she had done when Aunt Angélique was present. He wondered, as he sat down on the bench beside her couch, whether, if he had kissed her, she would have rubbed off the kiss as soon as his back was turned.

To-day her terrifying self-possession seemed to have quite forsaken her; she was as tongue-tied and awkward as the boy himself. At first this was an immense relief to him; then it flashed upon his mind that he had frightened her and made her unhappy by what he had said last Saturday about Father Joseph. He sat fidgeting with the handle of the basket; nobody but a brute would upset a white-faced scrap of a thing like that;

but once it was done, what was the good of talking about it?

"Will aunt be out long?" he asked helplessly.

"I don't think so; she is generally back by four."

"Oh, then, I'll stay till she comes."

Two or three more minutes dragged miserably by. Well, this was no use; if he waited till Aunt Angélique came in, there would be no chance of saying anything at all.

"I say," he muttered at last shamefacedly; "I'm awfully sorry . . . about Saturday, you know."

She looked up. "About Saturday? What Saturday?"

"Oh, well, saying things about Father Joseph, and all that. Of course, it isn't any business of mine. . . ."

He had scrambled through the words in a hurry, with averted eyes. Now he risked a glance at her; and at the sight of her face the apology died on his tongue. He threw out his hands with a gesture of impotence.

"Well, I can't help it; this place is like having a feather-bed on top of you! It's nothing but Father Joseph and Sister Louise and the Mother Superior; and everybody's so beastly good. . . . I say, do you really like them all?"

"I hate them!"

Her eyes blazed at him out of the white face with a horrible vindictiveness. She dashed a weak clenched fist against the arm of her couch.

"I hate them! I hate them all! They come here and kiss me, and bring me their loathsome goody books; and I have to say 'thank you,' and make things for the Mother Superior. . . ."

She crumpled up the toilet bag and flung it on to the grass. René sat still, appalled at the storm he had roused.

"Well, but," he ventured; "why do you have to? Why don't you just say you jolly well won't? I'd see them somewhere before I'd . . . Look here" — his nostrils dilated again — "they don't . . . bully you, do they? Because if they do, I'll . . ."

"Oh, they preach at me! They're always preaching! Father Joseph comes here and preaches about Christian patience, and not minding things, and being glad to lie here for Jesus. He hasn't got hip-disease. And I do mind! And you should have seen the fuss Sister Louise made the other day over just a tiny bit of a toothache. Oh, I'd like to kill them — I wish I could kill them all!"

René put out a timid, clumsy hand, and touched the angry little fist.

"Do you know, I never knew anything about it; I didn't know there was anything wrong.

The pigs never told me till last week. Does it hurt much?"

She turned and stared at him silently. Then she flung both hands up to her face and burst out sobbing.

"Oh, don't!" René cried. He jumped up in a hurry, himself on the verge of tears, knelt down on the grass and threw his arms round her. "If Father Joseph gives you any more of his jaw, I'll punch his head, the old . . . Marguerite . . . Oh, I say, I wish you wouldn't cry!"

When Aunt Angélique came back, René was teaching his sister to play cat's cradle. He had begun by dragging off a length of the blue braid for a string; but the child had assured him that there would be "such a lot of preaching" if this were discovered, that he had searched his pockets and found a piece of whipcord. The old maid came up, smiling to see them such good friends.

"Well, my dears, have you had a pleasant afternoon? What, cherries? I hope you have not eaten many, Marguerite? And what about your braiding? Why, what has happened to it?"

She lifted the crumpled piece of needlework from the couch-table. René rose to the occasion immediately.

"I'm very sorry, aunt; I knocked it down with my sleeve and it got trodden on. I'm afraid the braid's broken. It was awfully careless of me."

Aunt Angélique smoothed the stuff out in her hands. "Dear me, what a pity! Never mind, my dear; he didn't mean to do it, and I daresay we can get it right with steam and a cool iron. Luckily it is not soiled. Must you go now? Yes; it's true you have a long way to get back. You left your horse at the inn, I suppose? Just help me carry in the couch. Oh, my dear, please rub your boots! Well, good-bye! Our love to the dear father and Henri, and many thanks for the cherries."

The brother and sister took leave of each other as ceremoniously as if he had been Henri. Then, when Aunt Angélique went out for a duster to wipe the step where his boot had marked it, he stooped over the couch.

"Don't you worry! I'll have a talk with father. We'll put a spoke in Father Joseph's wheel. And you shall have the pup whether she likes it or no."

She lifted herself quickly; and for an instant they clung together, with their arms round each other's necks. Then he laid her gently back, and turned to meet his aunt.

"I hope I haven't tired her. I'll come again soon. Yes; I'll be careful of the polish. Good-bye!"

CHAPTER II

"CAN you spare a few minutes?" René asked, intercepting his father at the study door. "I should like to speak to you if you're not too busy."

The marquis held the door open. "Come in."

The great walnut boughs outside the window filled the bare room and its book-shelves with a green and cloistered stillness. The marquis sat down in the big worn leather chair, and looked at his son with a smile.

"You grow like your mother," he said.

"Is Marguerite like her?" René was standing by the window, frowning at the walnut branches, and spoke without turning.

"Not a bit; she is said to take after me. All your mother's people were fair."

"Aunt Angélique is fair. Was mother like her?"

There was something dogged in the lad's voice that made his father look at him with a new expression.

"One would have known they were sisters. Their hair was the same colour; but . . . No, they were not alike; not really. That is your

46

mother's portrait, on the wall; but it doesn't do her justice."

It did not, indeed; the sweet maternity of Françoise had quite escaped the painter's eyes; he had seen only the features, and they resembled those of Angélique. René turned away from the picture resentfully. He had no use for dead saints; and he thought it a shame that Marguerite couldn't have a nice, live, sensible mother to look after her. The uproariously happy Gloucestershire cousins came up in his memory: Aunt Nelly wasn't over clever, but she did know how to make you comfortable, whether you were a boy or a girl. Dora and Trix were always on the giggle, and as fat and jolly as starlings. They didn't have to lie on couches making toilet bags for a lot of beastly women. . . .

He looked up.

"Do you know that priest that comes to Aunt Angélique's?" he asked, firing the question out of his embarrassment as if it had been a squib.

"Father Joseph? Yes; I have met him several times."

"Well, don't you think he's rather a sneak?"

The father's eyes settled on his son's face.

"What makes you think so, boy?"

"Oh, I don't know," René mumbled, shutting up again.

"I shouldn't wonder if he is," the marquis said

thoughtfully. "No; I shouldn't wonder if he is."

He frowned over his papers for a few moments; then asked: "You think Marguerite is . . . not getting as happy a life as she might have?"

"I think it's a bit piggish she can't have a pup if she wants one."

"A . . . what?"

"Well, you know, father, she's only a kid; and she hasn't got a soul to play with or anything — only aunt and a lot of nuns. Of course, if we could have her over here for a week or two — just for a holiday — there'd be dogs, and rabbits, and things . . ."

He was seized with shyness again, and stuck fast. The marquis looked at him, troubled and earnest.

"Yes, yes; but the journey? It's the getting backwards and forwards."

"We could rig up a thing so that she could lie flat. If we took the big hay-cart and put boards . . . Look here, this way . . ."

He crossed to the writing-table and took up a pencil. His father, watching him silently, pushed a sheet of paper towards him, and the boy at once began to make a diagram.

"You'd want strong boards, six feet two by twelve inches; and there are two trestles in the coach-house that would go underneath. One would want four inches taken off the legs."

"You have measured them?"

"Of course. Then we could drive in big hooks there to hold it firm, and sling the two ends of the couch so, with ropes. She wouldn't feel the jolting a bit that way. I should sit in the bottom of the cart to steady the couch if it began to swing, and Jacques could drive very slowly, and take it round by Villamont. It's longer, but it's a much better road."

"Is that so? You haven't been there yet, have you?"

"Yes; I went over the ground this morning. There's only one rough piece; and there Henri and I could lift the couch out and carry it."

His shyness had vanished the instant he began to draw. He had been too much absorbed in the diagram to be self-conscious; but when he finished explaining his ears grew red and he dropped the pencil and stooped for it hurriedly, knocking his head against the table. His father was studying the diagram. The lines were as neatly drawn as if they had been the work of a professional designer.

"René," said the marquis; and René emerged from under the table with the pencil in his hand.

"Yes, father?"

"Suppose you and I go in to Avallon one day, and have a talk with your aunt?"

E

René fidgeted with the pencil.

"All right. Only . . ." The end of the sentence came with a little burst. "Don't you think Henri's the one to talk to aunt? She'll think more of it if it's his notion."

The marquis smiled.

"Quite so, quite so. I see you have the wisdom of the serpent, my son."

René knitted his brows at this, wondering whether father was making fun of him.

"You and Henri are going round the farm together, aren't you, this afternoon?" the marquis asked.

"Yes; I think he's waiting for me."

"Then perhaps you had better take the opportunity to talk it over with him."

As the boy was leaving the room his father called him back.

"René!"

"Yes?"

"Your brother is a good fellow; a very good fellow."

René looked puzzled.

"Of course, father."

"Don't let him feel too much . . . out of things. He's very fond of Marguerite."

He glanced up quickly, met his father's eyes, and nodded; then went out, humming to himself in a broad Gloucestershire burr:

" For 'tis my delight
Of a shiny night,
In the season of the year . . ."

His voice was not yet quite formed, and jumped from a growl to a squeak in the middle of the tune; but there were already a few tenor notes, very pure and sweet.

In the evening Henri came into the study to propose the scheme to his father. He began with: "René and I think"; but seemed to be under the impression that it had originated with himself. The marquis, listening with the air of a person to whom a new idea is put for the first time, agreed to everything, and deftly introduced a suggestion that Henri should be the one to approach Aunt Angélique.

"It would come better from you than from either René or me. He is too young; and if I spoke about it, she might perhaps think I was not satisfied with her care of Marguerite. I should be very sorry to hurt her feelings in any way. You know how good and devoted she has been."

"Indeed, I do," said Henri earnestly. "But I am sure she would never misunderstand anything you said. René, of course, might be rather tactless, though I know he would not mean it. He has such an . . . abrupt way. I suppose that comes from living at an English school."

"No doubt," said his father. "Poor René has no diplomacy."

Accordingly Henri was despatched to Avallon, a serious and conscientious ambassador. Aunt Angélique, at first inclined to scout the idea as preposterous and impracticable, was soon won over by the evident sincerity of her nephew's assurance that the whole household at Marteurelles was longing to see her a guest there, and began to pack garments for herself and Marguerite.

Henri drove his father in to Avallon in the rickety old carriage which was to convey his aunt and her luggage to Marteurelles. On the homeward journey, Jacques and the two lads would be occupied with the hay-cart, so the marquis himself had undertaken to drive, thus saving the expense of hiring a man in the town. Angélique was somewhat distressed at the thought of her stately brother-in-law doing a coachman's work for her, but consoled herself by reflecting that he showed thereby the true humility of a noble nature. The whole family lunched at her house; and Father Joseph, coming in to say good-bye, was invited to share the meal.

The priest, in this house, was king. Angélique and the guests he had been used to meeting here had never questioned his supreme authority in all things. Even Marguerite, petted and tyrannical invalid as she was, shrank before his dominant un-humanness. But in the presence of the marquis his dignity wilted and fell off him, frostbitten. He became a mean thing in black petticoats, aggressive and humbled, aping gentle speech with a rasping voice and vulgar accent. The aloofness on which his power depended seemed a mere affectation when confronted with aloofness of another quality. In him it was an acquired thing, sedulously cultivated; in the marquis it was the spontaneous expression of a natural bent of mind.

Father Joseph eyed the chiselled profile of the unwelcome visitor, beside whom he always felt like a cab horse beside a race horse. He looked defiantly round the table, noting with secret satisfaction that not he alone seemed to have lost caste. Poor Angélique, presiding with timid and fussy hospitality at her own table, had never looked so ill at ease, so incurably middle-class. The courtly deference with which her brother-in-law treated her seemed only to throw into relief her apologetic consciousness of inferiority. As for Henri, the completeness of his humility saved him. He watched his father with the adoring gaze of a faithful dog, and was troubled by no doubts.

Father Joseph roused himself. He, a Christian priest, was allowing himself to be terrorized and frozen into silence by a notorious atheist, and that before young people. The marquis was

a scholar, a learned Egyptologist; these weak-
kneed folk should see that the Church could hold
her own. He dashed in memory through a few
articles which he had read in reviews, and, gathering up his courage, plunged into an impassioned
attack on the "new theories about the Deluge."
The Marquis laid down his fork. For one instant
the line of his eyebrows expressed unutterable
boredom; then he turned his head and listened
with a princely and gracious attention.

Father Joseph came to the end of his speech with
a truculent manner which his eyes belied. He
had hoped for contradiction, and would have
known how to meet it; argument, especially with
opponents who could be made to lose their temper, always gave him confidence. But the marquis heard him out in courteous silence; and,
when he had finished, took a strawberry with
white finger-tips, still not speaking a word. Angélique, glancing nervously from one to the other,
interposed with anxious eyes.

"I am afraid, Father, this subject is too learned
for anyone here but M. de Marteurelles. He, of
course, can appreciate . . ."

She paused, with a beseeching gaze at her
brother-in-law.

"You are too modest," said the marquis in his
softest tones. "It is just of the lay point of view
that Father Joseph has given us so complete and

instructive a presentation. That of a specialist is naturally somewhat different."

She smiled uneasily, somewhat puzzled, but feeling that it was kind of Étienne, himself so great an authority, to speak in praise of Father Joseph. The priest, flushing with annoyance, looked away, and met the bright malicious eyes of Marguerite. Then he saw her exchange a glance with René, and realized at once that there was a private understanding between the brother and sister, and that they both hated him.

He began to look at the silent boy, for the first time, with interest. Till now his disdainful glance had taken in only the evidences of Norse blood; the tall athletic build, the air of health and good-temper, the bright hazel colouring of eyes and sunburnt cheek and thick short curls; and he had thought: "Another Henri." Now, suddenly and with a queer thrill of discomfort, he recognized an inimical presence.

He looked again. Yes, René was not merely hostile; he was unapproachable. His aloofness was unconscious, but it was no less distinct than his father's; and, between them, they had filled the mental atmosphere of the room with ice. Father Joseph glanced at his watch, invented an appointment and took a hasty leave.

Angélique looked after him wistfully as he went out. He remained to her the personification of sanctity, as her brother-in-law was that of intellect; but she felt dimly that he had overstepped the limits of his province and made himself ridiculous. There was timid apology in her face.

"I am so glad you and Father Joseph should have had an opportunity to get to know each other better, Étienne. He is not so learned as you, of course; he has given up opportunities of study in order to stay here with his poor. Indeed, I feel sure that no riches could tempt him away from them; he has chosen holy poverty. I would trust him as I would trust the blessed saints."

The marquis took another strawberry.

"My dear Angélique, I am convinced that Father Joseph is incapable of putting your table knives into his pocket; but he does put them into his mouth."

Marguerite broke into a suppressed giggle, which brought a flush of distress to her aunt's thin cheeks. She glanced again at René; to own a brother with whom one could share a joke was so new and wonderful to her that she wanted to assure herself of it afresh at every moment. But René's eyes did not meet hers; he looked sulky and ill at ease. He was glad to see Father Joseph snubbed; that was all right. But he wished Aunt Angélique wouldn't make an idiot of herself, and he wished father wouldn't . . . . Anyhow, what had Marguerite got to snigger about, the spiteful little cat?

He had almost arrived at disliking her again. But in the cart she looked so small and pitiful, and so frightened at even the tiniest jolt, that when she slid a hand into his for comfort a lump came in his throat.

They got her to bed as soon as possible; and the next morning she was in high spirits and eager to see the rabbits. The journey had not injured her at all.

Within a month the line of her mouth had changed. This was her first holiday; and, from the rising to the setting of the sun, its days were full of wonder. Dogs and horses, rabbits and pigeons, all paid their daily court to the little queen on the couch under the walnut trees. Once, even the baby pigs were brought up, squealing; and the garden rang with unaccustomed laughter as Jacques chased them across the flower-beds and, out of breath but smiling triumphantly, came back with the runaways tucked one under each arm that they might "apologize to Mademoiselle."

On wet days the brightest room in the house was filled with flowers and mosses, birds' eggs, butter-flies, kittens, and all delightful things. Sometimes the child was carried into the great old-fashioned kitchen, where Marthe, bringing a pastry-board to the side of the couch, taught her how to mix tiny cakes for dolls' tea-parties. In fine weather the two big brothers carried the couch about the farm, or slung it in the hay-cart and carefully guided old Diane to rocky dells and water-lily ponds, or cool green glades in the woods. Then they would collect sticks and boil the kettle, while Marguerite, propped against her cushions and chattering radiantly, buttered rolls for an "English picnic." Sometimes father himself would lay aside his books and join the fun. Those were red-letter days indeed; partly because father was of all companions the most desirable, and partly because Aunt Angélique never interfered or nagged when he was there. Altogether she was much less fussy now; perhaps the change was good for her too.

Four entrancing weeks passed before she began to think seriously of returning to Avallon. Then Father Joseph came over to see his truant penitents and to hear their confession.

"It has been a most delightful holiday," said Aunt Angélique the next morning after lunch; "and we have been tempted into making really too long a stay. We ought to go home tomorrow, I think. Could you spare the horses, Henri?"

"Of course, aunt, I will spare the horses whenever you wish; but surely you need not go just yet? We were thinking of making an excursion to Blannay next week to pick wild gooseberries."

"Let us persuade you to stay one more week at least," said the marquis. "We have all enjoyed this month."

"It is very good of you, dear Étienne; but Sister Louise is counting on me to help with her poor. We have had so much pleasure; we must get back to our duties now, mustn't we, Marguerite?"

The little girl's mouth had set in a line so hard and sour that she looked, for the moment, like a haggard old woman. Aunt Angélique shook her head sadly.

"Oh, Marguerite, Marguerite! If you look so cross I shall think holidays are bad for you! What would the dear Mother Superior say if . . ."

"René!" Marguerite cried out. The tone of her voice brought all the hearers to their feet. René was beside the couch instantly, with a soothing hand on hers.

"All right, Pâquerette! Just keep quiet, and we'll see to it. Look here, aunt, if you really must go, can't you leave the kid behind you for a week or two? We wouldn't let her take any harm."

"My dear René! Do you suppose I should neglect my charge like that? Of course, I should not think of leaving her. You have no idea of how much personal attention an invalid requires."

"There's Marthe," René began; then broke off, looking at his father.

The marquis was silently watching Marguerite. He had seen her immediate response to René's touch and voice; and noticed that the boy, while talking, still kept a hand on her wrist.

"We will discuss the matter later," he said; adding softly to his sister-in-law: "I think this talk is upsetting her. Will you come into the study? Henri, perhaps you will come with us. I want your advice."

As they went out, Marguerite flung her arms round René's neck, with a wild burst of sobs.

"I won't go! I won't go with her! René, René, don't let them take me!"

"Look here, Pâquerette, don't cry! Father will manage it all right if you just leave him alone. But it's no use setting aunt's back up. It's only Father Joseph that has been putting her on to this. Father will smooth her down."

"He won't! He'll let me go. He doesn't want me!"

René turned pink.

"Marguerite, shut up; that's not true! Father's been a brick about it. . . ."

A hand dropped on his shoulder.

"Has he, boy? I'm none so sure."

"Ah, father! Look here, sir, we can't let aunt take her. It's . . . it's not fair. We shouldn't like it ourselves. . . ."

But his voice was drowned by Marguerite.

"I won't go! I won't have Sister Louise come hugging me again. Father, I . . . I'll kill myself if you send me back."

"Oh, chuck it!" said René, outraged, and red to the roots of his hair. "There's no use making a goose of yourself. There, Pâquerette, father won't let you go. I say, don't . . . don't cry like that! Why, what a little silly!"

He had gathered her closely into his arms, and was stroking her head with a gesture inherited from Françoise. The marquis touched him on the shoulder again.

"Tell her she shan't go."

He slipped out of the room and left the child sobbing convulsively in René's arms.

Having given his promise he stuck to it bravely, though the difficulties appeared, at first, overwhelmingly great. All his tact and charm of manner were needed to pacify Angélique, who was both deeply hurt at her charge's ingratitude and horrified at the iniquity of giving way to caprice and "naughty tempers." Marguerite's reputation for patience and piety was dear to the old maid's heart; and she was more distressed to find such backsliding where she had expected only model conduct than even to see that her own devotion was unappreciated. Her first impulse was to shake the dust from her feet and leave her brother-in-law to complete the moral ruin of which his irreverent remarks about Father Joseph had sown the first seeds. Gradually she was won over to a less harsh view of the case, and, wiping her eyes, began grudgingly to discuss practical possibilities.

At Henri's suggestion old Marthe was called up, and proposed that her own daughter, a young widow living in the village, should be engaged to attend on Mademoiselle. Rosine was sent for at once, and, being a clean and motherly body, with kind grey eyes and a soft voice, quickly won the approval of the marquis.

"Surely, Angélique," he said; "this will do for a temporary arrangement? René will be going to college, no doubt, in the autumn; I think, as he and Marguerite have become such friends, we ought to let them have the summer together. Rosine can do what is necessary for a month or two, and we can decide about the future at more leisure."

"Oh, no doubt Rosine can do what is necessary as long as all goes well. But the child is grievously fragile, and needs constant watching. Is that to be entrusted to an ignorant peasant-woman?"

"My aunt is right," said Henri. "We owe

everything to her; it seems to me nothing less than cruelty to deprive Marguerite of her devoted care, just for a momentary caprice like this."

The marquis hesitated. He had lived so long among his books that now, when confronted with a practical question which must be settled, he felt like a bat blinking in sudden daylight. It was always easier to him to give way than to hold his own against opposition; but if he were to give way here he would not dare to meet René's eyes.

"It cuts me to the heart to go against your wishes, my dear," he said, turning to Angélique with a look that disarmed her at once. "You have done more than I can thank you for. But I cannot break the first promise I have ever made to the child. We must simply take what risks there are, and hope that we can persuade you to forgive us and to come again soon."

Angélique melted into tears.

"Dear Étienne, as if there were anything to forgive!"

He backed a little, nervously afraid lest she might be going to seal the reconciliation by embracing him as she had just embraced Henri. Marguerite's furious and lamentable cry: "I won't have Sister Louise come hugging me again!" echoed in his memory; and, for the first time, he thought of his daughter with a thrill of true spontaneous sympathy.

Angélique spent the rest of the day in packing clothes, giving instructions to everyone, and hanging inconsolably round Marguerite. Having no confidence in Rosine's ministrations, she tried to fortify the child against the possible consequences of neglect by rubbing the affected hip with an ointment recommended by the Mother Superior. Marguerite cried because the rubbing hurt her, and Angélique cried too because she could not bear her darling to be hurt. The following morning she left Marteurelles, with affectionate farewells and an air of mild reproachfulness. Marguerite, sternly admonished by René "not to be a little pig," managed to keep up a decorous manner till the sound of wheels on the gravel told her that aunt, and Henri, and the luggage, and the prayer-books, had really started. Then she and the boy burst into a simultaneous war-whoop of triumph, which brought the marquis out of his study to know what had happened.

"It's all right, sir," René gasped, scrambling off the floor, and deftly kicking out of sight the cushion which Marguerite had thrown at his head. "Sorry we disturbed you; we were having a game."

"So I see. Marguerite!"

She had dived under the couch-rug at her father's unexpected entrance, and now peeped over the edge timidly, with bright eyes.

"Yes, father?"

"You find things a bit less dull since this boy came home, don't you?"

"Yes, father." Her eyes were growing wide and frightened, and her under-lip was beginning to tremble. He glanced with a smile at René's touzled head.

"So do I. Perhaps, if we are very good, both of us, he'll let us go on having games with him. Pardon me, my dear; I didn't mean to interrupt your pillow-fight. When your sister can spare you, René, I should like to have a talk with you. There is no hurry."

He went back into the study. Marguerite turned slowly and looked at René. Her eyes were quite piteous now.

"He doesn't want me. . . ."

"Oh, stuff, Pâquerette! You don't like people that are for ever pawing and jawing like Sister Louise; and now because father doesn't do it you think he doesn't want you! Father's all right; only he's busy. You'd look at people as if they weren't there if you were always thinking about mummies."

She shook her head.

"Go and find out what it is. I know he'll tell you I'm to go back to aunt next month; I know he will!"

René went to the study, frowning. He was

F

beginning to find things increasingly complex since Marguerite had left off playing good child and become real. As for father, it was all very well to think about mummies, but Marguerite had got to be thought about now, and she was not in the least like a mummy.

"Sit down," said the marquis, looking up with a smile. "Why, what has gone wrong?"

"Nothing."

"It's time we had a talk about things. Have you begun to think at all what you would like to do in life? Do you wish to study for a profession, or would you rather stay here with Henri in the country? I think you know that we are very poor people; still, if you care to go to Paris and attend the Sorbonne, it can be arranged."

René sat frowning at the floor. Presently he looked up.

"If I were to go to Paris, would you keep the kid on here, or send her back to aunt?"

"Marguerite? I have not yet decided. In any case I shall naturally try to do what will make her happiest. But we will discuss that afterwards. What I want to hear now is about yourself. Have you any strong bent in any particular direction?"

"Yes, sir. But it does depend on the kid. I can't go to Paris if she's to be packed off to Avallon and stuck down there for ever and ever."

"Very well, we will begin with her. Do you believe she was really unhappy at Avallon, or was all this just temper? I should like you to tell me frankly what you think."

René fidgeted miserably, at a loss for words.

"She . . . she did have to be so good all the time . . ." he began; and then looked up with a flash of angry disgust. "And it's true. That Sister Louise woman doesn't know how to keep her hands off; she's always pawing people over. Then there's Father Joseph, preaching. . . . And a girl can't do anything — especially if she's got a bad leg. . . ." He broke off.

"I see," said the marquis. "Thank you. We will put a stop to Father Joseph and Sister Louise, at any rate. Perhaps your aunt could arrange to come and live here altogether for a few years." He glanced at his book-shelves with a sigh. "We shall have to see what can be done. Now tell me about yourself. What is the thing you wish to learn?"

At this René was overcome by shyness, and could scarcely manage to stumble through his answer.

"Oh, well . . . I like geography . . . if it's all one to you, sir."

"You got on very well with that at school, didn't you? Is your idea to be an explorer, or a teacher of geography?"

"I . . . oh, I don't know; I'd do just anything that comes, so long as it's a bit scientific."

"You used to be pretty good at doing things with your hands, as a child, and seeing how machines were made. Have you left off caring about that?"

"No; I like anything you can make, or anything you can just go on and find out about. I'm an awful fool at classics; there seems to be such a lot of jaw in it."

"But what you like best is geography? Are you sure?"

"Oh, quite."

"And you would be happy studying it at the Sorbonne, if your mind were at rest about your sister?"

"I should just think I would. But won't it cost a lot? Henri didn't get to Paris. It doesn't seem fair."

"He could have gone if he had wished it. He was offered his choice, and preferred farming. There is no reason why you should not go. Of course, I shall have to sell a piece of land to raise the money; but I am quite willing to do that. No; you need not be distressed about it; Henri and I both feel that you have every right. Then it is settled that you go to Paris in the autumn? unless . . ."

The marquis hesitated for a moment; then, reluctantly, took up a letter lying on his desk.

"I ought to tell you that I received an offer three weeks ago. If you wish to accept it, I don't want to stand in your way. It is from your uncle. He offers . . ."

"Yes, I know; to adopt me altogether and send me to Cambridge with Frank."

The father looked up, surprised.

"He has told you of it, then? I understood that you knew nothing about the idea."

"I didn't. I had a letter from him last week."

The marquis paused to digest this. Henri had always regarded any letters which came for him as common property.

"Indeed? I suppose that was written after he received my answer. I told him I could say nothing till I knew how you felt about it. And what does he say to you?"

"It's about my going in for geography. Of course, he always knew I liked it, and now old Fuzzy — that's the science master, you know — has been telling him I ought to take it up. He said I was not to worry about our being poor, because he would send me to Cambridge if there were any difficulty. It's jolly of Uncle Harry; he always was a brick."

"Have you answered yet?"

"Yes, I wrote last Sunday and told him I couldn't go back to England."

"So decided?"

The marquis raised his eyebrows. René frowned again, and looked down at the floor.

"Well, how could I? There's the kid, you know. She'd cry her eyes out."

"That is very likely. For my part, I shouldn't cry if you went; it's not my way. All the same, I am grateful to you for refusing, if it interests you to know."

"Father . . . Oh, father, I am sorry; I ought to have asked you first."

"Not at all, my son; not at all. You are quite capable of managing your own life . . . and mine too, it seems. Well, then, we will count the matter as settled, shall we? It shall be the Sorbonne, and geography."

"Thank you, sir. You're . . . you're awfully good to me."

He rose and shook hands, turned to leave the room and paused at the door.

"Father . . ."

The marquis had sat down to his papers again. He looked up and asked carelessly:

"What is it, boy?"

"I . . . think the kid is . . . awfully pleased when you take any notice of her. Only she's a bit afraid of you; she's such a little fool . . ."

He escaped from the room in a hurry. The marquis sat looking at the shut door.

"My daughter takes after me, it would seem,"

he said, and returned to his papers. "I also am something of a fool."

For a few days longer the household was given up to holiday joys; then one morning René, coming into his sister's room after an early swim in the river, found her crying bitterly.

"Hullo, Pâquerette!" he exclaimed; "what's the matter?"

There was no answer. The child was shivering violently. Rosine came out of the inner room holding a finger on her lip, and the boy tiptoed across to her with his hands full of water-lilies.

"Has anything happened, Rosine?"

"I am afraid Mademoiselle is going to be ill. She is feverish, and her leg seems to be very painful; she won't let me touch it."

René stood still for a few seconds; then he signed to Rosine to leave him alone with the child, and went softly to the bedside.

"Pâquerette, do you feel bad? Look, here are the water-lilies you wanted."

"Don't — don't touch the bed! My leg hurts. . . ."

"Shall I call father?"

She caught his hand.

"No, don't go away — don't go away! René . . . oh, I feel so sick . . . René. . . ."

With much difficulty he persuaded her to let Rosine feel the hip. It was hot and swollen, and Rosine at once went to call the marquis, while René tried unsuccessfully to soothe the child.

Henri, at first, was tempted to say: "I told you so!" But he was sincerely attached to his sister, and after a moment had no thought but of how to help. He rode off at once in quest of a doctor, and during the examination stood outside the door of her room in mute distress.

"I had better go to Avallon and beg my aunt to come back," he said, when told that a gathering was forming in the diseased joint. "I believe she would consent in an emergency like this."

The marquis, for his part, was prepared to go in person to Avallon, if necessary, and humbly entreat Angélique to return; the actual sight of pain which he could not relieve distressed him beyond endurance. He was shaken out of all sense of proportion, and ready to think, with Henri, that the child should have been sent back with her aunt; that any degree of unhappiness or mental starvation was better than the risk of illness without the accustomed nurse. But when he tried to soothe Marguerite by telling her that Aunt Angélique would soon come to her, she burst into a terrifying fit of rage.

"I won't have her; I won't have anyone but René! She shan't come near me — I hate her! I hate her!"

The state of hysterical excitement into which she was working herself was so bad for her that the doctor ended by advising her father to give way, for the moment at least, and try whether René and Rosine could do the nursing between them. As Henri had started for Avallon, Jacques was sent off in a hurry to catch him up on the road, and when they returned together René was already established in the sickroom. He was secretly appalled at the responsibility thus suddenly thrust upon him; but, beyond grave attention to the doctor's instructions, nothing was visible in his manner; and if he passed through a hard experience during the next fortnight, no one knew it but himself. Rosine proved a careful and sensible nurse, and between them they satisfied the doctor.

As for the marquis, these were the worst days which he had known since the dreadful time when Françoise died. As then, he could neither work nor sleep; and would listen miserably outside the shut door of the sickroom, starting at every noise and overwhelmed by the sense of his own uselessness.

Late one night, when he looked into the room, he found René sitting beside the bed whispering to the child, who lay holding his arm with both hands and crying.

"Mademoiselle is rather excited to-night,"

said Rosine. "I shall sit up. There is no need for M. René to stay; he is very tired, I am sure."

The marquis went softly to the bedside and touched René on the shoulder. The boy, without looking round, silently motioned his father away.

"You had better go to bed, M. René," said Rosine. "Mademoiselle will be all right with me."

Marguerite clung tighter to her brother's hand.

"I'm going presently, sir," René whispered. "Leave her to me for a minute, please."

The marquis stooped to kiss her forehead.

"Good night, my darling." But she only shrank away.

"No, no; I want René! I want René!"

Three hours later the marquis crept down the corridor in dressing-gown and slippers to listen at the sickroom door. The sound of weeping struck on his ears, and he opened the door cautiously. Rosine was dozing in her arm-chair; René sat in the same cramped position as before, holding the child in his arms. She was clinging round his neck with both hands, her face hidden on his shoulder. The boy looked white and tired, and like his mother as she had looked not long before she died. The marquis stood watching for a moment, then shut the door again and went away.

When Henri lunched with his aunt at Avallon in the following week, and told her what had happened, she started out of her chair with clasped hands.

"My poor little darling! Oh, I might have known something would happen! A gathering, indeed! She has never had such a thing in all these years. And I not there! I must go to her at once."

"But, aunt, it is all over; she is nearly well again now."

"And you never sent for me! Who nursed her? Rosine?"

"She and René managed it between them; I think they did everything very well, though, of course, it is not the same as having you."

Not for the world would he have told her that Dr. Moreau thought her rubbing with the Mother Superior's ointment had probably caused the trouble.

Angélique turned away and began to clear the lunch table. Her lips trembled slightly. After eight years of devotion she had been ousted from her place, quietly, imperceptibly, without a struggle; just superseded by a boy of eighteen.

The household at the château spent what little remained of the summer uneventfully. Marguerite had grown not merely paler and thinner since her illness, but also more serious. The fairy holiday was over, and René would soon be going to Paris. It was clear to everyone that some arrangement must be made shortly; and under this necessity she was developing a new independence of character. She no longer sobbed or screamed or threatened suicide; but gravely repeated, when the subject was broached, that she would never go back to Avallon.

Father Joseph and the nuns used their utmost influence to prevent Angélique from letting her house and settling in Marteurelles. She was useful to them in many ways; and they would not give her up without a fight. Ultimately the difficulty ended in a compromise. The house at Avallon was kept on, and Angélique divided her time between two homes.

"The chief objection to this arrangement, so far as I can see," said the marquis to René, "is that it will make Marguerite's lessons so irregular. That seems to me very undesirable."

"Do you think lessons from aunt are much good to Marguerite? She isn't a baby now; and you know, sir, she's pretty sharp, though she is a girl. She can always see through bad logic."

The marquis sighed.

"I am afraid you are right; but what can I do? To engage a capable resident teacher for her would cost more than we can afford. I dare not sell any more land; we have little enough as it is."

"But, father, why don't you teach her yourself?"

"I!" The marquis sat up straight and stared. "I? My dear René!"

René, with an obstinately set mouth, looked out of the window.

"Of course," he began slowly, "if you don't think . . ." There was a pause.

"What I think is scarcely the question," the marquis murmured resignedly. "The question is, what would the result be? I have never taught a child in my life; and I am getting rather old to start on a new vocation, even at the bidding of so very capable an autocrat as my younger son."

René wheeled round, overcome with distress.

"Father!" he cried out; then looked away again and added rather huskily: "I didn't mean to interfere, sir. Perhaps I've been too cheeky; but, you see, we wanted to get things done."

"And as you certainly do succeed in getting things done and I don't . . .? You need not apologize; you have amply justified your interference. Well, I will try what I can do. Shake hands on it, boy."

René got up hastily, with flaming cheeks.

"Father, you're such a trump whenever I want anything . . . but I wish you didn't always make one feel like a cad."

The marquis laughed.

"Do I? We are quits then; do you know what you make me feel like? A mummy."

CHAPTER III

WITHIN the next seven years many things changed at Marteurelles. The household gradually divided itself into two sections; almost, René thought sometimes when he came home for the holidays, into two camps. Father and daughter formed a defensive alliance in the study; aunt and nephew consoled one another in the salon, outsiders both.

Marguerite had risen up in revolt against all authority, and had completed her emancipation with a thoroughness which appalled René's conventional young soul. She would have nothing to do with prayers or pious books, and utterly refused to confess her sins to any priest. She had worried her father into teaching her Latin and Greek, that she might read scholastic philosophy; and now, instead of making toilet bags for nuns, picked the dogmas of the Church to pieces with relentless logic and an impregnable lack of imagination.

"She is horribly clever," the marquis said to René one day. "She learns so fast that I have all I can do to keep pace with her demands. To teach her is like being cross-examined by a criminal lawyer; she seizes the weak point before one has time to enunciate the argument."

"Only the weak point? Never the strong one?"

"Very seldom. It is the most destructive mind that I have ever come across. If she had been a boy and not a cripple, she would have a career before her at the bar; but what use will her brain be to a bedridden girl? She would be happier like your Aunt Angélique."

"Is aunt happy now, do you think?"

"I believe so. She was rather depressed for some time, as you know, and worried about all our souls; but she has grown reconciled to things the last year or two. Marguerite is growing up, you see, and getting more tolerant."

"Or more self-controlled," René answered, sighing. He was thinking of the day, four years ago, when Aunt Angélique had asked him to sing, and he had begun the old folk-song:

> "*L'amour de moy s'y est enclose*
> *Dedans un joly jardinet,*
> *Où croist la rose . . .*"

"Don't!" Marguerite had shrieked. "Don't! I hate pretty gardens; it's like Avallon!"

Angélique had left the room in tears, Henri following with indignant sympathy. Even René had not refrained from murmuring, "I say, you needn't be a little cad!"

The result had been one of the terrible scenes
which all the household dreaded. Apart from
the utter impossibility of defending oneself, in
any way, against a helpless invalid, Marguerite's
occasional fits of rage were of so terrific an intensity that they seemed, like explosions, to exhaust the air and fill the house with poisonous
emanations of hatred and misery. Also, they
had the unhappy quality of wounding the victims
just in their affections. One of her most un-
governable outbursts had been on the solitary
occasion when Henri, in a tender mood, had addressed her by René's special pet name: "Pâquerette." Her small clenched hands had flown
up to strike him. For a moment she had been
speechless with fury, hissing at him like a snake.
"How dare you! Ah, how dare you! I'm
René's Pâquerette, not yours; you never wanted
to call me pretty names till he came home!"

For a few years after her return to Marteurelles
she seemed to have no control over these emotional
hurricanes; but as she grew older her will-power
developed. Now, at eighteen, she was remark-
ably self-contained and reticent; and the marquis
had begun to realize that, notwithstanding the
intellectual companionship which had grown up
between him and his daughter, there was a wall of
glass shutting him out, and that, as a human being,
she was, and chose to remain, a stranger to him.

He wondered sometimes whether the bitter disappointment which she had suffered was the cause of this impenetrable reserve. During the first two years of her life at Marteurelles her bodily condition had steadily improved; she had become able to walk on crutches, and her little white face had filled out and grown rosy. Then a gradual change had begun; no one could understand why. It was now four years since she had stood upright, and her vitality seemed slowly failing. There was no acute pain; but the dull aching of a deadly weariness crushed her like some monstrous weight. It already needed all her force of will to work up fictitious high spirits for René's benefit, that his holidays might not be spoiled.

René had just come home for the summer vacation. He had done as well at the Sorbonne as at the English school; and, having made many friends and no enemies, had obtained, immediately after graduating, a post as cartographer in a government office. For so young a man this was considered an excellent beginning, though the salary was, as yet, small, and the work somewhat monotonous.

"May I come in, Pâquerette?" he asked, tapping at his sister's door on the morning after his arrival. "I want to talk secrets."

"Come in; I'm quite ready. And please ad-

G

mire me; I have put on my best frock because it's your first day."

Her couch was by the open window, and flickering shadows of walnut leaves danced about her head. Her best frock, like most other things in the poverty-stricken house, was plain and shabby enough; but she had pinned a fine old lace scarf round her throat with her one jewelled brooch, and tucked a white rosebud into her black hair. The worn and chiselled face that she turned to greet him looked all eyes.

"Ah, but it's good to have you back again and all to myself for the morning! Father's in the study, and aunt and Henri have gone to church. I want to yell and pillow-fight for joy, as if we were children again. Last night, with everyone in the room, I would not count that you had come. I told myself: 'This is only a pretence; he'll be here on Sunday morning.' No, stand off a little; let me have a good look at you. One, two, three lines on the forehead! You wicked boy; what is it? Have you been worrying over anything?"

"No; just aching to see you, that's all."

He sat down by the couch and lifted her hands to his lips. They were singularly beautiful hands: thin and waxen, but exquisitely shaped. For some time both brother and sister remained silent, too happy to talk.

"Sweet marjoram!" she cried out with her face against his coat. "So early in the season! Where did you get it?"

He pulled a handful of crushed blossoms from his pocket.

"I had forgotten it; I picked it for you on that sunny bank by the church."

"You have been to church? Aunt and Henri wanted you to go with them."

"I went to early Mass instead."

"So as to get home to me?"

"Partly that, and partly because I always like to go to church alone. Aunt gets in one's way somehow; there is a sort of duty air about her on Sundays, and it makes me feel irreverent."

Marguerite's fingers were playing with the buttons of his waistcoat. Presently she lifted her magnificent lashes.

"Do you always go to church? In Paris, too?"

"Generally. If anything keeps me on Sunday, I try to go one day in the week."

She sighed.

"But I suppose if one believed in . . . I mean, I suppose, to Christians . . . it is a question of duty, isn't it? Oh! I beg your pardon, dearest; I oughtn't to have asked you that."

René burst out laughing.

"How funny you are! Why shouldn't you ask me, if you want to know? Only it's such a queer notion, to make a duty of things. If I didn't want to go to church I shouldn't go."

"I wish you would tell me why you go — if you don't mind."

"Well, why do I come here?"

"But surely that is different. When you love people, you want to be with them."

René had not yet lost his youthful trick of blushing. His ears turned pink as he answered: "But, you see, Pâquerette, I . . . I love God."

She pounced at once on the weak point.

"Your analogy is wrong. If God is anywhere, He is everywhere equally. And you don't want the people you love in the middle of a crowd; you want them alone. Why must you talk to your God just in an ugly church with a lot of tawdry finery about and a fat priest leering over his missal at his neighbour's wife? Yes, but he does; the whole village knows it, and yet they all go to hear him say Mass."

"I don't think about the priest and the finery; I just forget them. But I believe you are right; it's not only a question of loving God; it's a question of loving other people. The presence of one's neighbours gives one courage to approach Him; He overwhelms me so when I'm alone with Him. In church, you see, everybody is saying 'Thank you' together, and one can get it out without feeling such a cheeky little worm."

"René, I wish you could explain to me what there is in life to say 'Thank you' for. Has He given you so much?"

"What for! Why, for every ray of sunshine and every blade of grass; and for summer holidays, and sweet marjoram, and geography . . . and most of all for you, La Marguerite des Marguerites. I want to give thanks to God for everything about you, from the tips of your hair to the tips of your fingers."

"Including my leg?" she flashed at him instantly.

The next moment she regretted saying it. His head dropped on to the hand he was clasping. He was silent so long that she began rumpling his hair with thin fingers, to console him.

"Don't, dear. You needn't mind so much. If I have got used to it, you can. I can't have you angry with God as well as with father, just because of my stupid leg. As for me, I have no use for any fathers, earthly or heavenly."

Her face had grown hard.

"I understand all about the sweet marjoram, just as I understand how good father has been over teaching me Greek. It would be very nice to be able to respond; but Father Joseph and Sister Louise stand in the way. I suppose it was much the same thing with God as with father; they both thought that sort of company good enough

for a crippled girl. And the queer part of it is
that father has grown to care about me now, when
it's too late. Not as he cares for you, of course;
just as a reflection of you. I believe he would
give up Egyptology to have you fond of him."

René looked away from her.

"It's no use," he said huskily. "I'm not angry
with father; I am awfully sorry for him. He
couldn't help being himself; and he's been a brick
to me these last years. I'd care for him if I could.
But when you're a child there are some things
that go right in, and you can't pull them out again
after you're grown up, however hard you try. It
seems silly, but you just can't."

He sat looking at the walnut trees.

"You see, when we were little, and left to
the servants, after mother died. . . . No, you
wouldn't remember; you were a baby. They
used to tell a lot of fairy stories. There was one
about a child whose parents wanted to get rid
of him because they were poor; so they took him
out and lost him in the wood. I used to imagine
the little thing wandering alone. . . . Then we
were told I was to go to England, and Marthe
began to cry. She didn't know I was within
hearing. She said to Jacques: 'Sending the
child to those English ogres!' Well, I'd heard
about ogres, and I put it all together and thought
I was going to England to be eaten. Of course,

when I got there, and Uncle Harry met me at
Dover with a bagful of cakes, and then we got
home and found Aunt Nelly, and supper in a cosy
corner by the fire, and the boys so jolly — I forgot all about it, or thought I had. Then I left
school and came back here, and I saw father and
liked him so much . . . I liked him tremendously.
Then they told me about you, and it all came back,
and I knew I'd only been pretending to forget.
I'd never really forgotten it at all. I'd known
all the time that father just wanted to get rid of
us."

"I see," said Marguerite. "I never understood
before why you persist in calling yourself 'Martel.'"

"Ah! I don't persist; only I just happened
to register my name so at the Sorbonne, and it's
too late to change now. You don't think it has
hurt father, do you?"

"I believe nothing in the world has ever hurt
him quite so much."

"Pâquerette! Did he tell you he . . . ?"

"Father? Don't you know him better than
that? He'd never say a word. Only Henri
began about it one day, and father stopped him
in a kind of sharp, sudden way. I've never heard
him speak like that about anything. He just
said: 'Your brother is quite right; it was perfectly justifiable.' Then he got up and went out
of the room, looking like an old, old man, and as

white . . . He looked round at me as he went;
he knew I understood."

"Oh, Pâquerette, I wish I'd known in time!
It was only . . . You see, Uncle Harry has been
so good to me, just as if I'd been his own son;
and I thought father wouldn't care one way or
the other. I've been an ass, as usual. There,
what's the use of talking about it now? I can't
undo it. Tell me about yourself. What have
you been doing all these months?"

"Various things. I have been reading a little
Greek, off and on."

"Off and on? That means you've been worse
again?"

"Don't look so miserable, dear; it's just a sort of
general weakness. I suppose it won't ever be any
better now. But I'm lucky in one way; there's
not much pain — just stupid backaches and head-
aches. You have an absurdly exaggerated notion
of them because I made such a fuss for every
trifle as a child."

"Did you, my pearl? I never found it out."
She laughed, with wet eyes.

"Of course you didn't, you old silly! When did
you ever find out anything about me that was not
perfect, except my fiendish temper? I believe
you even think me pretty. Confess now, you
do! Collar-bones, and sallow complexion, and
all?"

"Not pretty; beautiful. Take a glass and look at your eyelashes."

"Oh, well, I'll concede the eyelashes."

"And the eyes."

"And the eyes if you like. Now let me hear the secrets."

He was silent awhile.

"It's only one secret."

"Yes? It must be a big one to take so much getting out. Why, René, I do believe you have fallen in love!"

"No, it's not that. Look here, very likely it will come to nothing at all. Don't count on it; it's only a bare chance. There's a man in Lyons who has discovered a treatment for hip-disease. I heard about it last month, and I've been corresponding with him. He says some cases as old-standing as yours have been cured by his method."

"Cured!"

The colour went up into her cheeks.

"Oh, they are lame, very lame even; but they can get about."

She looked away from him. Then she turned and took his hand.

"Dearest, don't let us make up fairy tales to ourselves. Even if a few persons in Lyons have been cured by some famous man, that is no help to me here in the country with little provincial doctors."

"Dr. Bonnet is coming from Lyons next week to see you."

"René!"

"Well, why not? We may as well know all we can."

"But it's mad! He will only say there is nothing to be done; everyone has always said that. And where on earth shall we get the money to pay his fee? We are poorer than ever this year; the harvest was so bad last summer, and father's book cost a lot to publish."

"I have plenty of money."

"Out of a salary of a hundred and fifty francs a month?"

"No, out of my old allowance and Uncle Harry's birthday presents. I have over two thousand francs saved up."

"How long has that taken you?"

"I forget. Pâquerette, think! If you were cured and I got a good post — it's possible next year — we'd take a flat together in Paris, and . . ."

"Oh, René, René, don't! It won't happen; it will never happen. The world isn't made that way."

"Ah, but it is! It's the same world where sweet marjoram grows. Why shouldn't you have your share like other people?"

She put her arms round his neck.

"I have my share already; I have you."

The other members of the household were notified in due course that Dr. Bonnet was expected, and when he arrived the family physician was in attendance for the consultation. The great man asked many questions before seeing Marguerite at all; then followed a minute and exhausting investigation, after which the two doctors retired to confer together, and finally came back into her room, where the assembled family was now waiting to hear the verdict.

Dr. Bonnet's view of the case was more favourable than anyone had expected. The increasing weakness which had so much alarmed her friends was due, he said, to an accidental complication, which a course of treatment would gradually and easily remove. Till this was accomplished and her general health restored, it would be useless to attack the disease itself, as that could be done only by surgical methods which she was not at present strong enough to endure. He had already shown Dr. Moreau how to deal with the complication; but the radical cure, if it was to be attempted at all, must be his own work, and he was not prepared to guarantee success.

"I believe it to be worth trying," he added. "But you ought to understand first that it will mean a very long and painful experiment, and that the result is doubtful. It is a chance, and

I believe a good one; but that is all. I do not press you to accept my suggestion, especially as my colleague is against it; but I have enough hope to justify me in offering to try."

The marquis sat with a nervous hand at his lips and looked away. He was terrified lest he should be asked to advise. Of all bugbears, the worst, to him, was a sudden demand for a momentous practical decision. Angélique turned with clasped hands to her niece; her faded eyes were filled with tears.

"What a hideous idea! Surely you will not contemplate . . . My poor little pet! It is . . ."

"Hush, please, aunt; we have not yet heard what Dr. Moreau thinks."

It was René who spoke, in a hard, strained voice. He was standing between his aunt and the couch, as if to bar her approach. She drew back timidly and sat down again.

The family doctor expressed himself strongly against the scheme. It would be a useless cruelty, he said; would put the girl through a grievous amount of suffering and even some danger; would keep them all in suspense for months together, and would probably end in disappointment. "Dr. Bonnet tells me he has had a few marvellous successes lately, but I would ask him at what cost? And how many failures?"

At this Angélique broke out again. "Étienne!"

she cried, and burst into tears. "Étienne, you
must not let them. . . . It is atrocious—
atrocious! Étienne. . . ."

He did not answer, but he raised his head and
looked at Marguerite and then at René. They
were looking at each other. He rose, and, as he
had once done years before, gave them the only
help he could: that of leaving them alone together.

"I think there are too many of us in the room,"
he said. "Probably my daughter would like to be
quiet for awhile. It is for her to decide. Shall
we go downstairs, gentlemen?"

They went out, Angélique weeping, and Henri
consoling her with whispered assurances that the
monstrous proposal would never be carried out.
As he spoke they heard the door locked behind
them.

René remained shut in with Marguerite for
nearly an hour; then he joined the company in
the salon.

"Thank you, father," he said as he entered; and
the others wondered for what. He went up to
Dr. Bonnet.

"My sister wishes me to tell you that she is
willing to try the experiment. She fully under-
stands and appreciates the certainty of pain and
the risk of failure; but she is prepared to face
whatever must be faced for the chance of being
cured . . ."

"René," Henri broke in with indignation; "you have persuaded her! It is an infamy!"

"She doesn't understand what she is doing!" cried Angélique. "She is a child still!"

"Indeed," the family doctor added, "I fear Mademoiselle will repent it bitterly."

The marquis said nothing. He sat, as pale as ashes, looking at René, who went on in the same steady tone:

"Our only doubt is whether we can meet the expense involved. What do you think the cost would be?"

"I cannot give you any definite estimate. She would have to come to Lyons, of course, and live a quiet invalid life there for some months, with constant attendance and very careful nursing; and I think one of her own family should be with her all the time. The journey would certainly be expensive, and there would be considerable outlay for appliances."

René took a sheet of paper and began to put down the various items, the surgeon mentioning approximate figures. When the fees were added to the list he ran his pencil down it, wrote in the total and handed the paper to his father, who looked at it silently and, after showing it to Henri, handed it back with a sad droop of the head.

"It is impossible."

"It means utter ruin," Henri whispered to the marquis. "We should have to sell almost everything. Even if she were cured, we should be penniless. I doubt whether the house itself would not have to go."

René sat still with the paper in his hand. He was almost as pale as his father.

"Thank you," he said, rising. "I will go back to my sister now."

"Thank God we are poor!" Angélique cried out, when he had left the room. The marquis winced in spite of himself. What had a man from Lyons to do with the poverty of the de Marteurelles?

René came out of Marguerite's room to take leave of Dr. Bonnet, and accompanied him a little way in the carriage. The surgeon, curiously impressed by brother and sister alike, offered at parting to undertake the case — "if it would make the difference to you" — for half fees. René shook his head.

"It is very good of you, but my sister would not care to accept that. Also the expense is prohibitive, apart from any fees at all. But, if our circumstances should change a little later — say in three years, or so — and we were able to raise the money; would you still be willing to undertake the case?"

"Undoubtedly."

"Good-bye for the present, then; and many thanks."

Leaving the carriage, René went for a long walk alone and came in late for supper, grave and taciturn. After the meal he went up to his sister's room and found her alone.

"I'm going to bed early," he said. "I'm very tired. Is there anything you want?"

"No, thank you; good night."

They parted dumbly, without a caress or a sign of emotion on either side. In the night René paced his room, and the girl wept passionately in the dark. Her sense of proportion had completely deserted her; she was, at the moment, incapable of realizing that the discovery of a removable complication had in any way improved her lot. Nothing counted but the unnecessary struggle of stringing up her resolution for no result, and the overwhelming fact that René had left her to herself after such a strain and such a disappointment. Just to-day, to go off and leave her. . . . Just to-day, when she needed him so!

For some days little was to be got out of either René or Marguerite. Both were unusually silent; the girl tragically, with a hard mouth and sombre eyes; the young man with an air of one whose thoughts are preoccupied. Angélique tried earnestly to help them with affectionate and pious advice; no amount of experience ever taught her which persons to leave alone. Henri looked wistfully at them; he longed to offer sympathy, but, having learned to go cautiously with creatures so incomprehensible and so difficult, respected, without understanding it, the privacy of their grief. As for the marquis, he understood well enough, and held his tongue.

With each other they were no less reserved, till René broke silence one evening, when they found themselves alone together.

"Pâquerette," he began under his breath, and paused. "Pâquerette, I want to tell you . . ."

She gave him no help, and he got the words out with an effort:

"I'm going away soon."

"To Paris? Before September?"

"To . . . Very far off. I shall be away for a long time . . . three or four years."

She sat up. He had never got used to the sight of the strained and awkward movement; it always hurt him to see; and now he looked away.

"Where are you going?" she asked harshly.

"To South America. There's an expedition going out to explore, and I'm to be geographer."

She was silent, breathing quickly.

"When . . .?"

"We leave Marseilles the first of October."

"No, no; when did you take the post?"

H

"It was offered just before I came home. I refused first, and then . . ."

He looked up, saw the accusing eyes on his face, and turned his head away.

"And then accepted," he finished lamely.

"When?"

"Last week."

"After Dr. Bonnet was here?"

"Yes. They have written now, engaging me definitely. I . . . It's not so very long, really; it only seems so at first."

Her eyes were still devouring his face.

"It's well paid, I suppose? Is that it?"

He made no answer.

"Is that it? Tell me the truth, anyway."

"Yes, that's it."

He rose, and began to walk up and down the room.

"Look here, we've got to face things as they are; I see no other way to raise the money. And after all, what is it? Crowds of people go to the tropics. Look at the English; they go to India and think nothing of it. We shall be back in four years; possibly even in three. They might . . ."

"No doubt; but as you're not going with them it doesn't much matter to us when they come back."

Then she held out her arms to him, laughing and crying at once.

"Did you think I'd take that from you? Why, what an adorable goose it is! South America, of all places!"

"Pâquerette, it's quite settled."

Her breath stopped with a gasp. As he came and stood beside her, she caught his wrist with both hands.

"But you can't . . ."

"But I must. I didn't tell you till it was finally settled, just so as not to have a fight about it. I've signed the conditions and they've sent me money for preliminary expenses. Ah, don't . . . Pâquerette, don't look like that! But I shall come back!"

He freed himself from her arms and ran for water; her face terrified him. When she was able to speak again a long duel began, exhausting, shattering to the nerves of both.

"You have no right!" she cried. "It's for me to choose what the chance of being cured is worth to me; it's not worth this!"

"You said it was worth going through Bonnet's treatment."

"What is Bonnet's treatment to this? The price is too heavy; I won't pay it. To lose you for four years . . . and a savage country, where you might be killed any day. . . . Where is it? Chili? Paraguay?"

"Ecuador: the north-west tributaries of the

Upper Amazon. We go from Guayaquil, across the Andes and down through the foot-hills to Brazil."

"North-west tributaries . . . But that's the unknown district, surely! You may be eaten by wild beasts or massacred by savages. . . . Ah, you shan't go!"

"But, my darling, we shall be armed. It's a big expedition, led by an experienced man, a retired colonel from the Algerian war. With the guides and carriers and all, we shall be twenty or thirty persons. And it's not like the fever-swamps of Central Brazil; we shall go right over the mountains. You'll see I shall come back all right; and when you get cured . . ."

"René, I'll never take the money! You don't see what you are asking of me: I'm to accept a cure, or a possibility of cure, that may have cost your life. I won't take it; your safety is more to me than my leg."

"Put it the other way; think what you are asking of me. Am I to stay in safety and know you are missing your one chance?"

"No, you're to stay and know I'm keeping my one joy. René, I have nothing in the world but you. I can't lose you . . . I . . . can't. . . ."

She broke down suddenly; and René choked and bit his lip under the strain. But he was quite immovable.

"It's all settled, dearest; let us leave it now. You're making yourself ill for nothing."

She gave up the struggle at last, overcome by sheer fatigue, and hid her face against the pillow in speechless misery. Then René went into the study and broke the news to his father. He was in a hurry to get it over; after the appalling scene that he had just been through with Marguerite, nothing, surely, could hurt any more to-night; and the sooner the family knew, the sooner would everyone be reconciled to the inevitable. For all their sakes the kindest thing was to tell the truth at once.

He was not quite prepared, however, for his father's manner of taking the blow. The marquis, sitting at the desk, heard him without a word, and when he had finished sat quite still for some time, shading his eyes with one hand.

"Does she know?" he asked, at last.

"Yes." There had been no mention of Marguerite, or of any motive for the course which René was taking; but a pretence of not understanding would have been childish.

"Have you succeeded in getting her consent?"

"No, I must do without it."

"Have you told Henri?"

"No, nor aunt. I wanted you to know before I tell them."

"Can I be of any use to you by being present when you tell them?"

"It would be very good of you, sir. And . . . if you would keep them from worrying Marguerite after I go? She's taking it so awfully hard."

"I will do my best. They will want to know why you are going."

"I . . . don't want to talk about why."

"Naturally. Then, for the avoidance of future discussions, which might be very painful to Marguerite, shall we suggest ambition? An explorer's career is one of some fascination to a young man with his way to make in the world. Disappointed love might perhaps go down with your aunt; but it doesn't seem to fit you very well."

"Scarcely. Thank you, sir; yes, ambition will do. I'm not ambitious, but I might have been."

"Yes," the marquis answered; "most of us are not . . . various things we might have been."

He rose and leaned on the desk, supported by the spread finger-tips of both hands. The edge of the paper on which they rested fluttered a little.

"In case I should not see you again after you go — if anything should prevent your returning, for instance, or my staying — I should like you to know that I should have been . . . glad to be your brother, instead of your father. I might, perhaps, have been less conspicuous a failure in the part, and I should certainly have appreciated any fraternal feeling you might have bestowed on me. No doubt, though, you would have found me out, sooner or later. I have a fairly clear perception of some things. It is the prerogative of certain kinds of failures to see clearly. Shall we go to your aunt and Henri?"

They went downstairs, René struggling with an absurd tendency to choke. Never in his life had he felt himself quite such a callous brute; it seemed inhuman not to be able to say anything. And yet, what was there to say?

After that silent descent of the stairs, the protestations, entreaties, and tears which filled the next hour were easy to bear. Yet he was glad when bed-time came; it had been a tiring experience. "It's a bit too much to have all your teeth drawn in one evening," he murmured, as he tumbled into bed. "Even Isaac of York had only one a day pulled out."

Between then and the first of October it seemed to him that more teeth were pulled out than any man's head should contain. Every detail of his preparations was a fresh source of tears on his aunt's part, of furious opposition on that of Marguerite. The arrival of the formal document appointing "René François de Marteurelles, dit Martel," geographer, geologist, and meteorologist to "the expedition for the exploration of the northwest tributaries of the Upper Amazon, under the command of Colonel Duprez," raised a storm

in the household. The marquis alone had nothing
to say.

Uncle Harry came from England to see his
nephew, and after spending three weeks in the
château, returned to Gloucestershire, puzzled
and sad. "I don't know what's the matter with
them all," he said to his wife. "They're quite
friendly and pleasant; and you might as well be
picking your way among egg-shells all the time.
That crippled girl's eyes follow you about the place
as if she hated everyone that comes near her
brother. And Étienne! He entertains them all
politely, and makes cheerful conversation, with
a face as if there were a ghost behind his shoulder.
I tried to get out of the boy what is making him
go, but he only looked at me. There's something
tragic underneath, I'm convinced. He used to
be such a straightforward, jolly lad."

René, indeed, had taken refuge in silence. He
had arrived at feeling that anything would be
more endurable than this period of waiting. He
counted the days till the first of October; by
then the wrench would be over, and he would be
able to fix his mind on his work. Yet when the
actual time of parting came, it seemed to him
that he was quite unprepared, that he had not
realized at all what the last interview with Marguerite would be like. She had maintained to
the end her irreconcilable opposition; now, when

the day had come, she abandoned useless argument and entreaty, and merely clung to him, too desperate for speech.

He got out of the room somehow, and stumbled through the other farewells, feeling like a thing made of wood. Henri accompanied him as far as Marseilles, the marquis having made a trivial excuse to stay behind and fulfil his promise of protecting Marguerite from Angélique's caresses and tears. Had he but known it, his careless: "No, I think you had better go instead of me, Henri; I have been troubled with rheumatism lately," brought him nearer than he had been at any time in the last seven years to winning back René's lost affection.

*   *   *   *   *   *

The harbour lights of Marseilles faded in grey distance. René went down into his cabin, whistling a cheerful tune. Happily, he had plenty to do. He was learning Spanish, and had determined to spend five hours a day in studying it during the voyage. What with that, and all his work to prepare, and a diary to keep for Marguerite, the ship would have rounded the Horn before he would have time to mope.

Meanwhile, being an excellent sailor, he soon found his time fully occupied in unpacking and arranging for sea-sick companions, and by his thoughts in taking mental notes of their charac-

ters. By the time the African coast was left behind, he had learned something of the men whose
life he was to share. Had he failed to do so, it
would certainly not have been for want of information. The difficulty, indeed, was to get a
chance of forming any independent and unbiassed
opinion of his fellow-explorers, amid the mass of
gossip about each other which they poured into
his ears. No sooner did he settle down on deck
in the mornings with his Spanish grammar and
dictionary, than the fat voice of Stéger, the Alsatian botanist, would slide in among the strings of
verbs that he was laboriously committing to
memory.

"Have you ever seen anything like the cheek
of those two puppies? It's as good as a play to
watch them show off."

"What puppies?" René would murmur with
his eyes on the verbs.

"Why, the subalterns. They're so cocky over
having got furlough to join us that they think
themselves full-blown explorers. They'd never
have got it if de Vigne hadn't been nephew to
the Minister of War. The scamp persuaded his
uncle old Duprez couldn't get along without him
and his dear friend Bertillon. Good Lord!
Bertillon, that was making mud-pies and getting spanked by his nurse when Duprez retired
from service!"

"Scarcely so lately as that."

"Let me tell you, my dear fellow, our respected commander's no chicken. He won't see fifty-five again, and between ourselves, he'd have been better employed airing his orders and his memories of Austerlitz in the Tuileries Gardens than trying to head an expedition to the Jivaro country. In the place we're going to, it's more important to have the inside of your head shine than the outside of your waistcoat, and poor old Duprez is none too well furnished with brains. Well, he makes up for it in dignity. Did you hear him come down on Lortigue the other day for omitting to say 'Mon Colonel' in addressing him? If he knew what they all call him when his back's turned! 'Le Pion.' Not bad, is it?"

So the stream of tittle-tattle would flow on till René made an excuse to go below. He did not want to hurt Stéger's feelings, but he was not in the least interested in the commander's little weaknesses, and he did want to get on with his grammar. Once, retiring between decks to escape from Stéger, he was fastened on by the two subalterns and the big Gascon, Lortigue, whose passion for sport had brought him out to risk his life for jaguar skins. The great, contented, vigorous animal, well-fed and well-groomed, came lounging up at the sight of René's close-cropped head, parting lips too red over teeth too white behind the glossy black moustache, in cheerful welcome of a brother athlete.

"Got away from Choucrôute, have you?" he asked, mimicking Stéger's heavy German accent. "No easy job, eh? It sticks fast, that sort of thing, with its mouth all full of dough and its slack muscles. Why, there comes Guillaumet, out at last. Pah! the creature's like a blow-fly maggot! I declare, Martel, except you and me and the two boys here, there's scarcely a man among us with a decent biceps. What a crew to explore a savage country!"

"Come!" said René; "it's not so bad as that. Perhaps M. Guillaumet doesn't look quite hard enough for the life, but one can never tell beforehand, and the others are certainly all right. I should think Stéger would stand roughing it as well as most people; and the commander's wiry enough. As for Dr. Marchand, he looks as if sheer energy would carry him through anything."

"Oh, Marchand! That's quite another tale. If he could keep off the drink, Marchand would be a great man. They say he was one of the best doctors in Paris before that miserable business. Fancy throwing away a fine career like that, just for a silly woman!"

René frowned.

"I know nothing about Dr. Marchand's pri-

vate concerns. Have you read his book on ethnology? It's very interesting."

"Is it?" said Lortigue, yawning. "Well, as I
was saying, when he found his wife's lover . . ."

"I am sorry to interrupt you," said René in
his clearest tones; "but I think the colonel wants
me."

As he walked away, Dr. Marchand's great,
grey, lion head appeared at the top of the hatch-
way stair, and Lortigue, unabashed, advanced to
meet him.

"Hullo, doctor! Has Guillaumet done with
being sea-sick? What will you bet we shall be
nursing him all the way across the Andes, for one
thing or another?"

The ethnologist, balancing a heavy body on
small feet, glanced sullenly at the three idlers from
under shaggy brows.

"Get to work!" he snarled for all answer. The
subalterns laughed, quite good-humoured.

"Why should we work, doctor? We can't all
be Martel."

"No, don't you wish you could?" said Marchand, and turned to look after René. "But you
can get something to do. One can see you don't
know the tropics. If you lounge on deck all day
long, picking your neighbours' affairs to pieces"
— his eyes opened wide, sudden and piercing,
then half closed again — "you'll be as flabby as

Guillaumet himself by the time we reach the Napo."

"Not I," said Lortigue. "No flabbiness in me when once I get to shooting-ground."

"Nor in Bertillon or me," said de Vigne. "We came out for sport."

Marchand's stern mouth relaxed into a grin. It did not make him look any more amiable.

"Came out for sport, did you? Well, well, my little dears, by all accounts you're likely to get your fill of it before we see home again. Guillaumet came for sport too, he tells me."

"Guillaumet? Why, he doesn't know the stock of a gun from the barrel. Everybody knows why he came; because his father half financed the expedition just to get him out of Brussels till the scandal had blown over about Mme. . . ."

"Scandal again!" Marchand interrupted. "Eh, my lads, have you no room in those empty pates of yours for anything but other folks' business? Leave that sort of talk to Guillaumet; it's good enough for the likes of him."

The boys burst out laughing merrily, with a fine display of healthy young teeth.

"And you, grandpapa, leave preaching to the Colonel; it's good enough for the likes of him."

"The colonel's worth fifty of you all," Marchand muttered, and shouldered roughly past

them. He had the manners of a bear, and the
gift of making everyone pardon him.

In the evening he came up to René, who was
leaning over the deck-rail watching the glittering
fringe of spray sweep backwards from the ship.

"It's not as bad as all this really, you know,"
he began without any preamble, between two
puffs of his pipe. René looked round.

"Yes, yes, my lad, you know what I mean,
discreet as you are," Marchand went on, nodding
at him over the pipe. "But when you've kicked
about the world as much as I have, you'll know
that most men have better stuff in them than
they show on the voyage out. Just now you see
them at a disadvantage; their friends, and especially their friends' sisters, have been telling them
they're heroes, so naturally they can't do anything but loaf and gossip and make idiots of
themselves. They'll be all right as soon as there's
trouble."

He stopped, with his startling, keen gaze on
René's face.

"There will be trouble, you know?"

"I suppose it's a dangerous piece of country?"

"Well, the Jivaro Indians are not easy folk to
deal with. But the Colonel knows his trade. I've
been out with him before. Yes, and the boys are
all right too. If only we weren't saddled with
Guillaumet. . . . Still, on the whole, they're

good fellows enough, and they'll stand by each other at a pinch, for all the rubbish they talk. You feel a bit sick at it all just now; that's natural. But they'll settle down in another month or two, and do their work and let you do yours. How's the Spanish?"

The abrupt question pulled René up. He had been speculating how Marchand knew that he was feeling "a bit sick at it all."

"Middling," he answered. "I haven't much head for languages; but no doubt I shall manage it in time. What are we going to do about the native tongues, doctor? Is there anyone among us that knows them?"

"Unluckily, there isn't. We shall have to depend on a lot of slimy half-castes to interpret; that's the nuisance of it. We shall engage our guides and carriers in Quito, so, to get on with them, we must find someone who talks Quichua. Then, for the interior, we shall want an interpreter who knows Tupi-Guarani, and he ought to have at least a smattering of Jivaro. The worst of interpreters is that they always desert when anything goes wrong. I wonder why people that know languages are mostly such a worthless lot. The interpreters were the worst bother we had in the Atlas mountains."

"You were out there with Colonel Duprez, weren't you?"

"Yes. This is my third expedition. I suppose I shall stick to exploring now, for the rest of my time. We were in Abyssinia before."

"Together?"

"Yes; it's only through Duprez I took to exploring. We're old friends; we were at school together. Take us back thirty years or so and we were like the two cubs there; just as inseparable and just as pleased with ourselves and the world. Good night; I'm going to turn in."

He sheered off with his heavy obstinate slouch; and, passing the two subalterns, who were chattering and giggling together as usual, made Bertillon jump out of his seat by a careless tap on the shoulder from electric finger-tips.

"Having a good time, boys?"

"Hullo, grandpapa!" said de Vigne. "Come and take a hand at *écarté*, will you?"

But Marchand was gone. René, still leaning on the deck-rail watching the foam, heard Bertillon say: "Let him alone; he's in the blues tonight. Didn't you see him shove the wine aside at dinner? Anyway, I must go down too; I never made out that copy of the ammunition list."

There seemed to be no getting away from Dr. Marchand's private affairs. René had heard a good deal about them in Paris; but he took little interest in sensational gossip at any time, and,

I

after learning that the doctor was to be one of his fellow-explorers, had carefully avoided further enlightenment.   This did not prevent various fragments of the story from reaching his ears one night, when Guillaumet, lying in the berth above him, retailed them for Stéger's benefit, to an accompaniment of indignant interruptions from Bertillon, who declared it "disgusting piggishness" to make fun of things of that sort. Lortigue chimed in with corrections, and they contradicted each other roundly over the facts, which none of them knew in full, or would have understood had they known.

In earlier life Marchand was an eminent brain specialist in Paris. He had inherited a fortune from his thrifty, hard-headed, hard-working father, a shopkeeper of Amiens, whose useful gift for technical invention had blossomed, in the son, into true scientific imagination. The practice brought big fees and growing fame, and Marchand, with his pride of intellect and lower middle-class Picard blood, valued both; but always more and more of his time was given to original research. An impassioned worker, absorbed in his unfinished discovery, he was long regarded as a typical example of the callous and successful scientific brute that cares for nothing but money and vivisection. His utter disregard of the feelings of rabbits and guinea-pigs was notorious in

Paris; the fact that certain experiments which needed a human subject had been tried on himself with equal thoroughness escaped popular knowledge.

Curiously enough, the most drastic of these had nothing to do with his discovery; it belonged to his student days, and to the investigations of a famous surgeon, Professor Lemprière, in whose research laboratory he was working at the time. When the professor had interfered to cut short an experiment for which it seemed to him that his junior assistant was paying too much, the ill-mannered and ungainly youth had jammed his hat sulkily on to his head and walked out of the laboratory, muttering uncomplimentary remarks about "sentimental idiots that shirk." He had then shut himself up alone, and "got on with the job."

When the results thus obtained were ready for publication, he had driven a spluttering and heavy pen through his name on the professor's title-page; not from any lack of arrogance, or any doubt of the value, to an ambitious beginner, of the words: "By Claude Lemprière and Raoul Marchand"; but on grounds of strict logic: "unless you mean to decorate your title-page with the names and virtues of all the guinea-pigs." He remained unresponsive to the almost parental affection with which the professor and his wife repaid what, in the innocence of their hearts, they regarded as his heroic and generous self-sacrifice. He liked the Lemprières well enough, but the element of personal emotion which they had introduced into the matter bored him. His interest had been in the problem for its own sake.

When over forty he amazed himself by falling deeply in love with a convent-bred orphan girl half his age. After their marriage she rapidly developed into a leader of Parisian society; her social gifts were undoubtedly remarkable. Her husband, at first but scornfully tolerant of the shifting crowd of young men who buzzed about her, became instantly and gravely respectful when she explained to him that her object in having a salon was to help young doctors to a wider mental outlook, by bringing them into contact with the finest minds in the profession. He did not think Célestine's intellectual mission to the lower ranks of medicine likely to bring her anything except disappointment; but he was too earnest a worker himself to despise any genuine experiment, however absurd or childish, tried by a very young person. "She has the right to make her own mistakes, and learn by them. She'll find those tame poodles out in time; and, meanwhile, if Ferrand or any of the rest of them tries to be impudent, I shall be here to protect her."

Célestine claimed no protection and confided no disappointments. That inscrutable reserve

of manner which from the first had set her, in his
eyes, apart from other women, remained unchanged by all the vicissitudes of Parisian life,
by marriage and by motherhood. Even the
death of her child did not wring from her a sign
of emotion; and Marchand, who had begun by
only loving her as a woman, learned to respect her
as a human being. He, too, had shown no grief,
and he knew what his self-control had cost him.
The touch of the tiny fingers, when he had slipped
a daisy into them secretly before the coffin-lid was
closed, had shaken him, for a moment, out of his
self-confidence. That was his first experience of
the unknown, real Raoul Marchand, whose deep
inherent melancholy he had overlaid with so
much scientific curiosity and so much professional
success.

Shortly afterwards she asked him to think of
her, in future, as a sister, since she did not wish
ever to have another child. He took the sentence
quietly enough; it was Marchand's way to meet
pain quietly; but he loved her, and sheer pressure of work had kept his life so chaste that his
maturity retained the passionate vehemence of
youth. The longing for a son of his own ached in
him like a bruise; just at first he could not find
breath to answer her. "I know I can trust you to
understand," she murmured softly; and at that
he turned, and patted her shoulder as a father

might have done. "Oh yes, my dear, I understand."

He locked himself into the study, and fought
his battle out alone. Then he put his own hurt
aside, to ponder how he might comfort Célestine.
She must have taken the baby's death harder
even than he had guessed. In the night a shy
hope crept into his mind: the dear discovery
was like a child to him; if she too could learn to
know and love it, might it not console her as it
consoled him? But when he tried to tell her of
his experiments, a shock of icy horror froze his
tongue; he had felt the same frightful sensation,
though more slightly, the first time that he held
her in his arms. Before he could speak again,
she was talking placidly of trifles. He pulled
himself up sharply. "This won't do," he thought;
"I must take more exercise. A brain specialist
can't afford to have the jumps. I'm an egotis-
tical fool, anyway. How should she be interested?
It's not my child the poor soul wants; it's her
own."

"Raoul," she said to him the next week; "you
began to tell me something about your work. Do
you think there is anything I could do for you?
Copying, for instance, or sorting your notes?"
He was silent, and she added under her breath:
"I think, perhaps, it might help me."

Marchand stooped and kissed her hand. There

were tears in his eyes. He had thought her indifferent; and see, she had but been protecting him against herself, lest he might give her his pearl before she was sure that she could wear it worthily.

For three months she acted as his confidential secretary; in the fourth her interest flagged. A little later the sleek young doctor whose colleagues spoke of him as "that cur Ferrand, that blackmails women," jumped into easy notoriety by bringing out a book containing a garbled version of the theory after which Marchand had been patiently groping for years. Many records of observations had been stolen outright; and, though their bearing was but imperfectly understood by the thief, his book met with enough success to clear his path towards a fashionable practice, soon rendered lucrative by his admirable bedside manner.

Finding that her lover's unskilfulness in manipulating the information supplied by her had betrayed its source, Célestine at first feared that her husband might cause a public scandal, or make a fuss about the paternity of the baby, which, as it happened, had been really his own, and which, anyhow, was dead, and no longer a nuisance. Hitherto her boundless contempt for a person so easily fooled had kept her from noticing details about him; now, when he entered her room with

Ferrand's book, she looked at the still hand holding the open page, and wondered that she had not
seen before how strong it was. Sudden terror
seized her, lest the desecration of his domestic
hearth might rouse even this dull clod to strangle
her. The desecration of his unborn work was too
light a thing to trouble her memory.

He made no fuss and asked no questions. He
explained to her, quite kindly, that he considered
it more satisfactory for them not to meet again;
that she would receive half of his very comfortable
income, with unrestricted liberty to live where,
how, and with whom she pleased; and that he was
prepared to corroborate whatever version of the
cause of separation she might think fit to circu-
late. Having made these points clear, he retired
to his study; and, while she packed her dresses,
employed himself in burning his manuscripts.
He made a clean sweep of them; not all his work
had been stolen, but all must have been handled.
With the papers went into the fire certain wee
pink and white woollen boots which had been
locked away in a private drawer. Even the baby
had been Célestine's; the identity of the other
parent mattered little. Three days later he was
picked up in the street opposite the Palais Royal
in a state of helpless and swinish drunkenness.

Célestine was thus spared the necessity of cir-
culating any story at all. Everybody understood

how much she must have suffered in silence before her husband's secret vice drove her to the
extreme measure of leaving his house; no one
need wonder, now, at her unyouthful reserve.
General indignation was felt at the cruelty of old
Professor Lemprière and his wife, who cut her
dead by tacit mutual consent, and offered no explanation to anyone. Indeed, they had none to
offer; Marchand was inaccessible even to his best
friends, and they held no clue to the riddle. Yet
the professor had partly guessed it. He was quite
sure that no habitual drunkard could do such
work; and scarcely less sure that Ferrand could
not have written that book unaided. Mme.
Lemprière acted on instinct merely; it was enough
for her that she could always trust Marchand, and
that from the first she had shivered when Célestine
approached her.

But in all the large circle of acquaintance these
two were the sole exceptions. From everyone
else Célestine received much sympathy; and accepted it discreetly, with a pathetic lowering of
her crystalline and candid eyes. The only thing
which she was ever heard to say about the subject
was that people meant kindly, but that it hurt
her when they spoke against the man who, "whatever he might be," had been the father of her dead
child. As for Marchand, he drank as if he would
drink himself to death: there were moments

when he was as dangerous to approach as a caged wild beast. Professor Lemprière, undeterred alike by torrents of foul abuse and by a bottle flung at his head, made several brave attempts at rescue; and gave up the struggle in despair.

After nine weeks Colonel Duprez came to Paris, and heard of the scandal with which the town was still ringing. He at once went to the house, comforting the terror-stricken servants by the mere sight of his military gait and cross of honour, and forced his way into the den of what had been Marchand.

Its horrors appalled him less than they would have done a more imaginative person. He had seen other men mad drunk in his time; noting, with a practised eye, the impossibility of grappling with such strength and fury, he coolly fetched more brandy, and waited outside the door till the unclean rage passed into unclean sleep. Then he took up his station in the room; and, hour after hour, sat patient and soldierly, mounting guard over the sodden heap that snored on the bed.

Late in the evening Marchand woke, shameful to behold, but sane enough to recognize his visitor.

"Raoul," said the colonel in his regimental voice; "I start for Abyssinia on the sixteenth of next month, and take you with me. You will begin to prepare your outfit immediately."

Marchand, still prostrate on the bed, slowly put up both hands behind his neck and looked the decorated uniform up and down with a sullen gleam of bleared eyes.

"You always were a fool," he murmured wearily; "but even you might manage to see when a man's damned."

"I can see when a man's my friend," said Duprez.

Sick and bedraggled as he was, Marchand flared up at this. And what the hell did the thick-headed popinjay mean by calling itself his friend?

"Not your friend!" cried the colonel, forgetting his Olympian composure. "Why, I thrashed you when you were six!"

A vision passed before the drunkard's eyes: a bleak and foggy morning, and a mite in blouse and new school satchel trotting past the great cathedral steps, straining short legs to keep pace with the big boy who might thump him on occasion, but who wouldn't let the others do it. The colonel, again professional dignity personified, waited in stolid silence.

"All right, Armand," came at last in a whisper.

Marchand returned from Abyssinia apparently cured, and published some valuable ethnological observations; but he broke out again, no one knew why, and went abroad with Duprez a second time. After that he kept from the drink, and, as his blemished reputation rendered private practice no longer possible, drudged at hospital work; while his wife cultivated Christian resignation, in the becoming and elegant half-mourning suited to her widowed state. Ferrand's ascendancy over her had become so great that all her other lovers were discarded; every social connection which she could muster was made use of for his advantage. "Dr. Ferrand has been like a brother to me," she would say to wealthy invalids; "with all that great practice and all his research work he finds time to think of cheering a lonely woman. It's not till one is in real trouble that one learns how much kindness there is in the world."

His success assured, he deserted her for a rich bride; and she revenged herself by pouring out the truth from the witness-box of a court of justice, which she had entered on a frivolous pretext. Had murder not seemed to her underbred and disagreeable, she would probably have poisoned him; being physically fastidious, she preferred to destroy the career which she had herself built up, and leave him to drag out a penurious and dishonoured existence.

The next morning Marchand, who lived alone and seldom read the newspapers, wondered why everyone at the hospital, from doctors to doorkeeper, looked at him with a timid commiseration.

Presently a junior physician stumbled through a few hurried words of sympathy. Marchand laid down the stethoscope; for an instant his lightning glance swept over the faces of his colleagues.

"Something for me in the morning papers, eh? Let me see."

They stared at each other, aghast.

"The paper!" he flashed out; and the *Presse* was brought in haste.

They held their breath while he read the report of the trial. When he had finished, he turned back to the beginning and read it through again. Suddenly he tossed the sheet to the shrinking junior.

"Well, if you've got time to waste on newspaper gossip, I haven't! Who put on that poultice?"

There were both nurses and patients in tears by the time his round of the wards was finished, but never had the quality of his work been finer. No one again ventured to offer any verbal sympathy; but when he left the building, Professor Lemprière followed him into the courtyard, and silently laid a hand on his sleeve. He flung it off with a furious oath, shoved the old man aside, and went out at the gate like an angry bull, with his head down. At his own door he was met by a messenger, who summoned him to the Morgue to identify his wife's body. She had completed her work by throwing herself into the river.

"All right," he said carelessly. "Get along and tell them I'm coming."

Long after dusk he reached the Morgue, too drunk to identify anything.

For six weeks he was almost continuously drunk; then, hearing that Duprez had undertaken the command of an expedition to the Amazon, he volunteered to join as physician and ethnologist.

Guillaumet's version of what he knew of this story was somewhat modified by his idea of its humorous possibilities. Seen from his point of view, Marchand appeared as a supremely comic figure. René, unwillingly overhearing, discarded certain highly-coloured details as due to the peculiar personality of the narrator; and, thinking over what he had heard in Paris, decided that one point, at least, was clear: if Colonel Duprez had succeeded in dealing with such a situation, he must be less of a fool than he looked.

This was hardly fair; the commander did not even look altogether like a fool. Years of danger and responsibility had given to his eyes a grave directness of expression which the conscious dignity of the mouth could not nullify. His carriage would have been really fine had he not tried to make it so; when he could forget Amiens and the little grocer's shop which his father had kept there, he looked what he was: a man who had both done much work that was good and punished much that was bad.

René had begun by disliking him, for no better reason than the way in which he spoke to the servants, and the disappointment he had shown because the marquis had not come to Marseilles. His passion for the aristocracy was so childlike and sincere that it might have been pardoned; but the elaborate politeness to Henri, following immediately upon the cutting off of a half-franc from the pay of a porter who had dropped a trunk, set René's teeth on edge.

"M. de Marteurelles," said the commander one morning after breakfast; "would you do me the favour to come into my cabin for half an hour? I wish to talk to you about a few points connected with your duties."

"Whenever you like, colonel," said René, rising. "Shall I come now?"

As they walked to the cabin together, he added: "By the way, I'd rather be called 'Martel,' if you don't mind. Yes; my people keep to the old name, but I was brought up in England, and I've got used to the contraction. I was called 'Martel' at school, you see."

The commander turned light steel-coloured eyes upon him with cold disapproval.

"I hope you do not drop a historic name in consequence of any . . . subversive modern ideas?"

"It has nothing to do with ideas of any sort," René answered. "It's just a matter of habit."

Annoyed as he was, he had no thought of administering a personal rebuke; the immediate wilting of the colonel's dignity made him feel uncomfortable.

They talked for some time of nothing but work, and René soon found that a good deal more than he had undertaken was to be quietly shifted on to his shoulders.

"Dr. Marchand tells me you are studying Spanish," said the colonel. "That is well; it will be most useful to you. But you will soon pick it up when we land; and meanwhile I think it would be a better preparation to employ the time in acting as my secretary. There is a good deal to be done, and it will be excellent practice for you."

René was silent a moment. This was more than he had bargained for; but it was no use to begin by offending the commander under whom he was to serve.

"I thought," he said at last, "that M. Guillaumet had arranged to . . ."

"M. Guillaumet certainly joined us on that understanding, but I do not find his talents adapted to secretarial tasks. It is true that they are not strictly within your province, M. Martel; but it would be a convenience to me if you would take his place."

"As you like, colonel," René answered rather stiffly. He did not mind the extra work; it was good to have plenty to do; but he wished the colonel had said straight out at once: "I'm in a difficulty, will you help me?"

When he left the cabin, Guillaumet was coming downstairs, followed by Marchand. The Belgian's pale eyes narrowed malevolently at the sight of René.

"Ah, M. de — Marteurelles, is it? So you are preparing to act as the colonel's secretary, I hear? Well, I wish you joy!"

"Thank you, M. Guillaumet," René answered, looking him in the eyes. "I am called 'Martel,' if you please."

As he stood aside to let the older man pass, he heard a spiteful murmur behind him: "Milord is on the high horse this morning!" and Marchand's answering growl: "Keep away from its heels, then, you fool!"

He glanced round, and Marchand met his eyes with a brilliant smile and a shrug of the shoulders. He laughed and nodded in answer, ran up on deck and shook himself like a big wet dog.

"Brrr . . . what air! And what a voice. . . ."

Then he laughed again, restored to good humour by the memory of Lortigue's exclamation: "Pah! The creature's like a blow-fly maggot!"

K

CHAPTER IV

"WHY, grandpapa, what on earth is wrong now?" asked Bertillon, looking up from the bag he was unpacking. "Not another mule gone over the precipice?"

They were shivering in a wretched hut on the pass. Icy rain beat on the roof and the huge rock walls above. The wind, blowing down from the glaciers, entered at every chink; to men who had just come up from the stifling swamps by Guayaquil, it seemed like the edge of a knife.

Marchand only snorted contemptuously at the question.

"Mule?" cried Lortigue. "I'd send somebody else over the precipice if I had my way. Just think of it, boys; that flabby rascal has deserted!"

De Vigne opened his eyes wide.

"Deserted! Who? The Maggot?"

The name had stuck to Guillaumet; he was now seldom referred to, behind his back, otherwise than as "l'Asticot."

"No such luck," Marchand muttered with his back to them, stooping to warm his hands at a smoky fire.

"No, no!" Lortigue answered impatiently. "The interpreter, of course. Sneaked out in the night; gone to join those fellows with the pack-mules that we met yesterday, I suppose."

"But why . . ."

"Oh, no doubt somebody's been frightening him with tales of the Jivaros. Anyway, he's gone."

"And what are we going to do, doctor?"

Marchand shrugged his shoulders.

"Just go back to Quito and engage another."

"Back to Quito!" Both subalterns were on their feet in an instant. "What, down that fiendish gorge again? Oh, good Lord! That's a bit too much!"

"It's nothing out of the way," Marchand answered coolly. "Interpreters always desert if they can; it's their nature. We must make the next one understand we shall wring his neck if he tries on any tricks."

"But to get down . . ."

"Only one or two of us need go back, of course; the rest will wait here with the beasts and baggage."

Lortigue glanced round the hut with a grimace.

"Pleasant hotel to wait in for a week!"

The commander thought at first of sending Marchand back with two natives, and waiting for him encamped in some sheltered spot, if any such could be found, on the mountain-side. Then it was discovered that some of the provisions supplied to the expedition by Quito dealers were unfit for food. This decided Colonel Duprez to have all stores thoroughly examined before Marchand started, in order that any mistakes or frauds might be rectified. The investigation disclosed such a state of things that he resolved to go back to Quito himself. At this juncture a horse and several mules were found to be suffering from infectious disease.

"MM. Martel, Lortigue, and Stéger," he said, coming into the hut at nightfall; "kindly prepare yourselves to start with me for Quito early to-morrow morning. The rest of you, gentlemen, will remain here and wait for us, under the command of Dr. Marchand."

The ethnologist took him by the arm and drew him out into the pelting rain.

"Well, you'll have one man that will work without being made to, that's something. As you're going, you'd better take Guillaumet along with you."

"Guillaumet? But you are joking! We had all we could do to drag him up the gorge."

"We shall have more than we can do to drag him across the interior. Something's got to be done with him; we can't very well throw him over the cliffs, and if we leave him behind by force, his people will make a row. The only way out of it is to frighten him into deserting of his own will. If we pull him up and down these hills a bit, just as a preliminary, perhaps he'll find the climate of home is better for him, eh?"

"I should have thought, Raoul," said the colonel, severely, "that you knew me too well, after all these years, to think I would lend myself to such a scheme."

Marchand grinned at him, unabashed. "My good Armand, of course I do! When did you ever lend yourself to any of my nefarious schemes? He shall stay behind with me; and if he tumbles into the torrent in your absence, it won't be you that will be responsible. My reputation's gone, anyhow."

The colonel made no answer to this, but presently returned to the hut alone and included Guillaumet in the marching orders. To everyone's surprise the "Maggot" raised no objection. A belated coast steamer had caused the expedition to miss the monthly European mail, which would doubtless have arrived by now, and Guillaumet hoped for a favourable answer to the letter which he had sent from Valparaiso, imploring his father to let him go back to Brussels.

After two days of exhausting struggle against wet rocks and swollen torrents, the colonel's little group reached Cumbayá, at the head of the Quito

Valley, where they accepted the hospitality of
a friendly official, the place being within an easy
ride of the town. René tumbled into bed, bruised
and aching from head to foot, yet grateful to the
deserter, but for whom he would have had to
miss the precious home letters.

To engage another interpreter proved a difficult
matter. The mere words: "Pastassa River"
were enough to frighten away applicants. Lately
one of the wild Jivaro tribes, exasperated by the
interference of whites and the dishonesty of
"civilized" Canelos Indians, had raided a mission-
station as low down as the Napo, and the few
survivors of the massacre had carried panic with
them across the Andes. "Man-eating" and
"devil-worshipping" monsters stalked through
the popular imagination, hideous in war-paint
and feathers, boars' tusks driven through their
upper lips, and blackened heads of Christians at
their girdles.

The offer of pay in advance only changed the
nature of the difficulty. Applicants now began
to pour in by the dozen; but it was evident that
they intended merely to secure the money and
desert at the first opportunity, and few of them
would have been worth keeping had they wished
to stay. The colonel's time was fully occupied
with fraudulent shop-keepers and horse-dealers;
so, as Marchand had foreseen, the task of sifting

the riff-raff of Quito fell upon René. Lortigue, Stéger, and Guillaumet, meanwhile, amused themselves in their several ways; one with a horse and gun, one with a pipe and hammock, and one with a handsome quadroon.

The belated letters arrived on the fourth day. Guillaumet, receiving from his father a stern refusal to take him back till he had retrieved his character, sank into a state of apathetic dejection. For René there were affectionate farewells from Angélique, Henri, and the English relatives; a few quiet lines from the marquis, telling him that Marguerite had already started on her preliminary treatment; an ill-spelt scrawl from Jacques, written in the name of all the servants and several of the country folk at Marteurelles; and from Marguerite herself a cheerful diary, full of family news, extracts from the books she had been reading, thoughts about Greek poetry and eighteenth-century French prose. A bit of paper containing some dried blossoms of sweet marjoram fell from between the sheets.

As he put the flowers back, he saw that a few words were scribbled in a shaky hand across the inside of the paper:

"Oh, René, René, don't get killed — Think, if you never come back to me — What shall I do — what shall I do?"

He was still holding the letter in his hand when

the impudent face of a half-caste servant named
José looked in at the door.

"Some more interpreters, sir."

He roused himself with an effort, and the daily
grind began again. This morning José introduced
more impossible candidates even than yesterday's
set; dirty, drunken, incompetent, and insolent.
For three hours René sifted patiently; he was
feeling irritable and depressed, a rare thing with
him, and was the more careful not to let himself
be betrayed into speaking sharply. Presently
he was called to the colonel, and found that, the
rain having stopped for the moment, their host
had proposed a shooting-party. Lortigue was
eager to go, but the colonel hesitated, urging the
necessity of getting their business done and returning to the pass.

As usual, it was René who offered to stay behind
and interview interpreters and tradesmen. He
was growing used to having Lortigue's and
Stéger's work thrust upon him; and found it
easier to meet exploitation halfway than to assert
himself against persons whom he disliked.

"You are indefatigable, M. Martel," said the
colonel. "I shall feel quite at ease with you in
charge."

The barely perceptible lift of René's eyebrows
made him look, for a moment, like his father.
When the pleasure-seekers had gone, he went

back into the other room, and, with a hand in his pocket feeling over Marguerite's letter, tried to fix his mind on the praises of the next applicant, which José poured into his ears.

"The right man at last, sir. I know him well; he comes from my village. Speaks three, four, six languages; and of an honesty . . ."

"What has he paid you?" René put in, smiling.

"Me? But nothing! But, I assure you . . ."

"Well, bring him in."

The paragon turned out to be a villainous half-caste of no linguistic accomplishments, and was soon dismissed. As he was slinking out of the house, Lortigue, whose gun had proved defective, galloped back to fetch another; and, with a vigorous outcry, seized him by the shoulder.

"Here, some of you boys! Hold him tight!"

"What's the matter?" René asked, coming out at the noise.

"Oh, Martel, where did you find him? That's the fellow that stole my cigar-case last night. Now then, my man, turn out your pockets!"

When a few spoons and other small articles had been taken from the dirty pockets, the thief was kicked out by Lortigue and allowed to go. René looked on, wincing. He knew that such persons did not particularly mind being kicked, and quite realized the absurdity of his own squeamishness: but scenes of this sort made him feel sick. He turned resignedly to the grinning boy.

"Well, José, is that a fair specimen of your village?"

"My village, sir? But I never set eyes on him before! They're honest folk in my village."

"You get a nice lot to deal with, Martel," Lortigue remarked, as he came out with the gun. "I'm glad I haven't your job. And that boy José doesn't seem much to boast of, either."

"Oh, he's no worse than any of the other folk round here; they're all alike," said René. He stood for a moment watching Lortigue ride away; then went back into the house and sat down. "I won't see any more of them till after lunch," he thought. "I must have one hour's rest from this sort of thing." He turned to call José.

"Be off, now!" an angry voice shouted just outside. "We don't want your sort hanging about here. You'll be stealing something next!"

José was evidently venting on some one his annoyance over the affair of the last applicant. A low voice answered him, quick and tremulous; René caught only the word "Interpreter."

"What next!" cried José, indignantly. "Why, if you'd seen him kick out a respectable, well-dressed man just now! And to suppose he'd see a ragamuffin like you!"

René lifted the curtain of the doorway.

"What's the matter, José? Is that another?"

"A scarecrow, sir! A real scarecrow. I knew you wouldn't wish to see him."

"It's not your business to judge. Where is he?"

"I sent him away, sir. I thought . . ."

"Well, another time, don't think; do as you're told. Just go and bring him back."

Then he remembered that he had lately scolded José for failing to think. He dropped the curtain and sat down again. "Oh, Lord!" he thought; "I'm getting like poor old Duprez! To speak that way to a servant who daren't answer me back. . . ."

The curtain of the doorway had been lifted and dropped again, quite noiselessly. René, looking round and seeing the applicant standing before it, sat up straight and opened his eyes. This was indeed a scarecrow.

After all, there really was some excuse for José; a more forlorn and draggled bit of human flotsam would have been difficult to find in all Ecuador. The very extremity of the creature's distress aroused disgust rather than pity. René looked down from filthy rags to bare and bloodstained feet; then up again at a deformed left arm, a half-naked shoulder so sharp that the outline of the bone showed through the skin, a tangle of black hair tumbling over the eyes of a famished wolf. A half-caste, of course; yet that mahogany skin seemed more tanned than naturally coloured, but surely no white man could be in such straits. "What on earth has happened to the fellow?" René thought; and looked again, with awakened curiosity, at the face. There was nothing to read on it but hunger. He shrugged his shoulders, and began the usual examination.

"Did you come to apply for the post of interpreter?"

The man had not spoken. He was standing still, holding the curtain and breathing rather quickly. He answered now, in a whisper: "Yes."

"What languages do you speak?"

"French, Spanish, English, Quichua, Guarani, and . . . several others."

René smiled. He was used to magnificent pretensions, and had usually found them dwindle, on investigation, to corrupt Spanish and a little broken Quichua.

"Have you ever been employed as an interpreter before?"

"Not regularly, but I have often had to translate for people. You would find me fairly quick."

His Spanish was certainly better than that of most half-castes, and his voice singularly gentle. Instead of the usual blatant and vulgar intonation, there was a hesitating softness about his speech.

René had no curiosity to test his French, and the interrogation continued in Spanish.

"What references have you?"

"I have none."

"What, no one that can speak for your honesty?

"No one knows me. I don't belong in this part of the country. I came up here from the south."

"But where have you come from now? Quito?"

"No, Ibarra."

"How did you get here?"

"There's a foot-path across the hills to Guallabamba. I heard you wanted . . ."

"From Ibarra! With your feet in that state? But it's sixty miles, man!"

"I . . . they were all right when I started; it's only the stones. The river is in flood."

René looked him sharply up and down.

"You crossed the hills in this weather? Alone?"

"I was afraid of being too late. This is nothing; it will soon get right again. I'm not so very lame, sir, generally; I could keep up quite well."

He had been standing in the doorway all this time; and now came hastily forward in his eagerness. He was certainly lame enough at this moment, whatever he might be generally; and he put a hand on the table to steady himself. René glanced down at it; he had noticed the

scarred left hand with stumps where two fingers
had been cut off, but this was the right, and un-
injured. He looked for the blue stain that marks
the half-caste's finger-nails.

"Why, he's white!" he thought, with surprise.
The hand was sunburnt almost to coffee-colour,
but it was impossible to mistake the finger-nails;
there was no dark blood there.

"And such a high-bred hand," was René's next
puzzled thought. "He can't belong properly
among the tramp crew. I wonder, is it drink
that's brought him to this? If not, we might do
worse than try him."

He looked more closely at the face. Its devouring intensity of expression arrested his attention; he found himself gazing at it with a sense
of discomfort, of startled annoyance. What had
the fellow got to look like that about? No, it
would never do; how could one saddle oneself
with a man that had such a face? He would be
cutting somebody's throat some night, or sneaking
out of camp to hang himself. It was uncanny.

"I'm sorry," he said; "but I scarcely think you
would suit us. We wanted a . . . a rather different sort of person."

Not one of all the rejected applicants but had
tried to move him by pleading, or arguing, or
protesting. Till now, not one. This man came
a step nearer, looked him straight in the eyes with

a wide and tragic gaze, and turned his back without a word.

"Stop a minute!" René cried out.

The man stopped with a sharp quiver of the thin shoulders, turned slowly, and stood still, looking on the ground.

"I won't decide finally without seeing the commander of the expedition," René went on. "Don't build any hopes on it; I don't think you would suit us, but you may as well wait and see him."

He was possessed by a ridiculous and miserable sense of shame, as if he had done some abominable thing, as if he had meanly struck a creature unable to strike back. "Confound the fellow!" he thought. "I can't help it if he is disappointed. It would be absurd to give him the post; he'd only fall ill and be a nuisance. He's sure to turn out dishonest, and I believe he's consumptive too."

The man raised his eyes suddenly from the ground. They were not black, as they had seemed at first, but of a rare colour, a very deep and vivid blue.

"If . . . if you can't take me as interpreter, sir, could you give me any other work? I could do . . ."

"There is no other work. We do everything ourselves, except what the Indians do."

He put the tips of his fingers up against his throat. He was again breathing quickly.

"For instance, as . . . porter?"

"Porter!" René was too much overcome with amazement to do more than repeat the word. A white man, an undoubtedly sick man, so lame, so footsore, with a crippled arm, asking to be taken on among natives to carry weights . . .

"I . . . I've done it before, sir; I know how to get on with Indians. And I'm a g-g-great deal stronger than I look, indeed, m-m-much stronger. . . ."

He had begun to stammer.

"Why, it's sheer starvation!" René thought, with a wave of compassion. "The poor devil! He must be far gone."

"Well," he said; "we'll see when the commander comes in. Meanwhile, you must be hungry. The servants are just going to have their lunch; you had better go out to them, and I'll see they give you some too. You'll find them under a big . . ."

He broke off, and sat staring. Even through the dark sunburn, he had seen the man turn white.

"Oh, don't trouble, thank you; I've just lunched."

It slipped out hastily in French; perfectly correct French, with an accent slightly foreign but as cultivated as his own. He jumped right off his seat.

"But you . . . you're a gentleman!"

"What's that to you?"

The answer flashed back at him with tigerish swiftness. Recalling the scene afterwards, he asked himself whether he had not, for one instant, been in danger of actual stabbing or throttling. But at the time he realized nothing; he only stared.

It was the applicant who broke the silence at last, by saying, very softly, but in a quite clear and steady voice: "I beg your pardon; I will go."

René caught him by the arm.

"No, no; wait! But it was all a mistake, can't you see? Oh, look here, stay and lunch with me!"

The instant they were uttered he saw that the trivial words had taken the significance of a capital reprieve. The man wheeled round and stared at him, quite breathless at first; then broke into a little spurt of laughter.

"Oh, thanks, it's very kind of you; but I . . ." He stopped and glanced at his rags. "How could I, you know, without a bath?"

The sudden quivering of his underlip made him look pitifully young.

"Well, that's easy enough to manage," René said, catching at the first loophole of escape from an impossible conversation. "Here, José!"

José appeared in the doorway, grinning at the prospect of a row. René turned to him with a sense of enormous relief.

L

"This gentleman would like a bath."

"Sir!" José gasped, and looked from one to the other.

"A warm bath, at once, in my room," René went on blandly. "Fetch some clean towels and plenty of water. I will wait lunch till the gentleman is ready." He led the stranger into his bedroom. "Will you come in here? I will find you toilet necessaries, and . . . oh, yes, you'll want some clothes."

He unlocked a bag and knelt before it, talking fast and keeping his eyes down.

"I'm afraid my things won't fit you; they're all too large. But you will manage somehow. Where are the socks gone? And a shirt, and . . . there, I think that's everything. I will wait for you in the other room."

He rose, leaving the key in the bag. "What an ass I am," went hammering through his head; "what a preposterous ass! He will steal everything he can lay hands on, of course, and it will serve me right. But what can one do?"

In the doorway he turned to say: "Call José if you want anything." Then he saw that the man was not listening to him, but leaning against the table, shaking helplessly. He came back, took him by the arm and made him sit down.

"You'd better have a drink," he said; and poured a little brandy from his hunting-flask.

The man pushed the cup away.

"No, it would go to my head; I've been . . . too long. . . ."

He sat up, putting the hair out of his eyes.

"It's nothing; please don't trouble."

René waited in the outer room, chafing at his own stupidity. To saddle himself with the company of a sick and starving adventurer, probably a criminal, obviously disreputable, avowedly used to consorting with natives; and all because the brute had a soft voice and fine eyes; it was little short of idiocy.

The stranger came out at last, transformed almost beyond recognition. Apart from his emaciation he was naturally a much smaller man than René, whose big clothes, hanging loosely on the slender limbs, made him look even younger and more fragile than he was. He seemed, indeed, scarcely more than a lad. His hair had been roughly trimmed and brushed back from his forehead, showing the singular beauty of the brow and eyes. As he limped across the floor and sat down, he looked horribly ill, so ill as to set René wondering whether he might not soon settle the question of what was to be done with him by dying; but, except evident bodily suffering and exhaustion, he seemed to have little in common with the tatterdemalion of an hour ago.

He apologized for keeping his host waiting so

long; and followed him into casual talk with the
air of a person taking refuge in it. His French
was a little rusty from disuse and quaintly full
of Latinisms, also he stammered a good deal;
but the quality of his voice gave a curious dignity to the halting speech. The slightly formal
locutions suggested much reading of the classics;
one might think he had been fed from childhood
on Pascal and Bossuet.

"But you are eating nothing," René exclaimed
presently. The guest pushed his plate away with
a shiver of repugnance.

"You must pardon me. One can't eat much
after starving."

René looked at him closely. "Then it was
actual starvation?"

"Ah, yes, but not so long; only three days, and
I had some bread at the beginning."

"What would you have done if you had missed
us?"

There was no answer. René went on hurriedly,
feeling tactless and awkward.

"I don't understand how you managed in the
hills at night."

The blue eyes turned suddenly black.

"You just get used to it. It's only . . . being
alone."

"But it must be bitterly cold, sleeping up there
in this wet."

"Oh, you don't sleep."

René rose from the table.

"Then hadn't you better lie down now and sleep till the commander comes back? You must be quite worn out. José can make you up a bed."

When the hunters came back at nightfall, the stranger had recovered his self-possession, and answered Duprez's questions in a clear unfaltering voice. He had been sleeping all the afternoon, and had been able to take a little more food.

The commander was in no pleasant humour. Lortigue had proved a better shot than he, and had then made matters worse by boasting all the way back. Also, the rain had set in again, and everyone was wet and tired. Colonel Duprez put on his glasses and looked the applicant over as a judge might look at a convicted criminal.

"M. Martel informs me that you have come across the hills from Ibarra, M. ——?"

"Rivarez."

"Rivarez? A Spanish name, I suppose?"

"I come from the Argentine."

"And . . . have been wandering about here, alone, and apparently in distress?"

"I took part in the fighting . . ."

"Against the Rosas despotism?"

"Yes; I got wounded and crippled, as you see, and was taken. Then I managed to escape on a trading vessel, and got to Lima. I hoped to find a friend there, and stay with him till I could communicate with my relatives. I had come away without any money; the pursuit was very hot. When I reached Lima, I found my friend had just sailed for Europe."

"When was that?"

"About nine months ago. I waited in Lima, supporting myself in any way I could, and got a letter taken down to Buenos Aires to my people, asking them to send me money at once. When the ship came back it brought me a message from an old servant that the house had been raided and burned by order of Rosas, and all my people murdered. Then I came up into Ecuador, hoping to get employment at the silver mines; and in Ibarra I heard you wanted an interpreter, so I came to offer myself for the post."

"How is it you speak the local tongues, if you are from the south?"

"I picked them up since I came here. Languages never give me any trouble."

"And your French?"

"I was educated by French Jesuits."

"Do you believe this rigmarole?" Stéger whispered to René. They were sitting together, listening to the interrogation. René frowned and made no answer. His private conviction was that the whole story was a tissue of falsehoods; and he was annoyed with the stranger for lying and with Stéger for detecting him, but most of all with himself for being annoyed. It was nothing to him.

"It must have been a very difficult matter to cross the hills with the torrents so swollen," Duprez went on suspiciously. "How long did it take you?"

"Four days."

René made an impatient movement. Confound the fellow! If he must lie, why could he not at least lie consistently? At lunch he had said "Three."

A flicker of the eyelids told him that his movement was noticed. Then the soft voice added: "Four days, was it? No, three."

The interrogation went on interminably, Duprez laying little obvious time-worn traps to catch imposture, and the stranger evading them all with hesitating voice and anxious eyes.

"Thank you, M. Rivarez," said Duprez at last. "I will trouble you to wait for a few minutes in the other room. You shall be called in presently to hear my decision."

The applicant went out, looking straight before him. Passing René, he glanced round swiftly; but René was staring down at his boots.

"Now, gentlemen," said Duprez, "I shall be glad to hear what impression this individual makes upon you all. As he is white and evidently a person of some education, it is clear that we cannot engage him unless we are prepared to let him eat and sleep with us; therefore, though the final decision must, of course, rest with me, I desire to take into consideration as far as possible the wishes of those present to-night. Have you any suggestions to offer?"

There was a little pause. Stéger and Guillaumet looked at each other, and René still kept his eyes on his boots. Lortigue, lounging sideways on the table, picking his teeth and yawning, remarked:

"Well, if you ask me, colonel, I should say the fellow's a rank impostor, and a shameless one at that. A more impudently faked-up tale I've seldom heard."

"That settles the question," Stéger whispered, nudging René with his elbow. "Whatever Lortigue says to-night, the old man will say the opposite. They've been sparring all the way home. We'd better vote in the fellow's favour, or we shall get nothing but black looks for a week."

"Your opinion is very positive, M. Lortigue," Duprez said icily. "May I ask on what indications it is based?"

Lortigue put the toothpick back into his mouth.

"Oh, I don't pretend to know much about indications, colonel. I'm a sportsman, not a detective. But I know an impostor when I see one."

Duprez turned his back with silent dignity.

"And you, M. Stéger?"

Stéger looked up with his air of Germanic candour.

"Of course, colonel, I speak in deference to your judgment; but for myself I fail to see why M. Lortigue has so bad an opinion of the applicant. His story seemed to me a quite credible one."

"Oh, he's glib enough, I don't deny that," Lortigue threw in scornfully.

Duprez, ignoring the interruption, asked of Stéger: "Then you would be glad to see this person engaged?"

"I think so, sir, if you think well of it. Personally, I feel rather sorry for his misfortunes. If I may say so, it seems to me that any victim of such a monster as Rosas has a certain claim on our humanity, especially as Rosas is also an enemy of France."

"Quite so.   M. Guillaumet?"

The Belgian's loose mouth widened. He was prepared to support any theory which would put off the evil day of facing again the dangers and exertions of the pass.

"For my part, I am inclined to agree with M. Lortigue. It is a dangerous thing to take a man who has no references; I should advise that we stay here a few days longer, and find a respectable person."

The commander turned to René.

"M. Martel, you have seen more of this applicant than we. In a sense we may consider him your protégé. I presume that you agree with M. Stéger?"

René hesitated miserably. It seemed to him hard luck that the casting vote should rest with him. He wished the man anywhere but where he was, and had been half hoping that he would be unanimously rejected; but to vote against him now would be like uttering a death-sentence.

"It seems to me," he said at last, "that we have no choice. I would much prefer a man with references; but when we get one he deserts. We are going into danger, and not everyone will go with us. Whatever he may be, this man is willing to come. Possibly he is disreputable; but we are not proposing to admit him to our personal intimacy, only to put up with his presence because we want his services. As for waiting, we have been here four days and found no one. If we wait much longer, the waters will be so high that we shan't get the baggage animals down from Papallacta alive. They are rising with every day. I think, if he knows his work, it would be well to take him."

The applicant, recalled, came in with a set face, very pale under the tan.

"M. Rivarez," the colonel began, "you realize,

I am sure, that it is a serious matter to engage an employee without any reference or testimonial."

"Yes," he answered half audibly. A little bead of sweat broke out on his forehead.

Duprez continued: "On the other hand, as a humane person, as a Frenchman, I am unwilling to abandon a white man in distress. I have decided to give you a trial, subject, of course, to your proving competent in the local tongues. But you must understand that I do so partly against my better judgment, and chiefly on the recommendation of M. Martel."

"But, colonel!" René broke in.

"Am I mistaken?" the colonel asked, fixing him with a severe gaze. René understood at once. If the venture should turn out badly, the blame would be his; if well, the credit would be the colonel's. He coloured hotly, and bit his lip.

"What I said," he began, "was that . . ."

He stopped short. He had caught the man's eyes. For a moment they looked at each other in silence.

"I am certainly in favour of the appointment." He got through the words in a hurry, and looked down again at his boots.

"Precisely," Duprez assented; and went on: "It is understood that you have no claim upon the expedition, but join it merely in the character of a paid employee, who, if unsatisfactory, can be dismissed without compensation at the first safe place. You will undertake to obey orders implicitly, and to share without hesitation in the inevitable hardships and risks of the journey. It is my duty to warn you that they will be considerable."

"I am prepared to take risks."

"Then we will call in some of the Indian carriers and hear your languages."

The examination proving satisfactory, a contract was drawn up. The stranger signed himself in a rather shaky hand: "Felix Rivarez." He flushed deeply as he handed the paper to Duprez, then looked away and stammered:

"And . . . ab-b-bout an outfit? I have n-n-nothing but these clothes of M. Martel."

Duprez put on his patronizing air.

"You will, of course, succeed to the equipment bought for the former interpreter, including his mule and gun. But I am prepared to spend a moderate sum on necessary clothing. M. Martel is going into Quito to-morrow to buy a few additions to the stores; you had better go with him, and he will superintend your outlay."

"If you will pardon me, colonel," said René, "I should be grateful if one of the others might relieve me to-morrow. I'm a poor hand at bargaining; and besides that, I have been on duty every day and have had no time to replace the papers that were lost with that mule."

"I am sorry, M. Martel, but the papers must wait till there is more time. I wish everyone to be on duty to-morrow, as it is the last day; I intend to start the next morning. And I am sure you are quite competent; all I wish is that you should see the strictest economy observed in all purchases made by M. Rivarez."

Rivarez did not lift his eyes from the ground. The expression of his face filled René with vexation. Had the man no pride at all, that he took everything so meekly?

They started for Quito on horseback early next morning, taking José with them to mind the horses and carry back the parcels. René was obstinately taciturn during the whole ride; he disliked the task that had been thrust upon him, and was full of unreasoning irritation against his companion, not so much for putting up with slights and exploitation, since it was evident that a man in circumstances so desperate had no choice, as for having got into a position which compelled him to put up with them. Rivarez, for his part, finding René disinclined to talk, rode beside him in silence.

"Go on in front, José, and find out why those coffee beans have not been delivered," René said as they entered the town. "You can meet us outside the saddler's shop." Having seen the half-caste out of hearing, he turned with a stiff manner to his companion.

"After you had gone to bed last night the commander told me he considers it essential that you should have a good outfit. Therefore, though, of course, he wishes you to observe reasonable economy, he has no desire to stint you in providing yourself with necessaries. He agrees with me that the list made out last night is insufficient."

He said nothing of who had changed the commander's view. Rivarez looked at his horse's ears. Then he asked softly:

"Would you d-d-do me the favour to ch-choose the outfit entirely yourself? It would make things . . . less difficult for me."

"I?" said René, stiffening more and more. "Really, I don't understand why you cannot choose your own clothes."

Rivarez laughed; a little bitter laugh, broken off short.

"How should you understand? You see, the commander . . . Oh, I beg your pardon, M. Martel. Don't help me if you would rather not, of course."

René understood in a flash. "I'll do anything I can, with pleasure," he answered awkwardly, and relapsed into silence.

When they came out of the saddler's shop, José

was standing at the door, gossiping with a villain-ous-looking negro fruit-seller, who instantly began pestering René to buy his wares.

"Not from you, my man; last time I was here you sold me rotten fruit and false weight. José, take that parcel from M. Rivarez."

As Rivarez turned to give up the parcel, the fruit-seller stepped forward and confronted him. René heard a low, gasping cry; and, wheeling round swiftly, saw the negro's impudent and ser-vile grin break up into a stare of angry contempt.

"What? That your new interpreter, José? Don't you see who it is? Why, look at his lame foot and his left hand! It's the clown that's run away from the circus. He'll get his bones broken finely if old Jaime catches him! Didn't you see there's a 'runaway slave' notice up?"

"Are you drunk, man?" said René. "Can't you see . . ."

"Mother of God, it's true!" José screamed. "I knew I'd seen him somewhere. And I had to get his bath ready . . ."

"M. Rivarez . . ." René began; and stopped with a catching of the breath. The statue beside him never moved; only stood with wide eyes looking out into distance, and the livid face of a corpse. The stream of José's indecencies and abuse poured on, beating in idle ferocity against a wall of silence.

"Came from Ibarra, did you? And who threw a rotten granadilla at you last Saturday, eh? Why, Manuel here! Who tripped up that crooked leg of yours and sent you sprawling because you didn't know your part? I did, and I'll . . ."

There he too stopped, staring at the dreadful face. For two or three heart-beats no one moved.

"You hound!" René cried out, turning on the half-caste in a choking fury of anger. "Ah, you cowardly brute!"

He dragged out his purse, and, panting with rage, flung down some coins.

"There are your wages; take them and go. Your things shall be sent here to-morrow; I'll have them left for you at the tavern there. And if I find you at the house when I get back to-night . . . There, go, go, go!"

He caught the bridle of José's mare. The half-caste fled, squealing and whining with fear, but taking the money with him. Manuel was already out of sight.

René paused for a moment to recover his breath, and turned slowly back. The unmasked impostor stood as before, staring into space.

"M. Rivarez," René said, and came a step nearer. "M. Rivarez!"

"Yes?"

"I . . . think we had better make haste. Shall we go to the bootmaker's first?"

"Yes."

René dragged his companion from shop to shop with frantic haste. He was in a fever to get back to the house before José could carry his grievance there, and to forestall any malicious gossip. The discovery which he had unwillingly made filled him with horror; he shuddered inwardly at the thought that it might reach Lortigue and Guillaumet. To him it seemed a hideous tragedy, incomprehensible, inconceivable; in their eyes it would appear comic, and they would doubtless amuse themselves with facetious inuendoes, perhaps with practical jokes. He looked furtively at the face of the wretched man; it was not quite so rigid and corpse-like now, and the deadly colour was slowly changing, but it was still a face of which he dared ask no questions. Yet there was one question that must be asked.

"I think we have everything now," he said at last.

"You will want another porter," Rivarez answered in a strained and difficult voice.

"It's too late now; we must manage with one less."

René paused for a moment; then said under his breath: "M. Rivarez . . ."

"Yes?"

"Has . . . that man they spoke of any . . . legal claim on you?"

M

"Oh, no; but nobody needs to have a legal claim on me; I haven't any friends."

They rode home in silence. José's mare, with the packages tied on her back, clattered along behind them, pulling at the halter. As they dismounted, Duprez came out of the house.

"Ah!" he said, catching sight of the led mare. "Then it was not stolen, after all."

"What was not stolen?"

"The bay. That half-caste fellow turned up here an hour ago on a strange horse with a tale of your having dismissed him. I put him under arrest till he could account for the mare."

"Where is he?"

"In the hut over there, guarded by the tall Indian."

René gave his bridle and whip to the native boy who was unfastening the packages.

"Catch hold of those. Colonel, may I speak to you a minute alone?"

Rivarez looked up quickly, and dropped his eyes again. "Good Lord!" René thought; "he thinks I'm going to tell!"

He followed Duprez into the house. "I have been obliged to dismiss José for gross insolence. I have paid him his wages, and a month over in lieu of notice."

Duprez's lips tightened. "I am accustomed to being consulted, M. Martel, before my subordinates

take such measures. If the man's fault was slight,
he should not have been so hastily dismissed; if
it was grave, he should have forfeited the notice
money."

"I beg your pardon, colonel," René answered
gently. "The fact is, the man's conduct was
insufferable, and I lost my temper."

Duprez melted at the soft answer. "Of course,
if the man was really insolent to you, it alters the
case."

"Did he tell you why I dismissed him?"

"He began a rigmarole about circus clowns,
saying you had made friends with a runaway
tumbler; somebody's slave or apprentice, I think;
but he got abusive, so I did not listen to any
more. What happened? Did you take the part
of someone he was ill-using?"

René caught at the opportunity.

"Yes; one has to interfere sometimes. It was
a sickening case. I'm sorry if I have caused you
inconvenience, colonel."

Duprez, quite mollified, presently consented
that José should be given his belongings and sum-
marily ejected from the place. He was much
pleased with the economical way in which the
outfit had been arranged, and at supper was mark-
edly gracious to Rivarez, rallying him on his pale-
ness and evident fatigue, and advising him to go
to bed early, as they would have to start at dawn.

"You seem very footsore," he added. "Ask
M. Martel to give you some of his soothing lotion.
It is wonderful stuff."

René fetched the lotion.   As he handed Rivarez
the bottle, the sight of Marguerite's writing on
its label sent the blood to his forehead.   He had
forgotten to answer her letter.   He went out of
the house, and tramped up and down in the dark,
consumed by bewildered and helpless anger.

In God's name, what had happened to him?
Had he gone mad, or was he indeed so slight a
thing that the first wandering mountebank he
met could pull up the habits of his life by the roots?

When one came to think of it, what had happened was the impossible.   A runaway clown
from a low-grade circus — oh, undoubtedly a
criminal hiding from justice; nothing else could
explain a white man putting up with the brutalities
of José and Manuel — a wastrel used to kicks
and blows and degraded enough to accept them;
a clumsy impostor that fools like Lortigue and
Stéger could detect at a glance — had come along
and looked at him; just looked at him.   And
for that, and because the creature possessed, or
seemed to possess, an abnormal capacity for suffering, he, René Martel, had delivered himself up to
be used as a tool in any and every way.   He had
done for this battered adventurer what he would
not have done for his own brother; had kept his

secret, lied for him, eaten dirt for him at Duprez's pleasure, lost all self-control for him as he had never lost it in his life, except once as a little boy, when a nursemaid had been unkind to Marguerite. Worse than all, he had forgotten Marguerite for him. Everything else he might have forgiven; this was too much. "Confound the fellow!" he whispered. "Damn the fellow!"

He walked off his anger and went in to write his home letters. It was late when he went to his bedroom, treading softly, not to wake the sleeping household. His irritation rose again at the thought that, after to-night, personal privacy would be impossible; the impostor's presence would be forced on him by night as well as by day; they must eat and sleep together, cheek by jowl.

"M. Martel!"

Someone was standing outside the door of his room. At the soft, hesitating tones the scowl on his face deepened, even before he came near enough to see the burning eyes of the circus man's runaway clown.

"Yes?" he said harshly. "You wish to say. . ."

"Only that I am very grateful to you."

René lifted his eyebrows. "For the lotion?"

After a pause the low voice answered: "Yes, for the lotion. Good night."

"Good night."

CHAPTER V

BEFORE the explorers were well across the Andes, the position occupied among them by the new interpreter had undergone a change. Marchand was, perhaps more than Rivarez himself, the cause of this.

At their first meeting, when the little party from Quito struggled through a blinding snow-storm over the pass to the hut at Papallacta, and entered, hungry, chilled, and panting with the fatigue of violent exertion in the rarified air, Marchand cast a swift look at each weary face; then, cutting short the commander's questions with a curt nod, pushed him aside, poured out some hot coffee and brought it to Rivarez.

"Here, drink this."

Duprez drew himself up a little. Much might be forgiven to Marchand, the only person in the world from whom he could take either a joke or a home truth good-humoredly; but this was gross discourtesy. The thought had barely formed in his mind when Marchand guessed it, and came back to him with a grin.

"Can't be helped, Armand; the social hier-

166

archy can wait, and that chap would have been on the floor in another five minutes. Guillaumet looks like a sick rat too. — Here, Bertillon!" He raised his voice sharply. "Help Guillaumet off with his things, and get him some coffee, there's a good lad." He turned back to Duprez, the grin melting into a delightful smile. "I'm sorry I interrupted you; but fainting-fits would be such a nuisance in a small place like this. We shall have plenty of it with Guillaumet before we're done; flabby heart and funk. That other fellow looks as if he'd been starving. Where did you pick him up?"

"I engaged him in Quito as temporary interpreter. He has not complained of anything, but if he's not strong enough for the work he'll have to go, of course, as soon as we can find someone else. Perhaps we shall be able to replace him at one of the mission-stations on the Napo."

"Oh, no, you won't," said Marchand softly, and looked at Rivarez. "He'll take a lot of replacing."

Later in the evening he sat down beside the interpreter, who was crouching over the fire in a pose of utter exhaustion, his head resting against a dirty wall. In the ruddy glow his face showed, drawn and sunken, with closed eyes. Marchand watched him for some time in silence.

"It's time you got to bed," he said at last, abruptly. Rivarez opened his eyes with a start and sat up; his face had immediately taken an expression of cheerful alacrity.

"Oh, I'm quite rested now, thanks. We were all a little tired when we got in."

"You needn't bother to put that on with me," said Marchand coolly, laying a hand on his pulse. "I'm a doctor, you see. What is it? Starvation?"

"A . . . a . . . little. I . . . Did they tell you?"

"They told me all they know, you may be sure. Good Lord, there's never any lack of telling. But the question is: how much do they ever know? Martel . . ."

He had mentioned the name by chance; but though nothing stirred in the face he was watching, he felt the pulse leap beneath his hand, and knew at once that there was something which René had chosen not to tell. He released the wrist, and went on deliberately: "Martel is the only one who hasn't favoured me with some version of your history since supper-time. But he has a gift for holding his tongue about other people's business."

Rivarez shot one swift hunted glance at him, and looked away.

"What I wanted to say to you," Marchand continued, with the air of a person who has observed nothing, "is just this: when a young

man goes in for adventures, and for making himself obnoxious to big fishes like Rosas, and so on,
he puts a pretty heavy strain on his nerves.
If you should find yours give you any bother —
nightmares or headache, or anything of that sort
— don't get worried and think there's something
wrong with you; just come to me for a tonic.
See?"

Rivarez began to stammer, with shaking lips.
"I . . . I . . . thank you very much . . . it's
m-m-more than good of you. . . ."

"Well, get to bed now," said Marchand, rising;
"and remember you're among friends."

From that moment he tacitly accepted Rivarez,
but for the difference in years and experience, as a
colleague on equal terms; and treated him with
the same impersonal and careless friendliness that
he showed to René. The other members of the
party regarded the new interpreter as a cross
between an upper servant and a poor relation,
whose social inferiority and doubtful respectability it suited them to condone for the convenience
of exploiting him. Stéger was the first to discover
that the presence of a person at once so quick and
so obliging was a useful asset for an ease-loving
man in a hot climate. During the descent from
the mountains, a box containing botanical specimens had been broken; and at Archidona, René,
coming in to the mission-station for supper, found

the Alsatian smoking in a hammock while Rivarez
sorted tiny seeds with slender, skilful brown hands.
Stéger took the cigar from his mouth, and nodded
lazily to René.

"I'm in luck, eh? Those wretched seeds have
got mixed, and I should never have managed to
sort them; my fingers are all thumbs. Makes
one's eyes ache, too, I can tell you. Whew, this
climate!"

René glanced at the clear-cut profile bent over
the seeds, and wondered that Stéger cared to
accept a fatiguing, unpaid service from a stranger,
so evidently more tired than himself. Lortigue
was differently impressed. He stood for a moment watching the rapid fingers, then remarked:
"You have clever hands, M. Rivarez. I wonder
if you could mount those small centipedes of mine
that always shed their legs?"

He went on in a tone that made René want to
knock him down, "Of course, I don't wish to
exploit you; but if you care to add to your salary
by . . ."

Rivarez looked up with a gracious little affectation of laughter, and a steel gleam in the blue eyes.

"Oh, surely, M. Lortigue, even a s-s-small centi-
pede may give something to a neighbour without
wanting to be paid for it, even if it's only a few
sup-p-perfluous legs. If you will bring me the
specimens, I'll see what I can do."

René caught Marchand's eyes and turned away, flushing deeply. Lortigue answered, yawning, "Oh, well, that's as you like, of course."

Soon other jobs, in need of willing fingers, were discovered by this man and that. "It's a shame to abuse your good-nature, but you are so clever at fixing these things," they would say; and Rivarez, though the colonel gave him plenty to do, always managed to fit in other people's work besides his own. Within two months there was scarcely a man in the company but Marchand and René who had not in some way taken advantage of his obvious desire to please; he was growing quite popular. Even the subalterns, at first loud in their wrath at the colonel thrusting upon them the society of a "nondescript adventurer," soon became reconciled to the presence of a witty and cheerful companion, who resented no amount of exploitation and never lost his good-humour in any hardship or annoyance. Yet all the while the haggard watchfulness, the remorseless concentration of his secret and unsmiling eyes, were horrible to see.

He was always on the look-out for opportunities to make himself indispensable, doing little services here and there, gliding past slights and petty injustice with the air of one too much interested in his work to think of trifles, yet noting each man's private failing or weakness and adapting himself accordingly. But, with all his suppleness, there was about him some quality which kept even Stéger from venturing too near, even Lortigue from repeating that first mistake.

With René his manner was gravely and courteously negative; doubtless he was not inclined to risk another repulse. René, on his side, remained stiff and ungracious; and daily reminded himself, with ever increasing earnestness, that the interpreter's affairs were no concern of his.

"Martel," said Lortigue one evening, as they sat by the camp-fire, "the colonel says he wants to stop here for a day or two and give the peons a rest. We think of riding over to the mission-station to-morrow; we're a bit tired of living on nothing but roast monkey and stewed parrot. Ugh! It made me nearly sick yesterday to see those brutes of natives tearing that live monkey to pieces. At least the Fathers will give us a Christian dinner, for once. The doctor won't join us; he says he has too much to do."

"So have I," said René. "I must get on with my map, and those geological specimens want sorting and ticketing; so I'll stay in camp with the doctor."

"Why don't you get Rivarez to do them? He's splendid at that sort of thing."

"Why should he do my work for me? He was not engaged to sort specimens."

"But he's here to make himself generally useful."

"How nice for him!" murmured Marchand, sucking at the eternal black pipe.

"I don't remember anything about it in his contract," René answered drily.

"Oh, contract! When one takes a man on half out of charity . . ."

Marchand grunted. "One is charitable, eh? One gives away jobs for nothing."

"There he is!" cried Stéger. "M. Rivarez!"

The passing figure stopped with a start; then turned a smiling face. "I wonder," René thought in quick parenthesis, "does he ever hear his name called without expecting a blow?"

Lortigue began before René could prevent him: "We are trying to persuade M. Martel to join us to-morrow, and he says he has to sort rocks. I have been telling him I felt sure you would help him to get them done some time; you are always so good-natured."

The interpreter turned slowly, without speaking, and looked at René, who made haste to answer the look.

"M. Lortigue is quite mistaken; I should not think of troubling you. You are so kind that we are in danger of forgetting how to do our own work."

"I thought you would wish to attend to it

yourself," Rivarez answered, and turned to Marchand. "You are staying behind too, doctor, I suppose?"

Marchand nodded, with the pipe-stem between his teeth.

"Yes; so's the colonel. Roast monkey's good enough for us; at least it doesn't chatter."

"After all," René said to himself, as he lay awake that night, thinking, as usual, about the interpreter, "I may have been unjust to him. If he really wanted to ingratiate himself, he would try to flatter and please either me, because he knows I could ruin him if I chose, or Marchand, because Marchand can twist the colonel round his finger; and he hasn't done it . . ."

Then the blood rushed to his face.

"Lord, what a gull I've been. That's his way of flattering us, to let us see we're the only ones he respects. He leads us by the nose, just as he does all the others, only he goes to work a different way. If you're an ass, he dangles a thistle before you; if you're a dog, he dangles a bone."

He was so much overcome by this discovery that he sat up to think about it. The night was clear, and the faces of his sleeping companions stood out, pale and ghostly, in the moonlight. Rivarez lay next to him, breathing quietly.

"Confound his impudence!" René thought. "How did he find out?"

He looked more closely at the still profile.

"I wonder how much he knows about us all? Quite a lot, no doubt, by this time. I don't know anything about him, even though I know what he has been. Yes, there is one thing I know: something must have hurt pretty badly to bring that line at the corner of his mouth. It doesn't show when he's awake. I wonder . . ."

He lay down, and turned his back.

"There I go again, always wondering! What have I to do with him and his secrets? They're probably none too clean."

Thinking the matter over seriously the next day, René came to the conclusion that it was high time for this foolishness to stop. He had been behaving like an empty-headed idiot, with no better use to make of his scant leisure than to waste it in idle speculation about the affairs of a stranger. Whether Rivarez was or was not an unscrupulous intriguer was, doubtless, a matter of great moment to Rivarez, and to his friends if he had any; to René, a casual acquaintance flung in his way by chance, it was of no consequence whatever. He had simply got into a bad habit of puzzling over the question, and must put it out of his mind once for all.

He took himself to task so sternly that for nearly a week he succeeded in keeping his thoughts off the subject. Then, one day, during the after-dinner rest, Guillaumet, lounging in a hammock with a cigar in his mouth, began his usual pastime of telling dirty stories. To-day they fell flat; the weather was insufferably hot, and everyone was tired. The callow "puppies" giggled feebly, but the colonel yawned and cursed the mosquitoes, and even Lortigue only grunted. René, pulling his sombrero over his eyes, vainly tried to shut out the irritating voice and get to sleep. Marchand turned over with a growl.

"Very pretty, no doubt; but you young people had better go and chatter outside. The colonel and I want to digest our dinner, and as for Martel, you're boring him to death."

"Of course," said the irrepressible Bertillon. "Don't you know Martel's a family man, irrevocably wedded to the most exacting of theodolites?"

Even Marchand laughed at this; René and his theodolite were fair game. A few days ago he had jumped, at imminent risk of his life, out of the pirogue into a river swarming with alligators, to rescue the instrument, which, happily in a sealed case, had been tossed into the water by a kicking mule. He had been fished out, half-drowned, but clinging triumphantly to the chain passed through the handles of the case.

Bertillon, who had a turn for caricature, jumped up for his sketch-book, and began a drawing, headed: "Miladi is displeased." The proud theodolite, as legal spouse, with her telescope indignantly apostrophizing the heavens, and a fry of young sextants and declination compasses about her foot, was shown in the act of accusing a meek and henpecked René, whose affections had strayed to the charms of the pluviometer.

René joined heartily in the laugh against himself, and the sleepy company woke up to examine the caricature and offer suggestions. Guillaumet's contribution was grossly indecent. His mind was a sewer; nothing could pass through it without contracting the taint which hung about it. René turned away in disgust, and lay down again in his hammock.

"Well, I'm going to sleep."

Presently the velvet stammer of Rivarez startled him into sudden wakefulness. "You never f-finished that f-f-funny story you were telling us, M. Guillaumet."

René opened his eyes wide. Rivarez, to find Guillaumet's stories funny . . .

Guillaumet, much pleased, started his anecdote again, and this time with more success; but Rivarez was not listening. He sat a little behind the others, looking down; the expression that his face had worn in sleep had returned to it intensified. The line of the mouth was more than sad

N

now; it was heartbreaking. René watched it from under his sombrero.

"If lying hurts him as much as all that," he thought, "why does he persist in doing it?"

Again he checked himself angrily, and again the next day and the next. But it was useless; he could neither tolerate Rivarez nor forget him. The man was always in his thoughts, and all thoughts of him were hateful.

Oh, it was absurd! Plenty of people were not nice to think about, so one didn't think about them. Guillaumet was unattractive, for that matter; but you just classed him with mosquitoes and half-castes and didn't bother. Poor old Duprez was trying at times, with his fidgets and his dignity; still, the momentary annoyance over, you put him out of your mind. But when Rivarez entered the tent, his presence filled it, though he sat in a corner with downcast eyes and held his tongue.

Under the tyranny of this obsession, René's sweet nature began to sour. He found it increasingly difficult to keep his temper with Lortigue and Stéger, to make allowance for Duprez's age and Bertillon's youth. "It's the climate," he would assure himself, "and the want of sleep."

He was getting into a wakeful habit, due chiefly to the fact of Rivarez being in the tent. Night after night he would lie down with resolutely shut eyes and his back to the importunate figure; and night after night he would turn over cautiously, and peer through his mosquito-net at the face he was learning to know so well, possessed by a devouring curiosity to see whether the artificial expression it wore by day had, relaxed into the terrible real one.

After dawn one morning, while the others were still asleep, he lay watching with half-shut eyes, asking himself once more, "But why, why should he look so tragic?" Then he saw the eyes move and the face immediately stiffen into its mask of cheerful indifference; and realized that he, too, was being watched. After that they spent long vigils lying side by side, feigning sleep, and conscious of one another's every breath.

A sense akin to terror was creeping over René. He took refuge in hating Rivarez. Various little personal peculiarities: the hesitating speech, the silent, feline movements, the utter immobility of the face in repose, the lightning swiftness of its changes of expression; were each in turn the objects of his furious and unreasoning antagonism. The fellow was uncanny, he told himself; he came up behind you as softly as a hunting Indian, his eyes had the shifting lights of sea-water; when they turned black, it was as if a lamp were put out.

Marchand had been more than usually gruff and gloomy of late. Since the expedition left France he had touched no alcohol; at last, one day René found him in the tent, flushed, hilarious, and glassy-eyed, pouring out foolish talk to Lortigue and Guillaumet. Rivarez sat in a corner, mounting butterflies. René stopped short in the doorway, looking at the miserable scene. It seemed impossible to interfere; yet he could guess with what bitter shame Marchand would look back to-morrow on words that could not be unsaid.

"But how do you come to know so much about the general, doctor?" asked Lortigue. "Was he a personal friend of yours?"

"A patient, my boy. His liver was in a bad state for years; that accounted for his temper. He always got on better with the War Ministry after I'd given him a few weeks' dieting. Not that he liked it; he used to grumble like an old rusty gate when I put him on gruel and hard exercise. But he was always grateful afterwards."

"Ah, perhaps if you had dieted him oftener he'd have got on better with his wife."

"That reminds me," Guillaumet put in. "You must have known the truth about that affair. You attended her too, didn't you? Was there really anything between her and that German attaché?"

"Dr. Marchand . . ." René began, stepping hastily forward; but Rivarez was speaking.

"Dr. Marchand, can you tell me why the natives think it unlucky to meet this moth?"

They had interrupted at the same instant; and now exchanged a glance of mutual understanding. Guillaumet turned angrily on the interpreter.

"Who wants to know what a lot of dirty savages think?"

"I do," said René.   "Is it just this moth in particular, M. Rivarez?"

"Yes; they give it a curious name: 'The Discoverer of Secrets.'"

Marchand was standing up now, with a trembling hand against his lips.

"Is that so?" he murmured.   "Yes, very curious, indeed . . ."

His eyes wandered with a scared look from Lortigue to Guillaumet.

"Am I interrupting?" said René.   "I came in to ask whether you have time to explain to me the emblems on those fish-baskets.   You said they had to do with some ceremony."

"Certainly, certainly," Marchand answered in a hurried voice.   "Very interesting, those baskets. Yes, I . . . I'm growing an old man . . ."

René got him away without further words, and for nearly two hours kept him talking of native implements and emblematic decorations.   At first he was slightly incoherent; but soon regained self-command, and by the end of the conversation was quite sober.

"Thank you, Martel," he said suddenly, as they

walked back to the tent. "You're good fellows, you and Rivarez."

He paused for an instant; then added in a choked and jerky voice: "Nasty trick, betraying people's confidence, eh? It's . . . catching, too."

René stooped to examine a flower; and when he looked up, Marchand was gone.

How long it would be till the next outbreak, Marchand himself had no idea; but he knew that, sooner or later, it must come. The longing for drink was like a live thing within him, dashing itself against bars; however he might beat it down and crush it back, its writhing never ceased, its cry was always in his ears. Surely, one day, it would be too strong for him.

Formerly his drinking bouts had been only after mental shocks, or when he had come suddenly upon associations of horror. A parterre in the Tuileries gardens, bordered with scarlet geranium and blue lobelia, had been before his eyes when he opened the book containing the stolen discovery; and, on his return from Abyssinia, the chance sight of such a border had caused a relapse. After that he had put geraniums and lobelias round his bed at night, and by the morning could touch their petals without shuddering. Then, once more, he had said to himself: "Now you are cured; get to work." Only the suicide of his wife had shown him his mistake. But now? The craving no longer waited for tragedies or associations; hot weather and mosquitoes were enough. The form of it was changing, too; from a mad, momentary longing to be dead drunk and forget, it was slipping into a constant desire for just a little alcohol to help him through his work.

All his infallible remedies had failed him alike. Before starting on each expedition, he had concentrated his thoughts upon the moment when the coast of Europe should fade on the horizon. "When you see that, the craving will go, and leave you at peace." And till this time the suggestion had helped; now, he had seen the coast-line fade, and the craving had remained, a spectre that his scientific exorcisms could not lay.

Trivial fancies had begun to dominate him, too. He might jeer at himself, by day, to his heart's content; but at night his sleep was haunted by the white reproachful ghost of the daisy that he had sent to rot in the coffin of Célestine's child.

As the explorers advanced, the country grew more difficult. About four months after passing the Andes they had to cross a river, shallow, but full of whirlpools and cascades. Before attempting the dangerous ford, Duprez called a halt, to give men and beasts a rest; and personally examined every mule and its pack, altering little details of arrangement with scrupulous care.

For the first time René began to understand
why Marchand thought the "Pion" a fine commander.

The guides waded through the swift water,
carriers following with the precious and fragile
scientific instruments. Then came the mounted
white men, and the baggage-mules last. René
and Marchand, who were among the first to cross,
rode up the bank to examine the instruments,
while their companions followed in turn. The
commander remained behind till the last, keeping
back Lortigue and Rivarez, one to help with
nervous mules, and one to interpret orders to the
natives. Glancing back over his shoulder, René
saw them at the water's edge: Duprez on a light-
coloured mule, Lortigue on a dark one, and Rivarez on the bad-tempered bay with the white foreleg, which had kicked off the theodolite.

"Come, Martel," Marchand called. "Let us get
to shade; this glare is dangerous."

As they rode up the slope, sudden commotion
and shouting behind them made René's mule jib.

"Hullo!" Marchand cried out. "There's an
accident."

René mastered his beast in time to see the bay
dash wildly up the bank, riderless. There were
still two figures on the other side, but he did not
see them; he was looking at the mule with the
white foreleg and the empty saddle.

"Marchand!" Stéger yelled, running towards them. "Come back, quick! Lortigue's hurt!"

The ice that bound René's heart melted and was gone. The landscape reeled before his eyes. Only Lortigue . . .

Then he looked across the river, and saw the two men waiting at the water's edge. He came to his senses instantly, and followed Marchand back.

Everyone had dismounted. Lortigue lay on the bank with closed eyes, the water streaming from his clothes. Bertillon and de Vigne shaded him with their coats from the heat of the sun, while Marchand knelt beside him unbuttoning his shirt.

"All right, boys," René heard as he rode up. "He's only stunned."

Lortigue recovered in a few minutes, and swore savagely at the bay. He had insisted on changing mounts with Rivarez, who could not manage the troublesome animal; and it had flung him off in midstream. He was unhurt, but so angry that Bertillon began to chaff him.

"Pity you couldn't see the pathetic spectacle we all presented, getting ready to mourn for you. Martel came up as white as a sheet."

"He must have taken you for the theodolite," said Marchand.

René looked at him with startled eyes. He was beginning to wonder how much Marchand guessed of the frightful and senseless thing that was happening to him.

"Only Lortigue . . ." If it had been his own brother who was drowning, his thought, at the moment, would have been, "Only Henri!" Except Marguerite herself, there was no one but Rivarez whose life meant enough to him for the fear of its loss to bring out the sweat like that: no one in all the world but Marguerite and this shady adventurer.

He asked himself whether he was becoming subject to an insane fixed idea. What was Rivarez to him that he should think about him day and night? And did the man know what influence he exercised over a fellow-mortal's mind? Was it intentional? Perhaps his will was being enslaved of set purpose; perhaps . . .

He pulled himself up. Of all the idiotic trash . . .

His education had not fitted him for dealing with so hard a problem. The English public school had made him very sure, less of what exists in the world than of what does not and cannot exist. Tales of one person dominating another's will were humbug and old wives' superstition. He assured himself courageously that the influence he feared had no existence; and it continued to make his life wretched.

Even as he watched Rivarez, so Rivarez

watched him. Again and again he would feel in
the marrow of his bones that he was being looked
at; and, stealing a glance towards the interpreter,
would see the haunting eyes fixed on him with
a gaze of such poignant and horrible intensity
that it seemed as if they must burn a hole. Sometimes he fancied that the man wanted to speak
to him privately; and, with a kind of terror,
avoided giving him an opportunity. The rigid
hostility of his manner towards Rivarez attracted
the notice of men less observant than Marchand.
Guillaumet remarked to the "puppies" that
Martel, though he might drop the "de" from his
name, and pretend not to care for class privileges,
was capable of most brutal aristocratic insolence.
"Look at the way he treats Rivarez. It's the
English Milord all over!"

After passing through much tangled and difficult swamp, the expedition reached an open, hilly
district, abounding in game and watered by a fine
river. Beautiful weather set in, with a cool mountain breeze, and Duprez made the sportsmen
happy by arranging a big-game hunt for the mor-
row.

When the morning came everyone was in high
spirits, and the younger men laughed and joked
as they ate their breakfast and filled their knap-
sacks. Even Marchand was almost gay. René
kept up his share in the talk, but his eyes

wandered to the smiling and haggard face of Rivarez. "He looks like a man who will laugh, and laugh, and go out and shoot himself," he thought.

"The peons seem to be enjoying themselves too," said Stéger, as a burst of strident native laughter came from outside the tent. "I wonder what the joke is."

"Not a pretty one if it's like yesterday's," said Bertillon. "They were making two tarantulas fight; pricking them on with thorns."

"After all, that's not so bad as cock-fighting."

Bertillon gave a little shiver of disgust. Though pathetically anxious to prove himself a man of the world by a fine display of cynicism, he could not always keep it up.

"Oh, that cock-fighting in Quito, with the knives tied on to the birds' feet! What fiends the half-castes are!"

"Well, all the English go to cock-fights, and prize-fights too, don't they, Martel?" asked de Vigne.

"Not all, I think," René answered. "Has anyone seen my cartridge-belt?"

He was nervously anxious to get away from the subject of half-caste sports in Quito. Lortigue winked at de Vigne, who went on with a face of innocent wonder: "But surely when you were in England you must have seen such things? I thought they had prize-fights every Sunday morning after church."

"Did you?" said René, quite gently; and de Vigne subsided, with red ears.

Guillaumet yawned and stretched his arms luxuriously. "Well, for my part," he said, "the prize-fighting is just the one thing in England that I should care to see."

"Naturally," Marchand murmured. Guillaumet continued:

"There's too much sentimentality nowadays. If we go on at this rate we shall all be milksops in a generation or two. I believe in manly sports myself; and, for my part, I was very sorry we were too late for the Easter bull-fight that strolling circus fellow got up at Quito. I was told it was a fine sight."

René held his breath. For an instant he did not dare to look at Rivarez; then he stole a glance over the bag which he was packing. The interpreter was stooping to fasten his boots, and his face was hidden.

"I don't think anyone need call me a milksop," said Bertillon hotly; "and I say a bull-fight's a filthy thing. Which way is it a manly sport to maul blindfolded horses?"

"Besides," added Lortigue, "they're too cowardly for proper bull-fighting at Quito; it's just senseless bull-baiting; twisting the poor brute's tail and chivying it about with fire-crackers, so I'm told. I dare say you've seen the sort of thing, Rivarez?"

The interpreter's black head bent lower over his boot-lace. "Yes," he answered softly; "it's a ch-ch-characteristic sight."

"That's just my point," said Guillaumet. "It's part of the genius of the Spanish race; all the fine races are fond of sport. Why, I remember, when I was a boy in Ghent, we used to have rat-fights, and very good sport they were. There's nothing like rats to fight; they'll hold on by their teeth as long as there's a breath left in them. All you have to do is just to light a match and . . . ."

"That will do, M. Guillaumet." Marchand's voice cut in, clear and icy. Its tone made René look up, and he saw that Marchand was looking, not at Guillaumet, but at the livid face of the interpreter. "We've had enough of rats for one day. Are you all ready, boys? It's time to start."

"Dear me," said Guillaumet, offended; "you are a tender-hearted lot!"

"Aren't they?" Rivarez put in with a little soft laugh that chilled René's blood. "But n-n-never mind the rats, M. Guillaumet; there are p-plenty of bigger animals that will hold on by their teeth if there's a l-l-lighted match behind them."

René fastened the bag, and rose. If he was to keep his temper and do his work, he must get away from all this for a little while. He took his gun and powder-flask.

"If you will excuse me, colonel, I won't join the hunt. I have been wanting to take some records of the direction of the river, and I think this will be a favourable day."

"I wouldn't go far along the river alone if I were you," said Lortigue. "Unless I'm much mistaken, it's a likely place for snakes and wild beasts."

"If you are really anxious to take the records to-day," said the colonel, "one of the others had better go with you in case of accidents."

"Oh, it's quite unnecessary, thank you; I'm not going far. All the details I want can be seen within half a mile of camp. I'll just look round and choose a position, and then come back for the peons and instruments. It would be a pity to deprive anyone else of the shooting; you know I am not much of a sportsman."

Rivarez looked up from the boot he was lacing.

"If you want any help, M. Martel, I should be quite willing to miss the hunt."

"Many thanks," René answered coldly; "but I really think I shall get on better alone."

He put on his sombrero, and went out to prevent further discussion. Once alone in the scented brushwood, he looked round him, and drew a long breath of relief. Here, at least, he was safe from seeing Rivarez first wince at Guillaumet's jokes, and then pretend to enjoy them.

That was where it stung. If the man had really liked brutalities and foul hints it would have been simple enough. But to see the higher nature aping the lower, wilfully trying to blunt fine instincts, to curry favour with a vicious lump of debauchery by the pollution of those beautiful lips . . . "Oh, why can't he be honest!" René groaned. "If he would only be honest!" Then he put the whole wretched subject away from him. He had come out here to forget it all, to be alone with clean things and to regain his peace of mind.

At the edge of a little thicket a gorgeous veil of passion-flower hung from a tree, sweeping the ground with trails of blossom. He went up to it, and stood for a moment trying to think only of its beauty, and of how Marguerite would have loved to see it. Then he raised his hand to lift a drooping spray, and instantly, out of the green curtain, flashed a cloud of rainbows; he had disturbed a company of humming-birds. All the bitterness faded out of his mind as he watched them; they were joy incarnate.

He walked on towards the river, singing to himself, for the first time in South America, the gay, tender, old French songs that he used to sing for Marguerite.

> " *Qu'il gagne bataille,*
> *Aura mes amours.*
> *Qu'il gagne ou qu'il perd,*
> *Les aura toujours.*"

The growth of brushwood left off abruptly. He had come out on to a smooth, grassy slope and saw the river winding, a broad band of silver, through a wilderness of flowers. It was long since he had seen anything so noble and so tranquil. He ran down the flowery slope to dabble his fingers in the clear water, and strolled on in leisurely enjoyment along the bank, humming Marguerite's favourite song:

> " *Qu'est-ce qui passe ici si tard,*
> *Compagnons de la Marjolaine ?* "

How she had loved the happy tune! "That song is a live creature," she had said to him one day; "but it's a creature that has never, never had anything wrong with its leg."

Presently he came to a brook running into the river. It was too wide to jump, so he took off his boots and waded through. The opposite bank, though low, was fairly steep. Just as he reached it a stone rolled from under his foot, and he saved himself from falling headlong into

o

the stream by catching at an overhanging branch. It broke in his hand; he scrambled up on to the bank, rather wet but unhurt.

The broken branch hung down the rocky bank, barring his way. He stooped to lift it, and, seeing something move, pushed the branch aside. Behind it was a small cave in the rock, smelling offensively and strewn with bones, and curled up on the floor lay the loveliest kittens he had ever seen; as large as full-grown cats, and yet mere balls of round-eyed fluffy innocence. "Jaguar cubs," he thought. "I'd better get away from here; the mother can't be far off."

He walked on along the river-bank, looking about him with vigilant eyes, yet mechanically humming to himself:

> "*Que demandent ces chevaliers,*
> *Compagnons . . .*"

A stealthy sound behind him checked the song on his lips. He turned with a leaping of the heart, and looked straight into the angry eyes of the mother jaguar.

As he raised his gun to fire, he felt it wet against his hand, and knew that his one chance for life was gone; the thing must have dipped under water when he stumbled. He had no sense of fear; there seemed, indeed, no place for such a feeling; this was not danger, it was death. Yet he pulled the trigger mechanically, and heard the hammer click on the wet steel.

" *Compagnons de la Marjolaine . . .*"

The song came back, and the river; not this river, but a tributary of the Upper Yonne, where he used to fish as a boy. Shallow stream and shining ripples, water-lilies floating, coot and lapwing in the rushes: all were clear in the instant before the jaguar sprang.

He did not hear the shot fired close against his head; yet he could not have been unconscious, for as the dying jaguar rolled over, dragging her claws down his arm, he realized dimly that he was still alive. But that was impossible; indeed, it was impossible. There must be some mistake. . . .

Someone lifted the huge paw carefully off him and helped him to sit up. He rubbed a hand over his face, and stared round him stupidly: at the gun lying on the grass, at the dead jaguar, at his boots, at the blood soaking his sleeve; then up at the white face of the man who had saved him.

"Whatever has the fellow got to be so upset about?" he thought. "Nothing out of the way has happened."

Then he tried to scramble to his feet; and immediately sat down again, overcome by giddiness.

Rivarez fetched him water, helped him to a spot where he could lie down, then cut off the torn sleeve and used it to wash and bandage the arm; all without speaking a word. The traces of emotion had quite vanished from his face by the time that René struggled up again into a sitting posture and looked round at him.

"Pretty near thing, wasn't it?" René murmured, with an imbecile wonder.

"Fairly. Will you have some brandy?"

"Yes, please, and a smoke. There are cigars in my left pocket. I suppose the matches are wet."

After they had smoked for a little while, René stood up, tried a few paces, and felt himself over. But for a good many bruises and the flesh-wound on the shoulder, which was only now beginning to burn, he was apparently unhurt.

"I'm all right," he said; "but perhaps I'd better get back to camp. This sort of thing does shake one up. No, I don't think I need an arm, thanks."

They walked back slowly, pausing to rest awhile near the hanging sheet of passion-flower.

"I haven't often seen so many of those orange-throated humming-birds together," said Rivarez.

René looked round. There was not a humming-bird in sight.

"Where?" he asked; and added in surprise: "Oh, then you saw . . ."

He broke off with an exclamation, seeing Rivarez turn first red and then white. There was a moment of silence.

"I am quite rested now; shall we go on?" said René.

He dragged himself up painfully, very stiff and sore, but seemed not to see the hand which his companion held out to him. Rivarez shrank into his shell at once, and they walked back to camp in unbroken silence. Being unable to remove his coat and boots himself, René reluctantly consented to let Rivarez help him and attend to the wound; then, still feeling sick and faint, he lay down on his bed in the hope of sleeping off the shock. Rivarez was leaving the tent when René opened his eyes with a start.

"But we forgot the babies!"

"The jaguar cubs?"

"Yes; my head was so muddled. . . . We shall have to go back for them."

"No; I killed them."

René sat upright and stared.

"Killed them!"

"Yes; before you recovered."

"But whatever made you do that?"

The other looked away from him, silent.

"Being knocked on the head is less unpleasant than starving," he said at last. "At any rate, it's quicker. I've tried both, so I know."

He went out as softly as a shadow.

René puzzled for a moment over this enigma, but soon gave it up and shut his eyes. His head was aching furiously. Soon he dropped off to sleep, and woke some hours later with a burning pain in the wound and a raging thirst.

"Felipe!" he called.

It was Rivarez who entered the tent.

"Can I do anything for you?"

"No, thank you. Is Felipe there?"

"I'll call him."

René, left alone, struck his hands together in a sudden blaze of anger. "Spying on me again!" Then he checked himself in horror.

"Oh, what am I thinking — what has come to me! It was only kindness. He was watching in case . . . Yes, yes; but the humming-birds . . . he saw the humming-birds. . . ."

A native servant came in, and René sat up with a hand over his eyes.

"Get me some water, Felipe, will you?"

"Here it is, sir; and M. Rivarez said I was to bring you some food and a cup of coffee."

"Where is he?"

"In the other tent, sir. And he said, if you could sleep, I was not to disturb you."

René drank the coffee and lay down again. The headache slowly passed; and his thoughts began to shape themselves.

There could be no doubt that Rivarez had followed him from camp. He must have made some excuse to the others for not joining the hunt, and slipped out privately to dog his footsteps. Certainly, as things had befallen, it was lucky that he had done so; but the idea was none the less repulsive. There was something uncanny about the whole affair; what object could he have in following a man who had expressly said he wished to be alone? And if the accident with the jaguar had not happened, would he have followed all day, skulking in the brushwood and making no sign? Was it because the place was dangerous that he had watched, silently playing invisible Providence to a reckless fool who ran risks through ignorance and obstinacy? "I don't want a nursemaid," René muttered angrily. "And anyway, why couldn't he speak out if he had any warning to give me?"

He sighed impatiently. It was galling to owe his life just to those underhand and secret ways that he so detested in Rivarez.

Hearing the hunt return at sunset, he got up, aching in every limb; and, with Felipe's help, adjusted his clothing. The prospect of meeting all the company and being asked innumerable questions about the details of the accident was hateful to him; but he had better go and get it over. Rivarez would be sure to have told them the main facts already. "I wonder, has he told them he was following me?" René thought.

Supper had begun when he entered the tent. One of the usual hunting disputes was in full swing.

"I tell you I shouldn't have missed if the sun hadn't been in my eyes," Stéger was saying.

"Ah, M. Martel!" said the commander. "And how did the observations turn out? Why, your arm is in a sling. Have you had an accident?"

Everyone looked round but Rivarez, who went on eating.

"Oh, I . . . slipped in crossing a stream," René answered hastily. "It's nothing much."

Rivarez looked up from his plate. "I hope the arm is not sprained?"

René flushed scarlet.

"Oh, no, thanks . . . it's nothing to matter. But I got a bad headache, and came back to camp. I must take the observations to-morrow."

"A touch of sun, no doubt," said Marchand, innocently, watching Rivarez out of the corners of his eyes. "I told you to be more careful in the hot part of the day."

The conversation turned on the dangers of sunstroke. After a moment, René rose, pleading headache, and went back to the sleeping-tent. He lay down, but instead of sleeping, he stared through the mosquito-net at the roof of the tent, and tormented himself with questions that had no answer.

Why had he told a lie? He had not the remotest idea. What hideous infection was upon him, that he must shuffle and evade like this — he, who had nothing to conceal? He had lied in Quito; but that was different. Then he had merely kept another man's secret, which chance had brought to his knowledge. But now it was he who had given Rivarez a secret to keep for him, who had gone out of his way to make one where none was needed. The whole thing was like a nightmare, senseless, incoherent as the fancies of an idiot. For all he cared, the whole of South America might know of his adventure. He had been attacked by a wild beast, and Rivarez had saved his life; that was all. Saved it, by the way, at considerable risk to his own; he must have been nearly touching the animal when he fired. A failure to kill at once would have been almost certainly fatal. And his gratitude had been to impose silence, as if he grudged a brave man the credit of a brave action. And Rivarez had acquiesced instantly, tacitly; had placed him under a double obligation; just Rivarez, before whom, of all men on earth, he would have wished to be blameless in his own eyes.

CHAPTER VI

RENÉ's arm soon healed; and the adventure
with the jaguar was not referred to again. The
distress and confusion of his mind were now increased by the miserable embarrassment of owing
rescue from violent death to a man with whom
he was scarcely on speaking terms. When by
chance his eyes caught the interpreter's, the hot
colour would go up to his forehead. "What a
cur he must think me!" he would say to himself.
"He saved me, and I haven't had the decency
to say 'thank you.'"

Two months passed. The explorers were slowly
advancing, with enormous labour and difficulty,
along a hitherto unexplored tributary of the
Pastassa River, known to be one of the chief
strongholds of the dreaded " head-hunting" Jivaros. Some of the peons had already deserted,
and those who remained were in a state of terror.
Once the wind brought from the distance a sound
of native drums and dancing; the peons cowered
together, shivering in fear and whispering: "Auca!
Heathen!"

Apart from actual impediments of cataract and

jungle and swamp, the hot and steamy atmosphere of the district rendered progress difficult. One evening the camp was pitched, between tangled forest and reeking bog, on a rocky outcrop by the river-side. Early next morning Rivarez asked permission to go out with the "captain of peons," an intelligent, semi-Christianized native, much attached to him, who followed him about like a dog. He was away most of the day, and on returning entered the commander's tent with Marchand. After dinner Duprez told the assembled company that he had "a statement of importance" to make.

Rivarez had brought him word, it appeared, that a Jivaro tribe had assembled by the river for the religious festival of initiating the young bravés into manhood. The ceremonies, which included fasting and mutual flagellation, had begun, and it was likely that when the later stage of dancing and drinking should be reached, the temper of the tribe would become dangerously aggressive.

"As they are ahead of us," said Duprez, "we cannot advance without disturbing them, which at this moment would be attended with some risk. M. Rivarez has implored me to retire to our last week's camp and wait there till the tribe disperses; and Dr. Marchand is also inclined to think such a course advisable. It is quite natural that they should take what appears to an old campaigner like myself a somewhat exaggerated view of the perils of the situation. I do not regard it as a sufficiently grave one to necessitate the loss of the progress so laboriously gained; but I am prepared to take all reasonable precautions to avoid collision with the savages. I have therefore decided to remain here quietly for a week, after which we shall be able to proceed unmolested."

He looked with the air of a schoolmaster at the younger men.

"Let me point out to you, gentlemen, that this enforced rest will afford you an excellent opportunity for reducing to order the material already gathered. Meanwhile, I wish to impress upon you all the importance of refraining from any action likely to cause disturbance. Dr. Marchand and M. Rivarez will explain to you certain local customs which you will be so good as to respect during our stay here. I understand that they are connected with the childish and ferocious superstitions to which these benighted savages so obstinately cling. M. Martel, I rely upon you to hold yourself responsible for the observance of all necessary precautions."

Marchand followed him out of the tent. When they had gone, Bertillon exploded into laughter.

"Oh, là, là! The long words! Attention, gentlemen! I have a statement of importance."

He jumped up and posed as the colonel, twisting his innocent face to an impertinent solemnity.

"The childish and ferocious superstitions of these benighted. . . . Get away, de Vigne, or I shall pull your ears. Not your moustache; it isn't long enough . . . benighted scare-mongers (saving your presence, M. Rivarez), render it necessary for us to stick fast in the middle of a bog till a naked hocus-pocus man finishes exorcising bogies. *In saecula saeculorum. Amen.*"

Stéger greeted this sally with vigorous hand-clapping and a throaty Teutonic laugh.

"Yes; it's all very well," said Lortigue; "but this is beyond a joke. If we're to be held up every time M. Rivarez chooses to bring word that a lot of mangy natives have got drunk . . ."

"And are dancing a sarabande, without a rag on them," de Vigne chimed in. Guillaumet took the cigar from his mouth with a scornful snigger. "My dear de Vigne, that would naturally enhance their claim to respect in the eyes of M. Rivarez. You forget that he is more likely to have a fellow-feeling with any sans-culotte, white or coloured, than with the class of society to which some of us belong."

Rivarez sat absolutely motionless. The smoke of the cigarette that he was holding rose from his hand, a straight, unwavering line. René, without speaking, left his place, and sat down beside him.

At that, the interpreter's lips shut a little closer, and the whitened nostrils quivered slightly; but there was no other sign. A cool, deliberate voice from the doorway made Bertillon start guiltily.

"So have I; the sans-culottes have better manners."

Marchand's big head and shoulders came through the aperture, square and threatening. He walked straight past the others, and laid a hand on Bertillon's arm. It was a formidable hand; too small for the massive build of the man, cushioned and broad and taper-fingered, with a lady-like smoothness of skin that gave it, to the unobservant eye, a podgy, ineffectual look, startlingly contradicted by the grip of a steel vice.

"I thought you were a decent lad," he said.

Bertillon, crimson to the roots of his hair, flamed into vehement remonstrance.

"It's not fair, grandpapa! Because you've taken a fancy to Rivarez, you back him up in all this stuff; and we're to be stuck in this filthy swamp and eaten alive by mosquitoes . . ."

"Instead of being roasted alive by Jivaros. Just so."

"Oh, come, doctor," said de Vigne; "we're not a young ladies' seminary. Surely we could give a fair account of ourselves against a handful of natives, even if they did turn spiteful."

"Which do you mean by 'natives'?" Marchand

asked sweetly, his ruthless grip still bruising Bertillon's arm. "The Quito half-castes that you can kick, or forest braves with the pagé's 'devil-drink' in them, and all their war-paint on?"

"I don't know much about 'devil-drink,'" said Guillaumet. "I know the effect of ordinary drink on some white people is not to make them very clear-headed."

Bertillon wrenched his arm free, and sprang up.

"Ah, that's dirty! Let's be gentlemen, any-way!"

"All right, boy," said Marchand; and put the hand back on his arm, this time kindly. "Suppose we keep to the point."

"Well, then," said de Vigne; "the point is that niggers are niggers, whichever sort they are, black or red, tame or wild. Bertillon and I could manage half a dozen apiece before breakfast."

"And half a hundred apiece?"

"But, doctor," Lortigue protested; "only the other day you told us these savages live in little scattered groups of just a few families together."

"I told you that about the Zaparo tribes on the lower Cururay. These Jivaros are a finer race; they have a system of signalling with war-drums." He turned to the silent interpreter. "How many fighting braves do you think they could together at an alarm?"

Rivarez unlocked his lips with an effort. "I'm

not sure; probably between two and three hundred."

"We are nine," said Marchand, looking at Guillaumet. "Nine at the outside. Well, boys?"

There was a pause. René spoke for the first time; his voice was low, and deep with suppressed anger.

"As the colonel has made me responsible for precautions, I should like to know just what I have to guard against. Perhaps M. Rivarez will be kind enough to explain about those customs."

The interpreter looked slowly, first at René, then at Marchand; and all three saw that they could count on each other. He began to speak, quite clearly, without stammering.

"I understand that we ought to keep out of their way, and make as little noise as possible; certainly not to shoot. But the great thing is to get rid of that bird before the peons see it."

He pointed to a dead hawk which Lortigue had brought in. The Gascon flared up.

"Get rid of it? I intend to have that specimen stuffed. It's a species I don't know, and . . ."

"I think I do," said Marchand, turning to Rivarez with knitted brows. "I suppose it's one of those sacred falcons? Which sort is it, the Caracara?"

"No: worse. It's the Acauan."

"The snake-eater?"

"Yes. You know what we may find ourselves let in for if anything should go wrong with a woman."

Marchand whistled softly, looking down at the mottled plumage; then raised his eyes to René's intent and quiet face.

"It's mixed up with a lot of magic, you see. It protects the tribe from serpents, and brings messages from the dead, and enslaves the souls of living women. Then they go into convulsions and die — really die, mind, of hysteria. They infect each other, and then there's a hell of a job."

"Of all the preposterous stuff . . ." cried Lortigue. "I'm to destroy my own property, because M. Rivarez has an attack of nerves and the doctor believes every old wife's tale . . . Martel! But . . ."

René had risen in silence, picked up the bird and carried it out of the tent. Lortigue rushed after him with a cry of fury; and found himself caught by a silken hand that left blue marks on his wrist, and put back, strong as he was, on his seat.

"There we are," said Marchand, in the tone that he might have used to a child of three years old.

"What have you done with it?" Lortigue gasped, when René came in again.

P

"Tied a stone round its neck, and sunk it in the river. I'm sorry; but it couldn't be helped."

"M. · Martel . . ." Lortigue could scarcely speak for anger; "you will give me satisfaction."

"I'm not a duellist," René answered; "and if you have any quarrel it must be with the colonel; I followed his instructions."

"Also," Marchand added in a gentle, unfamiliar tone; "any person who let off fire-arms here this week might find fire-arms let off on him. I'm not a duellist, either."

He cast a meditative eye on the pistol in his belt. Lortigue rose with a white face.

"Shall we finish our cigars outside? I am used to the society of gentlemen, not of strolling adventurers and cowards."

He went out with Guillaumet, Stéger, and de Vigne. Bertillon lingered, irresolute; but de Vigne looked back from the doorway to ask reproachfully: "Staying? You?" and he followed, with a shamed, unhappy glance at Marchand.

"Pack of idiots," Marchand growled, yawning as if half asleep. "Now, my children," he went on briskly; "we three have got to look after this camp. We'll take turns to watch at night. The peons are no use; they'd faint at the shadow of a Jivaro. The colonel will be all right by tomorrow; touch of gout, perhaps. Martel, you'd better take Bertillon under your wing. He's quite sound underneath; this is just kiddishness and bad influence. Get him away from Lortigue. Do you think . . ."

René interrupted him passionately. "Oh, don't ask me, doctor! I think nothing, but that I live in a sty among swine."

Rivarez looked up with a slow bitter, smile.

"And where the deuce did you expect to live?" snapped Marchand. "There, man, for the Lord's sake don't you be a fool too."

His voice had dropped suddenly to a caressing tenderness. René began to laugh at once.

"All right, 'grandpapa'; I'll try not to."

Early next morning he woke with a start, to find Marchand shaking him by the shoulder. Lortigue's hammock was empty.

"He's gone, and Bertillon with him. They've taken guns."

They looked at each other, silent.

"Rivarez is gone too."

"He's patrolling. They must have given him the slip somehow. Martel?"

"Yes?"

"If those two bring in another Acauan, what shall you do?"

"Sink it in the river, I suppose. What else can I do? I can't sink them after it."

Marchand looked at him; a frightening look; and went silently to the commander's tent.

An hour later the truants appeared, put away their guns and sat down to breakfast. Sternly cross-questioned by Duprez, they declared they had gone to search for butterflies, and had taken weapons only in case of accidents. They had, however, some secret joke to share with de Vigne. While they were enjoying it Rivarez came in, white and depressed; he could eat no breakfast, and seemed scarcely to notice the contemptuous glances cast at him. As de Vigne said, he looked "sick with funk."

René spent a busy day over the map that he was making. During the night, while he was patrolling, Duprez came up to him.

"You can go to bed now; I'll watch."

René went to his hammock, wondering what methods Marchand had used. Before dawn a sound of whispering roused him; he woke with the word "Acauan" in his ears, and saw a figure steal noiselessly out of the tent. He sprang up on the instant, suspecting another surreptitious shooting-party; but Lortigue lay snoring peacefully beside him; it was Rivarez whose place was empty.

"I must have been dreaming of that confounded bird," he thought, and fell asleep again.

At breakfast Rivarez was missing. The deep roll of a drum sounded from the distance. "I suppose they're dancing," said Lortigue. Marchand did not answer, but his look made René shiver, and fancy the sound different from what they had heard before.

The commander came in late, and so white in the face that Stéger, meeting him in the doorway of the tent, cried out: "Why, colonel, are you ill?"

Duprez brushed past him.

"Gentlemen, we must prepare for an attack. An alarm has been brought by the captain of peons. Yesterday an Acauan falcon was picked up in the forest, dying of a gunshot wound."

He paused. Bertillon rose with a burning face.

"Colonel, I went out . . . I didn't think . . ."

"Be quiet, Bertillon," said the Gascon. "This is my affair. I am responsible, colonel; I persuaded Bertillon to come with me; and unluckily the bird was only wounded and got away. I am sincerely sorry if any trouble has resulted from a mere joke; the blame is entirely mine."

"Yes," said Duprez. "Unhappily, that won't help us. A girl has been seized with convulsions, and the pagé says the young women of the tribe will die. All the braves are preparing for battle."

There was a murmur of indrawn breath. Lortigue alone failed to understand; his placid scorn for "natives" died hard. He flashed a reassuring smile at the stern and silent company; then, meeting no response, became offended.

"I have already expressed my profound regret. Certainly I am to blame, though there was great provocation. But the danger can hardly be serious. M. Rivarez, of course, is timid, and imagines . . ."

The unfinished sentence broke off in a gasp; Duprez's lips had begun to twitch. René let his cup fall with a crash, and the coffee flowed along the ground.

"Where is Rivarez?"

He spoke in a loud, harsh voice, standing up, with a clenched hand on the tent-pole.

"He has gone to the natives."

"Alone?"

"Alone."

"But he'll be murdered!" Stéger cried out.

Duprez turned away, murmuring: "There was no other chance."

He gave them the details; quickly, quietly, not stopping to choose his phrases. For once, he was shaken into simplicity.

Rivarez had gone to try his powers as a peace-maker. He had painted his face in native fashion, and put on the great coronal of scarlet plumes from Marchand's ethnological collection, as the Jivaros were said to appreciate such a mark of respect. He had refused an escort, and left his pistol, taking with him only a few drugs from the medicine chest, and chemicals for the performance

of "magic." His chance of success, he had declared, depended on his being alone and un-
armed; and he had wrung from Duprez a reluctant
promise to keep silence till he had been gone an
hour.

"He is very confident," the commander added,
with little confidence in his own voice; then
plunged at once into practical matters.

"There is no time to lose. Raoul, you will
take command on the north side of the camp,
with Lortigue, de Vigne and half the peons.
Martel, you take the south, with Guillaumet,
Bertillon, and the other half. Stéger and the
captain of peons remain with me. You will shoot
any person attempting to enter or leave the camp
without a written permit from me. The ammunition will be served out . . ."

His orders followed each other, rapid and clear;
the emergency showed him at his best. Lortigue,
waking from his stupor of amazement, broke in
with a wild scheme for raiding the Jivaro camp.

"Savages can only attack; they can't defend.
If we rush the place before they have time . . ."

"Hold your jaw," said Marchand; and shoved
him aside. He was too much astonished even to
resent the insult. René took down all instructions in writing and left the tent; he had not
spoken at all. Bertillon, meanwhile, had been
standing still and growing slowly whiter; now he

came up to Duprez, who was talking to Marchand in an undertone.

"Colonel, will you let me go to them? I can tell them it was I that shot the bird. It's not fair Rivarez should have to . . . It's I that ought to pay the price if . . ."

"If it would help," Marchand interrupted harshly. "You can't even speak their language. There, stand out of the way; the mischief's done."

The commander had not troubled to answer; he was gone, with an impatient movement of the hand. Bertillon burst out crying, suddenly, uncontrollably, like a frightened schoolgirl. René coming back with peons carrying a case of ammunition, called to him sharply: "Here, Bertillon, unpack this. And make Guillaumet help you; he's under everyone's feet."

Guillaumet was in a state of abject panic, and worse than useless. Everyone else worked admirably, including the two culprits, who, after the first shock, recovered their self-control and did what they could to help. In a short time such preparations for defence as were possible had been made, and sentinels were watching all approaches to the camp. René patrolled the south side with keen eyes, and not a spare word for anyone. A black rage possessed him; he avoided looking at Bertillon for fear of being tempted to

kill him. The morning dragged on, and there
was no sign of peace or war.

At midday food was served out to the watchers,
who ate standing, with eyes on the forest. De
Vigne came to bring Rèné a message from Marchand, and stood beside him with an unhappy face.

"Martel . . ."

René was examining the river through a field-
glass. He answered without moving: "Yes?"

"You know Rivarez better than any of us.
What do you . . . think . . .?"

"I think nothing."

"But you don't believe he's . . . dead?"

"He's a lucky fellow if he is."

The boy drew back with a little smothered cry.

"If . . . Oh, but it's not possible! They
won't . . . they can't . . ."

"Why not? Do you suppose these people put
on white gloves?"

"Martel . . . Bertillon and I were at school
together. If . . . that has happened . . . he'll
shoot himself. . . . I know he will. . . ."

René turned to scan the river in the opposite
direction.

"He'll get off cheap, then. Take the glass and
watch the bend there till I come back."

He put the glass into the lad's hand and went up
to the nearest native sentinel, who had laid down
his carbine to kneel and cross himself.

"Get up! Take your carbine! You can say your prayers when you're off duty."

"Oh, sir," the man whimpered, picking up the weapon hastily, "will the bloodthirsty heathen murder us all?"

"They won't need to, if you neglect your duty again. I'll shoot you myself."

"Yes, sir," the sentinel gasped with round eyes. René went back to de Vigne, and took the glass out of his hand.

The afternoon passed as the morning had passed, dragging out hideous minutes into hours. In the still and scorching blaze the men waited, staring with hot eyeballs, listening with strained ears. René moved from sentinel to sentinel; vigilant, silent, unconscious of fatigue, indifferent to grief. He was like a machine wound up, that must go on working till it runs down.

Shortly before sunset there was a sudden commotion on Marchand's side of the camp. René cast a quick look round at his men, and felt for the pistols in his belt. A moment later Lortigue came tearing over the rocks and flung himself on Bertillon's neck.

"It's all right . . . he's back . . . he's made friends . . ."

They reached the tents in time to see a grotesque figure, with a face all stripes and circles, and a huge, tossing, fiery aureole, struggle out of the commander's embrace, only to be deliriously hugged by first one man and then another. Bertillon approached last, stammering entreaties for forgiveness. Rivarez laughed and submitted to be kissed on both painted cheeks; then turned and looked slowly round the eager crowd.

"But where is M. Martel?"

René had slipped away unobserved, and sat on a slab of rock at the water's edge, sobbing and choking, with his head down on his knees.

When the storm passed he leaned back against the rock and reviewed his position. It seemed to him as horrible as it was strange.

In six months this runaway circus clown had become the centre of his affections. That was preposterous and utterly absurd, but it was true, and this day's suspense had proved it to him. In all his life he had conceived of no such suffering; he marvelled how he had endured it and killed neither himself nor anyone else. Yet, though he had realized to the full the danger of violent death which threatened him and all his companions; though he had thought much of Marguerite, picturing to himself her misery, her ruined hopes, her desolate and widowed life; what had hurt most had been the thought of Rivarez alone among the savages.

Against his will, in spite of his passionate and continual protests, his love was irrevocably given to an impostor of doubtful antecedents and mysterious conduct, who surely cared nothing at all for him, except to use him as a tool. That was the miserable fact, and he must make the best of it.

When he came into the tent, supper had begun. Rivarez sat beside the commander, bandying jests and repartees with a radiant, excited company. He had pacified the frightened peons by removing his terrific head-gear, and had tried to wash the war-paint off his face; but it still showed here and there in evil-looking sticky smears and fantastic patterns half erased. One small toucan feather clung in his hair like a red flame. His manner was horribly artificial, and the jokes were as stale as ditch water; also he stammered so much that his speech was difficult to follow. After the meal he was called upon to relate the day's adventures. He began to describe, very humorously, his arrival among the angry savages; but stopped short in the middle of a sentence, with an empty and lifeless face. The next instant he looked round with an apologetic smile.

"I'm v-v-very sorry. Will anybody tell me what I was saying?"

Marchand rose and took him by the arm.

"We'll tell you that to-morrow; you're to go bye-bye now."

He went meekly, followed by René, who had

only now realized that he, too, was aching with fatigue. The excitement over, the whole company began to feel the effects of the long day's strain, and soon settled down to rest. René slept heavily; but from time to time woke out of frightful dreams, and, slipping on his clothes, crept out to rouse the weary sentinels, who were dropping asleep at their posts. Once, coming back in the half dark, he fancied that Rivarez was sitting up under his mosquito-net, and spoke to him softly; but, receiving no answer, fell asleep again.

Next morning, in the presence of the whole company, Duprez destroyed the contract engaging Rivarez as temporary interpreter, and drew up another which placed him on an equal footing with his companions. René and Marchand acted as witnesses.

"This," said Duprez, "is the only practical expression I can give at this moment to my esteem. Rest assured, however, that when we return to Paris — which, but for you, we might never have seen again — I shall not fail to make a public acknowledgment of our indebtedness to you. Should you care to accompany us to Europe, Paris and the great French nation will know how to welcome a foreigner who risked his life to save French citizens."

"Holy Virgin!" Stéger whispered to Marchand. "It's worse than a prize-giving in a village school. The bad boys will come in for attention next."

And indeed, once in the vein, Duprez went on to sermonize Lortigue and Bertillon. René stood counting the seconds till he had done; after yesterday, this solemn farce was scarcely bearable. Then he saw Rivarez, standing a little behind the commander, catch Bertillon's eyes and wink at him, as who should say: "Never mind the old man; he can't help prosing."

When Duprez paused at last, the soft purring voice of the hero of the hour glided into speech, with the effect of murmuring water after the rattling of dead sticks.

"All that you say of me is most kind and f-f-flattering, colonel; but, indeed, I was thinking of how to s-s-save my own skin. As for the little mistake of these gentlemen, surely you, who have served in the Great Army, can pardon an excess of contempt for danger. Have we not always heard that courage, in France, is not a v-virtue, but a weed?"

René set his teeth. Oh, if you have no pity for your own self-respect, have you none for those who love you? The misery of it; to stand by and see you — you of all living things — playing on an old man's childish vanity, laughing at him behind his back . . .

He looked at Marchand. "Ah, thank God!" he thought. "He loathes it too."

Duprez smiled.

"The first tradition of the Great Army was obedience to orders; but, as these gentlemen have given me their word of honour not to offend again, I will let bygones be bygones. All human faults may be pardoned, except cowardice."

His eyes swept majestically over the wilted Guillaumet.

After supper that evening Duprez ordered out several bottles of champagne, which had been included among the stores for great occasions; and, standing, proposed in a long speech the health of "our dear and intrepid comrade." Marchand lifted his cup, but at the smell of the wine turned pale, and hastily put it down again untouched. He had been all day in one of his black moods; a sullen and gloomy foil to the scintillating gaiety of Rivarez.

"But, doctor," exclaimed Lortigue; "won't you even drink the health of the Jivaros and their tamer?"

A jerk of René's elbow upset the bowl of rice and charqui over Stéger's legs.

"Oh, how clumsy of me!" he cried, jumping up. "Doctor, will you give me that spoon? I'm very sorry, Stéger."

Then he looked round, and realized, with a

blank surprise, that Rivarez was doing nothing to back him up. Marchand cast a long, malevolent sidelook at him, raised the cup, emptied it at a gulp, and held it out to Lortigue to be refilled. René sat down again slowly. He had been living for three days in a succession of nightmares, and this was but one more. His only feeling, now that the thing had happened, was a dull wish that Rivarez would leave off laughing. He had been laughing immoderately to-day, and there had been something hard and monotonous about the sound. To-night it was almost shrill. He was deeply flushed, too, bright-eyed and over-merry; but he neither ate nor drank.

Marchand was filling his cup for the fourth time when Duprez saw what was happening, and quietly moved the bottle out of his reach. René, watching, saw Guillaumet put another in its place. At that he rose again, and asked in a clear voice: "Is anyone coming out to see the river by moonlight?"

"We haven't heard the adventures yet," said Stéger. "Tell us all about it, Rivarez."

René remained standing by the doorway while Rivarez began to narrate as glibly as a professional actor, shifting from part to part with swift changes of voice and expression, and presenting in a farcical light a succession of figures: himself, the pagé, the hysterical girl, the excited relatives.

A little less ferocity in the caricature would have made it a brilliant piece of mimicry.

"When I got there, with my hands held out so, in sign of peace, the old gentleman was strutting round the house with a pipe in his mouth, doing incant-t-tations, and the lady inside, tearing her hair, and foaming at the mouth, and s-s-squealing: 'A-ca-uan! A-ca-uan!' for all she was worth. I had as much as I could do to p-p-persuade them I should manage the exorcising business better than the pagé; he wanted them to k-kill me first and talk after; n-naturally the poor old chap didn't like an outs-sider poaching on his monopoly. Who would? Think of an ama-t-teur coming in to Notre Dame and offering to teach the archbishop his business! Besides, there's a lot of theol-l-logical fervour about these fellows; you'd almost think they were Ch-Christians."

Duprez looked shocked, and frowned severely at the giggling Bertillon; but the boy was too happy to notice.

"Well, I started on the sacred signs, and invoked the Jurupary spirit, and talked about the four palm trees that are brothers; but it didn't make them any more friendly. So I tried vent-triloquism as a last chance; told them I'd bring up the Gurupirá to lead away the ghost of the bird, and give it to the Ypupiara."

"To what?"

Q

"They're f-forest demons; the Gurupirá takes human shape, and tempts people to follow it into bogs, and disappears. Then there's a thing called 'Ypupiara' — that means 'water-lord' — that lives in bogs and rivers. You try to r-run away from it, and really you're running towards it all the time, because its feet turn b-back from the ankle. . . ."

"I don't see the logic of that," said Marchand, accurate even now. "How does the direction of its feet make you run towards it?"

"Oh, well, I suppose th-that's what you'd call a m-m-mystery of faith. I told you they're a theol-l-logical folk. Anyway, you always end by running into its arms, and it strangles you. So first I made the bird's ghost come into the house and wail, this way . . ."

He dropped his face into both hands. A long piercing cry, more a laugh than a wail, sounded directly overhead: "A-ca-uaaan! A-ca-uaaan!"

"Then I did some pow-wow to call up the Gurupirá, and told them all to cover their faces."

He covered his own again. From afar came an unnatural voice, faint at first, then sweeping nearer and ending in a bellow just outside the tent. Then the cry of: "Acauan" sounded again and again, dying away in the distance. He looked up, laughing.

"By that time they were all on their faces,

and the poor pagé was nothing but a jelly. He knew the s-spirits wouldn't make those noises for him. Even the girl had forgotten to howl. So then I took a fiery devil out of her mouth . . ."

"How did you do that?"

"Just the usual conjurer's trick with the sleeve and a bit of tow. Then I gave her an opium pill, and told her to go to s-sleep, and wake up cured. That was the whole thing."

Through the laughter and applause of the delighted audience came the voice of Guillaumet. His opportunities for conversation had been few since yesterday. He had found himself steadily and quietly cold-shouldered by everyone; and already knew that Marchand had been discussing with the colonel the possibility of shortly getting rid of him by dumping him down at the first mission-station on the Marañon.

"How very fortunate," he said, "that you should have happened to know so much about conjuring and ventriloquism. One never knows what may come in useful. Where did you pick it all up?"

René caught his breath audibly. Had José succeeded in getting a hearer, after all? Had the Maggot known, and kept silence, all these months?

How stupid! Of course it was mere random malice. Rivarez had not even changed colour.

"Oh, I used to be rather fond of amateur theatricals."

"I suppose," said Guillaumet; "you have a natural talent for . . . a . . . what one might call . . ."

Rivarez threw himself back with a little affected laugh.

"Monkey tricks? Yes; I think I should have made q-quite a resp-p-pectable mountebank. Or I might even have done for the f-f-founder of a new religion; esp-pecially now I've taken to healing the sick and c-c-casting out devils. Raising the d-dead would be a tough job, though; besides, they might be annoyed."

René slipped quietly out and paced the rocky platform in the moonlight. He would not have believed it possible that any joke could hurt so much. In various wretched moments he had mentally accused Rivarez of many things, but never till to-day of insensitiveness. To suspect his best beloved of breaking half the laws in the Decalogue had been bad enough; to wince at his taste was worse.

A low sound of panting broke the stillness; a sound like the breathing of a tired runner. A figure was crouching on the rock at a little distance, its head down on the crossed arms.

"Who's there?" he asked, and approached it.

"It's . . . nothing. Wait a minute . . ."

The voice was unrecognizable; but the man put up a mutilated left hand to ward him off.

"Rivarez! What's the matter? Are you ill?"

He saw again the terrible face that he had seen in Quito.

"Yes. Don't tell the others. I made an excuse . . . I couldn't keep it up."

"But you ought to be in bed."

"I know. Help me; will you?"

He rose, clinging to René's arm.

"Can you walk? I'm strong enough to carry you."

"I can manage; thanks."

With René's help he walked a little way, very slowly, and catching his breath at every step; then stopped, with a hand over his eyes.

"Oh, this is absurd!" René said. "Put your arms round my neck."

As he stooped he felt Rivarez drop heavily against his shoulder. He lifted him from the ground, carried him into the commander's tent and laid him in the hammock; then sent Felipe to fetch Marchand.

Rivarez opened his eyes.

"M. Martel . . . What are you doing?"

"Taking off your boots. Lie still."

"Yes, but . . . oh, and you've put me in the colonel's tent."

"When did you begin to feel ill?" René asked, unlacing the other boot.

"Early this morning; no, in the night. I hoped it might pass over; but it's the real thing now."

"Is that why you've been playing professional entertainer all day?"

"I suppose so. Once a clown, always a clown, no doubt. I seem to have been buffooning ever since the deluge. Did I do it very badly? It's so inconsiderate to fall ill just now. Do you know, I hate to delay you all, but I shall have to lie up."

"Sir," said Felipe, putting his head in at the doorway, "the doctor has just gone out with M. Lortigue. Shall I go and look for them?"

"Yes, please."

Rivarez protested. "But there's no hurry. You needn't have bothered . . ."

"What do you expect me to do when a man faints?"

"That was just the pain. It's often happened; it was because I tried to walk."

"Then you've had this sort of thing before?"

"Good Lord, yes! Half a dozen times in the last four years; I ought to be getting used to it by now."

"What is it?"

"I don't quite know. One man told me it was a local inflammation; but very likely he was wrong — he drank like a fish. It hurts enough,

whatever it is. It comes from some internal
injury. They s-s-say you don't usually die of it,
unless you get periton-n-nitis. It was done when
this was." He touched his left hand.

"What do you do for it?"

"Just wait till it goes over, and keep your head
if you can. It doesn't last very long. I suppose
you'd be dead, or mad, or something, if it did.
It's only making up your mind to stand the pain
for a few days. It comes in big waves and
drowns you every now and then. You can get
on all right between, so long as you lie in one position and are careful how you breathe."

René thought for a moment. "The colonel had
better turn out," he said; "and I'll nurse you
here."

"You? Oh, no; Felipe can manage. I
wouldn't have you."

"Why?" ·

"But you d-d-don't understand. This is only
the beginning."

"All the more reason . . . ."

"You don't know what it's like; it would make
you sick. This sort of pain is a beastly sight.
And you, that hate ugly things!"

"You needn't worry about that; I've done
plenty of sick-nursing at times. My sister is a
chronic invalid. She has been bed-ridden nearly
all her life."

"Oh, that's hard!" Rivarez murmured with dilated eyes.

How it happened René scarcely knew. He found himself talking of Marguerite, and of his fears and hopes for her; telling things that he had never told to anyone.

"So that's why I came out," he added; and sat staring at the shadows. Rivarez broke the silence with a dreary laugh.

"R-rather like a g-gladiator show, isn't it? Thumbs down, all round. One would think the Lord must get quite a l-l-lot of sport, with so many of us."

When Marchand came in, flushed and smelling of wine, the patient set him laughing with a stream of gay anecdotes and epigrams; and turned his head to whisper desperately to René: "Get him away from me! Get him away! He's drunk!"

It was all René could do to get Marchand out of the tent. When they were out of earshot he asked: "Can't you give him anything to stop this pain?"

Marchand laughed. "My dear fellow, you're a sentimentalist. We don't give opiates for every trifle. Yes, there's a touch of inflammation; he probably got over-heated, riding, and took a chill. But it's nothing much, or he wouldn't have his repartees so pat."

René looked after him hopelessly as he went staggering away.

Some hours later, when René had seen as much as he could bear to see, he went to the other tent and roused Marchand; he would get an opiate this time if he had to fight for it. The champagne fumes had passed by now; and Marchand came back with him, very sombre.

"Yes, that's acute inflammation right enough," he said, after one glance at the huddled figure. "Get me boiling water and cloths for compresses. Just hold the light a minute first."

He stooped over the hammock, speaking softly and clearly.

"Listen; if you must have relief, I'll give it to you; but it will be better for you in the long run if you can do without opium. Can you?"

Rivarez, with an arm across his face, made a gesture of assent. Marchand put a hand on his chest to unfasten the shirt, and turned sharply to René.

"Martel, you've been spilling water."

"No," René whispered. Marchand took the lamp quickly from his hand, drew down the arm and looked at the face; then went at once for opium.

"My lad, you ought to have told me," he said when he had given it.

After a few hours the paroxysms began again. They were of so furious an intensity that the

various palliatives which Marchand, with René's
help, tried almost incessantly for two days and
nights, were of little use. Only heavy drugging
would have really helped, and that he wished to
avoid if possible.

"I should have had to do it with most patients,"
he said on the third evening; "but you have pluck
enough to help me out."

Rivarez looked at him strangely. "How long
shall I have it, do you think?"

"As long as there's a bit of you left; it's in-
grained."

Bertillon had just gone out, overjoyed at finding
the patient well enough to joke. There had been
no lack of sympathizing visitors; the difficulty
throughout had been to keep them away at the
moments when Rivarez was too ill to deceive
them. He insisted on keeping up a fiction that his
illness was a comparatively slight one; and whenever it was possible to admit them, the immediate
readiness with which he would put on his airy
manner, and, wiping his forehead hurriedly with
a drenched handkerchief, would turn upon the
entering guests a genial face, did not fail to amaze
the two watchers. His talk during these days
was often racy and amusing; and though it was
sometimes broken by fits of breathlessness, there
was little other sign of effort in his voice than a
slight increase of the stammer. He laughed

rather too much, but in a surprisingly natural way; and no one but Marchand and René guessed the truth.

Having got rid of Bertillon, Marchand called René to help him lift the patient, that he might examine the progress of the inflammation. René was a skilful nurse; but in the act of stooping he slipped a little on the uneven ground, and recovered his balance with a slight jerk.

"Oh, God!" Rivarez cried out. It was almost a scream, savagely bitten off.

René stood, frozen and sick, listening to the panting breath, till Rivarez looked up with a smile of gracious apology.

"I'm so sorry, M. Martel. It was just that I wasn't expecting it; you didn't really hurt me a bit. Would you mind trying again?"

He preserved the smile successfully till the examination was finished. Then, at a sign from Marchand, René drew back out of sight.

"He doesn't need to keep it up so hard when we can't see his face," Marchand whispered.

René hesitated for a moment, then asked softly: "I wonder if you could get him to drop this pretence, at least with you and me? It's such a cruel, unnecessary strain on him. Oh, it's all right to be plucky; but this isn't only pluck. I can't see why he tries all the time to persuade us it doesn't hurt; he's only making it worse."

Marchand growled at him like a bear. "No, you wouldn't see. As it happens, it's he that has got to stand the thing, not you, and he must stand it his own way. Anyhow, it's time for you to go and lie down if you're to sit up to-night."

René obeyed, without further speech. Even had he been able to lay aside the personal feeling which made it difficult for him to talk about Rivarez at all, he would still not have known how to express his real thought. It seemed to him that under all this superb display of courage lay something else; not stoicism, not pride, not consideration for others; a ferocious timidity, a paralyzing distrust. "What has he got to be so afraid of us?" he asked himself again and again. "He's saved all our lives; and he hides his pain away as if he were among enemies. He can't think we shouldn't care — he can't think that."

When he came back at nightfall, Marchand met him in the doorway.

"Martel, I'm going to sit up to-night; he's worse."

"Have you given opium?"

"A little; but it hasn't acted so far, the thing's too acute. I shall have to give a heavy dose if this doesn't stop soon. Go in, he's been asking for you."

He went in alone. Rivarez caught him by the wrist.

"Get Marchand to bed. I can't have him here. I'll explain afterwards."

René returned to Marchand, who was standing in the doorway.

"He has a fancy to be alone with me to-night. Does it matter?"

"It would matter a great deal to upset him. No, it's all right; I can trust you."

René took down a list of instructions.

"I don't want you to give the opium," said Marchand. "If this hasn't stopped within an hour, come for me; or sooner, if you see any sign of incoherence. It wouldn't take much now to make him light-headed. If he gets drowsy, don't leave him. I shan't go to bed just yet."

When he had gone Rivarez signed to René to approach him. His voice was now so faint that it was difficult to hear without stooping.

"I want you to promise . . . you're not to call him, whatever happens; not even if I ask you to."

"But he can help you. It's to give opium."

"He can get drunk; and Guillaumet can . . . I'm safe with you."

He began to speak more clearly, with a violent effort.

"I've lost my head, before, when it's been like this. How do I know what I may say? Would you like Marchand to know your secrets?"

René hesitated, remembering the moth and the fish-baskets.

"It's your right to choose," he said at last. "I promise not to call him, unless . . ." He stopped.

"Unless?"

"You must leave me some discretion. If I thought . . ."

"That I might die? No fear! Is it a promise?"

"Yes."

"Give me your hand on it. Oh, you needn't worry; nothing ever kills me."

After a long silence he broke out suddenly in a harsh, unfamiliar voice:

"Don't you know I can't be killed? Breaking my bones won't do it — that's been tried. Breaking my heart won't do it. Oh, it's no use, it's no use to kill me — I always come alive again!"

Soon afterwards he began to talk incoherently; now in Spanish, now in Italian, but mostly in English, which, to René's surprise, he spoke without the slightest trace of foreign accent. Once he asked for a cup of water, but when it was brought to him, pushed it back with a fierce outcry: "Don't come near me — you lied to me!"

To this phrase, or some variation of it, he returned again and again.

"You brought me to this — you did it! I trusted you, and you lied to me!"

"I wonder," René thought; "was it a woman?"

But the next time the phrase was repeated it began with a cry of "Padre! Padre! Padre!" and that too recurred at intervals during the night, alternating with broken scraps of strangely contrasting reminiscence. Often the words were inaudible or ran into one another; sometimes the voice was very faint; but separate sentences would flash out of the confused murmur with the vividness of lightning.

"Yes; I know it's broken. My foot slipped; the sack was so heavy. Oh, but that's all my week's money — I shall starve!"

A little later came: "Aix-les-Bains? It's a very tiring journey, isn't it? And mother does hate strange hotels. But if you really think it important, I suppose we could hire a furnished villa and take our own servants?"

Presently he began in a conversational tone: "I'm sorry, padre; I couldn't get on with St. Irenæus. No; it's not the Greek that bothers me, but it's such dreary reading; there's no humanness about it. Don't you think . . ." and broke off with a cry of sheer helpless animal terror:

"No, no! Don't set the dogs on me! Can't you see I'm lame? Oh, you can search me if you like; I haven't stolen anything. The jacket? But I tell you she gave it to me!"

Once he began counting on his fingers.

"Stéger's for me, and Lortigue . . . the centipedes did it . . . that's two. Guillaumet's for me; three. Only I must laugh . . . I mustn't forget to laugh at his jokes. Marchand . . . Oh, but Martel, Martel! What shall I do about Martel?"

After that he began to sing snatches of half-caste comic songs:

> "*Ah, you needn't make eyes at me!*
> *Did you take me for an ass?*
> *But I've found you out, you see;*
> *No more coffee for you, my lass!*

Now he would imitate the voice of a mincing, sniggering mulatto girl:

> "*Oh, get away, do, and don't tell me lies!*
> *Do you think I've forgotten how you behaved . . . ?*

The next lines were filled with senseless indecencies, gabbled through hurriedly in now a male, now a female voice. Doubtless all this had formed part of the circus repertory. To the circus he came back without end. That, and the pain, and the man who had lied to him, were a perpetual undercurrent through everything.

"What's Jaime so furious about now? Because

I fainted? But, man, I couldn't help it!" Then he would break into a sudden wail:

"Padre, why didn't you tell me the truth? Did you think I shouldn't understand? Oh, how could you lie to me — how could you lie to me?"

After a long string of indistinct or incoherent talk, the voice would drop to a frightened whisper: "Wait! wait a minute . . . it's coming on again. Yes, I'll tell you presently, I . . . can't just now . . . Oh, it's like a red-hot knife . . ."

Or he would burst out laughing; a horrible sound.

"Your reputation's quite safe; I shall never tell, and they'll hold their tongues too, now there's been a suicide about it. Think of the scandal in a respectable British family! Don't be afraid; I'm dead and damned, safe enough, and you'll be a saint in Paradise. God won't mind; it's His own trade, to save the world at other people's expense."

Then he would go back to the circus. "Do you see the fat negro in the corner there? It was he that started the row last week, when Jaime turned out the lights. He had the same woman with him then. Well, if I must, I must; give me a minute first . . . Oh, if you knew how it hurts . . . Yes, I'm coming."

Then the circus patter would begin again. Once, in the middle of a filthy negro catch, he

R

burst out with a tearing cry: "Oh, kill me! Padre, kill me quickly — it's gone on too long! Jesus, Jesus, You didn't have it as long as this . . ."

He flung up a hand and struck himself savagely on the lips.

"You idiot! What's the use of whining? He doesn't care any more than Jesus does. Don't you know there isn't anything to pray to? Kill yourself if you want to; no one else will do it for you."

Towards dawn the raving sank into an unintelligible murmur, then into silence. Marchand came in early; and, seeing his patient in a dangerous state of exhaustion, turned fiercely on René.

"Is this the way you do your work? Why didn't you call me?"

René looked away, and said nothing.

"You've been asleep!" Marchand hissed at him in blazing wrath. "And this going on all night . . ."

Still René looked away. Sudden silence made him lift his eyes; Marchand was staring at him with a face out of which the life was slowly ebbing. It was ash-grey when he moved at last to stoop over the half-conscious patient. René turned and went out without a word. "Oh, the poor devil!" he whispered to himself. "Oh, the poor devil — he's understood!"

That day the inflammation began to subside;

and the following night, all danger of delirium having passed, Marchand took the watch and René went to bed.

Tired out as he was, at first he could not sleep. He had stumbled upon the explanation of all the mysteries and contradictions that during the last half-year had bereft him of his peace of mind; and was now torn between shame at his unwilling intrusion into the privacy of his neighbour's soul, and horror at the groundless and cruel suspicions which had kept him from guessing the truth before.

It was all hideously simple. A mother's petted only son, scholarly, sensitive, and delicately bred, suddenly, in early youth, finding his trust betrayed; then a mad leap in the dark, alone and unprepared, into utterly new conditions of life; and the inevitable avalanche of disaster and despair: it was so simple that he had never thought of it. He had thought of murder, forgery, half the abominations of the penal code; of everything but an unequal struggle with a purely personal tragedy. He might as well have had such thoughts of Marguerite.

Marchand would never have repulsed this lost and desperate wanderer as he had done. "For the lotion?" Even at the time it had sickened him to see the hunted eyes dilate. "And all because he tried to lie in self-defence, and didn't know how to do it. . . . Lord, what a brute I've been, what a smug respectable brute!"

By the morning Rivarez was able to breathe without pain. During the next few days he slept most of the time, while René sat beside him working at his map. One evening, after a long and minute examination, Marchand told them that all inflammatory symptoms had disappeared. "I suppose you know you've had a fairly narrow shave of your life?" he added.

"Which life? I must have started with as m-many as a cat to take so much killing. I wonder how much of that sort of thing one can live through."

"Quite a lot," said Marchand, grimly; "and a good many sorts of things. But it's hard luck to know so much about that at your age." He glanced round; but René was counting miles, with his head bent over the map, and he went on: "If this should ever happen again, don't be superhuman; it's bad for the temper. No, I'm not fooling, so you needn't try to be witty; I'm giving you a warning. Of course, the way you've taken all this has been magnificent; that needs no saying; but I'd rather have seen you make a fuss, like other folk. You've been tearing your nerves to pieces, and not learning humility."

"Oh, humility! Surely there's no lack of opportunities for learning that."

"No," said Marchand, quite sombre now. "Not for most of us. We howl when we're hurt and go to the devil when we're betrayed, and at least we all go together: 'mau chat, mau rat.' Villon knew a thing or two. But your rock ahead, my son, is too much stoicism and too little human charity. You're a very wonderful creature; quite the most wonderful that I've met with yet, or am likely to meet. But you're made in the same image as the rest of us, and that's a dangerous thing to forget. There, did you ever know me preach so much before? And the poor colonel waiting all this time for his bézique! See what a tropical climate does when a man's getting elderly and liverish! Ta-ta, my children."

Rivarez looked after him with a puzzled frown. "Well, I don't know," he said; "I shouldn't have thought there was much howl about Marchand. It's queer, anyhow. Do you think anything has been upsetting him?"

"I shouldn't wonder," René answered laconically, with his eyes on the map. "The camp's been having an upsetting time lately. And twenty-five and a half . . ."

There was a pause. Marchand had left the atmosphere so heavy with suppressed emotion that it was difficult to begin talking; but silence only made the sense of oppression more stifling.

"Do you believe there is any danger from the

natives further up the river?" René asked at last, as he marked his map with: "Warlike tribe."

"Scarcely, unless we upset them. But we shall have to be careful."

"Oh, Lortigue's had a lesson. Still, things may happen. Suppose sickness broke out among them, and the pagé put it down to us?"

"That would be bad."

"You don't think you could pacify them?"

"No; but it's all guess-work. I didn't think I could before."

René's pen jerked across the paper, and stopped.

"Didn't you expect to succeed when you went to them?"

"I didn't think there was one chance in a hundred."

"Then what on earth did you suppose they'd do to you?"

"Well, I . . . ref-f-frained from speculating about that. Anyhow, w-w-what did it matter which particular thing they might do? Whatever it was, it wouldn't have been m-much worse than last Tuesday week, and it would p-probably have been over sooner."

René bit the feather of his pen, reflecting.

"I see. And what do you think got you out of the mess? Just their seeing you were not afraid?"

"But I w-w-was afraid."

"Well, then, your making them believe you weren't?"

"Partly. But ch-chiefly making them believe they were."

"Afraid?"

"Yes. They weren't a bit. But they thought they were. It's just as good."

"Or just as bad?"

"Oh, no! Thinking you're afraid is less than death; being afraid is more."

"Then is your idea that courage depends less on not being afraid than on not thinking you are?"

"Hadn't we better def-fine our terms? What is courage?"

"You ought to know."

"I don't, unless it's an enlightened kind of fear, with a little sense of proportion thrown in as make-weight."

"That's too subtle for me."

"Is it? You see, I was a phil-losophy student before I was a circus clown; the c-combination would make any fellow subtle. Well, for example: Marchand thinks I was courageous on Tuesday night, because I lay still and didn't mak a f-f-fuss. He'd lie still if it hurt less than wriggling. And how are you going to make any r-reasonable-sized fuss when you're being burned alive?

You've got either to shriek, like a pig having its throat cut, or to keep quiet. Then you get a r-reputation for courage."

René turned round.

"Look here, I want to ask you something. You know what I told you about my sister; if you were in her place, which would you choose: To be bed-ridden all your life, or to have . . . oh, I suppose an indefinite amount of hacking about, and perhaps be cured at the end? Only perhaps, mind."

He was too much absorbed in his own trouble to notice the hearer's face. He went on hurriedly: "You've pricked the bubble for me. She feels confident about it, and so did I till last week. I suppose Tuesday night has got on my nerves; I'd . . . never seen anything quite like that. How can I put her through I don't know what? She's so young."

Rivarez spoke at last, in a slow, strained voice.

"It's difficult to answer. You see, pain splits one's conscious self into two separate beings at war; the one knows a thing to be true, and the other feels it to be false. If you asked me that next month, I should say: Take any chance. Tuesday, if I could have answered at all, I should have said you could buy even certainty too dear. To-night I'm enough myself to know I'm not myself."

"I oughtn't to have asked you," René murmured, ashamed.

"Why not? It's all a question of illusions. It seems to me I couldn't live through that Tuesday night again; but I know that's an illusion. When all this happened, four years ago, it was like Tuesday night some part of nearly every day for weeks together; and you see I didn't go mad or kill myself. Of course, I kept thinking I should have to; but I didn't."

He added, hurriedly and stammering: "I suppose we col-l-lonials are t-tough."

"Oh, why will you lie to me?" René cried out in sudden despair. "Why will you always lie to me? I never ask you questions."

He broke off, wishing he had not spoken.

"That means . . . I talked?"

"You were light-headed. Am I to tell you what you said?"

"If you please. Ah, no, no! Don't tell me — don't!"

He put both hands over his eyes, shuddering. Presently he looked up and spoke quietly.

"M. Martel, whatever you may have found out or guessed, I can offer you no explanation. If you can, forget you heard it; if not, think what you must about me, but don't ever ask me to explain. Such as it is, my life is mine, and it's I that have to bear it."

"What should I think about you," René answered simply; "except that I love you?"

Rivarez turned his head and looked at him, very grave.

"Love is a big word."

"I know that."

"And do you . . . trust as well as love me? Though I have lied to you?"

"It makes no difference. You lied in defence of your personal privacy; you couldn't know you were hurting me."

"No; I didn't know. I won't lie to you again."

With that they left off talking; but René did not return to his map. He sat idly dreaming till Felipe came to call him to supper; then he looked up with a start, and sent the lad back to say that he would wait till Dr. Marchand was ready to replace him.

"But I shan't want anything; Felipe can stay with me. Please, M. Martel, go and have your supper."

"I wish you'd call me René."

Rivarez flushed with pleasure.

"If you like. But what will you call me? Felix? It means no more to me than Rivarez; they were both names I saw over shops in Quito. One must have a name."

The colour died out of his face again.

"S-s-since I came to South America I have been known by nicknames, chiefly. The half-castes are . . . clever at inventing nicknames."

"Felix will do for me. Oh, I'll go if you like, and send Felipe. Sleep well, my friend."

CHAPTER VII

MARCHAND played bézique with the colonel for two hours. He won five francs and fourteen sous, and put down the exact amount in a notebook.

"You're getting careless, Armand," he said. "You lost three francs last time by that same mistake. Good-night; I'm going to have a look round before I turn in."

He inspected the camp-fires methodically; then strolled down to the river-side, and sat among tumbled, moonlit rocks, looking at the water.

He was in no hurry. Even now, with the pistol cocked and lying across his knee, and a laconic scrawl, addressed to the colonel, ready folded in his pocket, he was prompted by a lifelong habit of scientific investigation to pause and think the matter over once more, as impartially as he would have considered the case of any stranger entrusted to his skill.

On the whole, suicide appeared the most reasonable way out of the deadlock. Till last week he had thought he might still conquer the drink craving, or at least keep it within such bounds that it would be only a misery to himself, not a danger to others. But if he had already come to this; if a patient in such extremity must forego relief lest he, a physician, should betray professional confidence; then it was time to make an end.

He had not gone under without a fight. Few of the experiments that had won him the name of a ruthless vivisector had been as ferocious as the methods of cure to which he had subjected himself. He had tried to starve the craving out of his nerves, to burn it out, to stifle it with furious exertion, to deaden it with fatigue. He had lain all night with a brandy bottle on his pillow, and corrosive acid smeared on the edges of the glass. All these things alike had failed to help; and now old age was creeping near, the bleared and garrulous old age of the nip-drinker.

Degeneration, degeneration . . . Yes, the pistol was his best refuge.

But the expedition? How were these raw lads to get through the fever swamps with no doctor, and not a man among them that knew the tropics except poor old Armand, failing in health and a fool into the bargain? Martel had some commonsense, but no experience; and, anyhow, he couldn't stand alone against Lortigue and Guillaumet. Then, for Rivarez it was a life and death matter; his chance of ever being strong again depended on skilled care now, though it might be the care of a doctor whom he couldn't trust.

At any price, one must see the boys through; that was clear. There was always suicide to fall back on afterwards, if need be.

No, he would have no sham consolations. It was now or never. It might be another three years before the boys could get on without help, and by then it would be too late. An old drunkard hasn't pluck enough left to shoot himself, or brains enough to see why he should; he has nothing but an appetite.

"All the same, you can't rat. There isn't any way out." He laid the pistol aside, and sat up, quite straight and still.

His head was clear enough now, at any rate. He could see the whole future mapped out before him. It was a pity one couldn't go under a little quicker, once the case was hopeless. It would come very slowly, and he knew the symptoms by heart beforehand. That's the worst of being a brain-specialist; it's all so familiar. Your bull's-eye lantern has searched every step of the descent into the pit; and when your own turn comes to slide down, you know both what will meet you on the way, and what waits at the bottom.

How far had he slid yet? And how long would the remaining stages take? How soon could he hope to be past caring? He ran a swift professional eye back over his case.

Age fifty-four; occupation healthy, but of late

entailing some fatigue and hardship in a tropical climate; family history excellent on both sides. Personal history: no previous illnesses; health sound except for an occasional touch of liver when overworked. Has always worked to limit of capacity. Has at various times tried experiments on himself, with drink and drugs, also with . . . No, none of those are germane to the case, but the ones with alcohol may have had something to do with it. How much?

Habits abstemious and regular till mental shock at forty-five. Drank continuously for nine weeks; went abroad; coast-line; all right for fourteen months. One attack after seeing geraniums; took drastic measures; went abroad again; all right for nearly six years. Bad relapse after another shock; drank for six weeks; went abroad third time. Coast-line failed; drastic measures failed; daisy; craving took chronic form. Has given way twice in thirteen months, once without any special cause. The new feature is the chronic character of the desire. First symptom of incipient degeneration. There is also constant fear . . .

It came like a blow on the head, scattering his thoughts in a shower of sparks. "Why, this isn't the drink habit! This is funk; sheer crazy funk. You've been drinking for fear of drink . . ."

He was standing up, somehow, with both hands
flat against the rock behind him to hold it steady,
and the moon jiggiting up and down in the sky.
Well, this was a fool trick for a man's nerves to
play him. He shut his eyes, and held them shut
till the hammer left off thumping in his chest;
then he resumed his interrupted analysis of the
case.

It was only since his coast-line panacea had
failed that he had been haunted this way; he had
left off analyzing then. And even so, in thirteen
months the terror had not driven him to alcohol
more than twice. Was this the incurable habit
that he had fought so blindly?

"But you haven't got it!" he cried aloud; and
laughed till the echoes of the rocks laughed with
him. "You haven't analyzed the thing, you
ass! It's a bogey you've been frightened at;
there's nothing there at all!"

He stooped for the pistol, set it at half-cock
and tucked it into his belt. He had done with
drink, and the fear of drink. The humour of the
situation kept him still chuckling grimly as he
filled his pipe. For a leading brain-specialist he
had made a pretty fool of himself. "All the same,
it's an interesting lapse," he murmured as he
walked back to camp. "Now, why was it I didn't
think of that before?"

*   *   *   *   *   *

The expedition returned to Europe in due course, but with two members missing. The dysentery of the poisonous tropical swamps had carried off Stéger, and de Vigne had been killed in a skirmish with native tribes during an attempt to cross the Ucayale wilderness. Guillaumet had taken no part in any adventures; he had been left behind, by common consent, in a mission-station on the Amazon, and rejoined the explorers only on their way home.

Over three years of incessant toil, hardship, and danger had left their mark on the company. The commander was now a decrepit old man; he had stuck bravely to his work, but all his desire was to get back to France, and have a few quiet years there before he died. His importance had not borne the long strain. The simplicity into which it had faded gave him, at the close of his life, that dignity to which he had so long aspired. During the last two years Marchand had virtually com-manded the expedition, with René and Felix for counsellors and helpers. All three had done their best to spare the old man's pride, keeping carefully in the background and offering him deferential "suggestions" which he was too wise to disregard.

To Marchand these years had brought salvation. Once laid, the spectre had never troubled him again; and, for the rest, the deadly nature of the responsibility thrust upon him by the break-down of his old friend had forced him to keep sober for so long that the physical desire for drink had worn itself out. He too had aged; but he was cured, and could go back to Paris without dread.

As for Bertillon, he had grown up, and no longer rushed into needless peril to prove the courage which no one doubted. Lortigue alone had learned nothing. The shock of the Acauan affair had long worn off; the memory had twisted itself, in his mind, into a reminiscence of an exciting adventure in which he and the interpreter had played equally picturesque and heroic parts. Neither danger nor humiliation could disturb for long his buoyant self-content; it rose after every drowning, unchanged and unchangeable.

René, bronzed and bearded, sat on deck, read-ing again the letters which he had found waiting for him when the ship touched at Madeira. Mar-guerite had not much family news to tell: old Marthe was dead, Aunt Angélique had been laid up all the winter, Henri was married at last, a new instalment of father's translations of papyri was coming out; that was all that had happened in four years, except to the girl herself. The complication was now finally cured, and her general health, in consequence, much better. She was far less helpless, and Bonnet, who had again seen her, believed her to be already fit to meet the strain of the radical cure. "And this too, like all my other blessings, I owe to you. Otherwise everything has been as always; I still read Greek, and help father with his work, and count the days that you are gone. But now the world is transformed for me; I can count the days till you come home. I wonder, are you very different? Shall I see a new René; and if I love him too much will the old René that I carry in my heart be jealous? Ah, but you can't really have changed; it's only the outside of you that can change. You are always René, and I am always Pâquerette. Nothing else matters."

At the end of the letter was a postscript: "My dearest, of course I want to meet your friend. He must come to stay with us some time, but not at first. Just at first I must have you all to myself."

Marchand came up to him as he sat with the letters.

"Martel, are you busy? I want a talk with you some time."

"No, I wasn't doing anything. Where is Felix?"

"In the colonel's cabin. It's about him I want to speak to you. Do you know what he's going to do after we get home?"

"At once, do you mean? I suppose he'll go to Paris with the rest of you."

"Oh, that's simple enough; not one of us will be able to do anything for the first month or two, but attend meetings and refuse invitations and answer idiotic questions. You needn't think you'll escape lionizing, any more than the rest of us."

René laughed, but his eyes were grave. "Guillaumet can have my share; I shall have other things to think about. Probably I shan't get to Paris at all this year. I shall go straight home to Burgundy from Marseilles, and then, I think, to Lyons. But no doubt Felix will go with you."

"Of course; but that's not what I mean. What is he going to do afterwards for a living?"

"I believe he has some notion of becoming a journalist."

"H'm. That's all right if he makes a success of it, but I won't have him a poor journalist. He can't afford it."

"You mean . . .?"

Marchand nodded. "Cheap lodgings and bad food would soon start those attacks all over again."

"But his health is so much better than it was; he's like another person. You've done wonders with him."

"Yes, he's immensely improved, without doubt; it's marvellous how he has recovered in the sort of conditions we've been having, and in that climate too. All the same. his constitution has been knocked about too badly to stand poverty now. For the future he's got to be comfortable if he doesn't want to break down. And he hasn't a sou except his pay."

"No, but it has been accumulating. He has enough to keep him for some time, and meanwhile he can get work."

Marchand smoked in silence for a while.

"I have more than I want," he began tentatively.

René stopped him at once.

"Don't say that to Felix; he wouldn't forgive you."

"He's difficult, I know; but I thought perhaps you . . . ?"

"If I had money of my own to spare, I shouldn't dare to offer it. Even the closest friendship goes only a certain length with him; he's a . . . solitary kind of being. I begin to think, sometimes, one isn't really of much use to him."

He broke off and sat looking at the water.

"It's a solitary kind of world, you see," said Marchand. "You may be able to save a man's life, on occasion, or look after his health a bit; and that's about all anybody can do for anybody."

Then he added, inconsequently: "My son died as a baby."

While smoking on deck with René and Felix the next evening, he told them that his banker had written to him, strongly advising a certain investment, which seemed to be both safe and exceptionally profitable; and asked whether they would care to make use of the opportunity for any part of their accumulated salaries. To René the offer was useless, as most of his money would soon be spent; but Felix accepted with a simplicity that made Marchand wonder whether the subterfuge had been necessary.

"Martel judges by himself," he thought. "This one's too big to be proud about money."

"I hadn't a notion what to do with it," Felix said gaily. "There's a beautifully settled feeling about being a shareholder; it's all of a piece with coming to live in Paris and wear a black coat and write for the newspapers."

Marchand looked at him from under frowning brows.

"Are you going in for respectability and a career, by any chance?"

"I'm not going to b-b-bother my head much about respectability, and a career is altogether too gorgeous a thing. I'm just going to live p-p-peaceably in my own little corner, and keep dry."

"A difficult combination, isn't it, when your own little corner happens to be a corner of Niagara?"

René looked up with a puzzled smile. He was used to hearing this clash of repartees between Marchand and Felix, and to accepting it good-humouredly, whether he understood or not; but this time he shook his head.

"That's unkind. If a man wants to keep dry, you shouldn't throw cold water on him."

"I shouldn't on you," Marchand retorted; "but if he wants to keep dry he'll have to dress in oilskins."

They both started at the bitterness of the voice in which Felix answered: "Oilskins are only good to drown in. For the future, my dear Pangloss, I shall 'cultivate my garden'; I've had enough of philosophy and Mademoiselle Cunégonde."

"No doubt," said Marchand. "Has Mademoiselle Cunégonde had enough of you?"

The red end of the cigarette that Felix was holding made a swift line of light in the dark.

"'She is a washer of dishes, she is ugly,'" he whispered to himself; and presently rose and moved away with his limping, yet stealthy tread. The end of the cigarette appeared and disappeared as he walked up and down the deck.

"She may be ugly, but she's strong in the arms," said Marchand. He turned to René with a fierce gloominess of look and tone.

"Hold on to him tight if you're his friend. He's in a dangerous way; he thinks he's going to settle down and be like other folk."

"My dear doctor," said René; "have you still not found out that if you and Felix want me to understand things, you've got to keep at the level of my intelligence? I haven't the ghost of a notion what all this talk has been about. If you're Pangloss to his Candide, who is Cunégonde? As for me, I can aspire to no nobler part than that of the old woman who looked on."

Marchand burst out laughing.

"No; you'll be the virtuous anabaptist, and be chucked overboard."

*   *   *   *   *   *

At Marteurelles the sweet marjoram was in blossom all the way up the drive. René tried to fix his attention on Henri's joyous stream of talk; but his heart was thumping like a hammer, and the smell of Marguerite's favourite flower nearly brought tears into his eyes. Even the sing-song Burgundian speech of the country-folk by the roadside was as music in his ears.

He looked up at the grey tower. From Marguerite's window a face framed in a black cloud of hair looked down at him. He stooped and picked a sprig of marjoram to bring to her.

It was the marquis who drew Henri gently aside in the hall, that René might go upstairs alone. Half an hour later a gay message was sent down, inviting the family to take coffee in Marguerite's room, "as I really cannot spare him." They all went up and found René, laughing and flushed, pouring cream on to the raspberries that Rosine had brought. Blanche, Henri's wife, stared in amazement; the plain, dowdy little sister-in-law was scarcely recognizable. There was a faint and lovely colour in her cheeks, her great eyes shone, and all her dusky masses of hair hung loose about her shoulders. She was tying up bunches of flowers.

"Everyone must be beautiful to-day. René, give the mignonette to father; he likes scented things. Oh, no, aunt; indeed you mustn't take it out; lavender is just right with grey hair. Put the marigolds into your bib, Rosine, and take one to Jacques for his buttonhole. Now, Henri, we want to hear all about everything. Where did you meet? At Dijon? Did you recognize him with that ridiculous beard? Oh, but you'll have to shave; I can't own a brother that looks like a wild man of the woods."

"But I am a wild man of the woods," René protested. "You haven't realized yet how uncivilized I've grown. Except Felix, I don't think one of us knew what to do with fruit-knives and table-napkins the first time we saw them again."

"Why 'except'?"

"I don't know. You'll see when you meet him. Felix was born dainty; he rides a mangy Brazilian mule as if it were a thoroughbred. He's like father in that way."

"What way?" Henri asked, with a perplexed face. Marguerite laughed merrily.

"Oh, you know; the 'born in the purple' air. If father were dressed in a beggar's cast-off rags he'd be taken for a prince wearing them for a masquerade."

"I'm not so sure," said René, looking down at his plate. "Rags are an effective disguise, whoever wears them."

"Which is Felix?" asked the marquis. "The man who saved you all from the savages?"

"Yes, sir, Felix Rivarez; he's my best friend. I hope you'll all meet him soon."

"It sounds like a Spanish name," Blanche put in. "What country does he belong to?"

René paused for an instant, with the lie burning his tongue before he uttered it.

"He is from the Argentine."

"A South American? And he has come over with you? Has he ever been in Europe before?"

"I don't think so."

The gaiety had died out of Marguerite's face. She looked up; and, meeting her father's eyes, saw that he, too, was asking himself why the mere mention of this friend from the Argentine should, twice within one minute, make René's voice jerky.

The next day the cases of curios were unpacked, and the servants were called in to receive their presents. René had forgotten no one. When the woven basket labelled with old Marthe's name was lifted out, he took it quickly from his brother, and, beckoning Rosine aside, put it into her hand.

"It was packed before I heard of your mother's death. Perhaps you will keep it for her sake. I'm very sorry, Rosine; she was good to us when we were children."

He came back to find Henri opening another case.

"Take care," he said. "Those are native weapons, and some are poisoned."

"What are you going to do with them?"

"They're not all mine. Most of them belong to Felix; I just packed them with my things. He's making a collection of weapons."

"Is this his, too?"

Henri took up a flat parcel, labelled: "Felix."

"No, that is mine. It's a crayon portrait of him, done by an artist that was on the ship with us."

"I may look, I suppose," said Henri, untying the string. Angélique rose to lean over his shoulder.

"Oh, let me see; I feel quite impatient to know him. Is he handsome? Spaniards often are, they say. Doesn't it seem strange, Étienne, to owe dear René's life to a man we have never seen? I'm sure we shall all love him. Oh . . ."

She had rattled on without noticing Rene's look. When she broke off with a smothered exclamation, Marguerite started slightly and dropped her eyes.

"What a strange face !" Angélique said. "Oh, no, Blanche, I don't agree with you. He's quite handsome; indeed, rather striking; but . . . Look, Étienne !"

The marquis was watching René.

"May I ?" he asked softly.

"Of course, sir."

He looked, and was silent. This was the man who had robbed him of his last chance. Some day, he had thought, when Marguerite was cured and happy, and all the miserable past forgotten, he might become René's friend, perhaps even his closest man friend. He knew better now.

"Thank you," he said at last, and laid the portrait on the table.

"Doesn't that face remind you of something, Étienne?" asked the old maid.

"Yes; in expression, not in feature. It's a picture in the Louvre: Lionardo da Vinci's St. John. I'm glad he's your friend, René, not your enemy."

"So am I, father."

Angélique was hurt; this seemed to her almost blasphemous.

"I have never seen the pictures in the Louvre," she said; "but I can hardly think any artist would represent the blessed saint like that. Oh, don't think I mean to disparage your friend, my dear; I shall never forget what we owe him. Very likely it may be just something in the drawing. The expression is so . . . it's like . . ."

René laughed in a queer, uncomfortable way.

"A cat, perhaps? The Belgian who went out with us said the little jaguaronda panthers that prowled about the camp reminded him of Felix. I couldn't see the likeness myself, but no doubt we all appeared in an unflattering light to poor Guillaumet; we weren't nice to him."

"Why?" asked Blanche. René shrugged his shoulders and answered in a dry voice: "We didn't like him."

The feather head-dress that Marchand had given to René caught Angélique's eyes, and she failed to notice that Marguerite had not looked at the portrait.

When René went to the girl's room to say good-night, she asked him to bring it to her; and, left alone, stared long and drearily at the beautiful, dangerous head. The artist had known much of his craft, though little of his sitter, and had drawn him smiling, half in shadow.

"Oh, I hate him!" Marguerite cried out, and covered her eyes. "I hate him!"

Then her hands dropped. Ah, how monstrous, to hate the man who had saved René from murder! And there was nothing hateful in the face. It might have been an angel's, if only he wouldn't smile.

She gave the portrait back to René in the morning, without comment.

"Thank you, dearest," he said gravely, as he wrapped it up. "You were right; you are always Pâquerette."

He could not have explained to her why he was so glad that she had refrained from talking about it, even from looking at it, in the presence of the others.

"Is he really as beautiful as that?" she asked after a moment.

"I can't judge; I have come too near. To me he is beautiful."

"And as . . . ?" She checked herself. The word on her lips had been, "Poisonous."

"Ah, well, I won't ask you questions. I shall know when I meet him, after Lyons. I shall know many things by then, shan't I, René?"

He looked down at the hand that lay in his.

"Pâquerette, my darling, are you sure you want to go to Lyons?"

She glanced at him with a smile, half whimsical, half tender.

"Is that all you know about me after all these

years? Why, you dear goose, do you think I'd give you up for four whole years, and have you risk your life for me, and then let it all be wasted just for the fear of a little pain?"

"It's not a little. Dear, you were only eighteen when you decided."

"Everything's a little when one has lain awake night after night and asked oneself: 'Is he dying of fever? Is he dead? Have the wild beasts eaten him?' I have dreamed of you drowned, and starved, and torn to pieces. I have seen father look at me and think: 'It was for her.' Four years of that doesn't leave one very young. I'm a great deal more than eighteen now; a great deal more than twenty-two. You can't frighten me with anything Bonnet can do."

He bent down and kissed her forehead.

"Then, if we are going, it had better be at once. I'll write to Bonnet."

"He is expecting us. I wrote a month ago, saying that you were on your way home, and that we should probably come soon. René, you will stay with me all the time, won't you? I'm not religious, you see. I haven't got any god to hold on to; I've only you."

They started for Lyons in the following week, taking Rosine with them; and, on arriving, Marguerite at once went under treatment. Dr. Bonnet, as rough and bearish in manner as Mar-

chand himself, soon began to show, to both
brother and sister, something of Marchand's
underlying gentleness. "That girl's the right
sort," he said to René. "She's got pluck."

Certainly she would need it. From the first it
was evident that the cure, even if all should go
well, must be slow and painful. After nearly
three months Bonnet told them that the method
on which he had been working was not proving
successful, and that he must try another experiment.

"Mind," he said gruffly; "I won't guarantee
that this one will be the last one, either. It's a
difficult case."

Marguerite silently put a hand over her eyes.

"Well?" said Bonnet, after a moment. "Do
you want to give it up?"

She threw back her head with a gallant peal of
laughter.

"Give it up? Why, you're as tender-hearted
as my brother! Do look in the glass, both of you;
did you ever see such doleful faces? I might as
well have my maiden aunt here, except that you
don't cry."

René looked round.

"You see, she has made up her mind to go on.
It's no use saying any more."

"Not a tiny bit," she answered in her gayest
tones. "No more use than it was for me to ob-

ject when you went to Ecuador. It's my turn
to be autocratic now."

*   *   *   *   *   *

Felix, meanwhile, seemed to be assiduously
cultivating his garden. During the long autumn
and winter that René spent at Lyons, a helpless
onlooker wearing out his heart in striving after
patience, letters came at intervals, from Marchand,
from Bertillon, from Felix himself.

Paris had been kind; the Acauan story, told by
Duprez at a public banquet, had been repeated
everywhere, and the velvet voice and racy tongue
had done the rest. Felix was already a social
success. Also two of the leading newspapers
had offered him permanent work at high pay;
he was not likely to suffer want. "For his health,"
Marchand wrote in January, "I am now far less
anxious. He continues to improve with every
month. When we arrived here I advised him to
put himself into the hands of my old colleague
Leroux, and am more than satisfied with the
result. As a patient, and apparently in every
other way, he remains a model of discretion;
follows scrupulously all instructions about exercise and diet and hours; works steadily, without overworking; cultivates influential friends
without cheapening himself, and makes a reputation as a wit without being ill-natured, and as
a connoisseur without being mean. By the way,

his collection of savage weapons is growing fast;
he is developing quite a gift for picking them up
in unlikely places. Some day they ought to be
worth money. Meanwhile, it's a harmless hobby,
and not too expensive. Of course, the women
throw themselves at his head; but it won't be that
way he'll wreck his life. At present he's engaged
in building it up, stone by stone. God help the
fool!"

René worried over this letter for a day or two.
This was the second time that Marchand had
hinted at some danger threatening Felix. Why
should anything go wrong with him? Surely
enough things had gone wrong already. Why
should he not now become, as his energy and
talents deserved, a successful man? But Marchand's mind had been warped by his own misfortunes; he had become unable to see the world
otherwise than as a place of traps and tragedies.
The mere fact that Felix was dear to him was
enough to rouse his morbid fears. And there was
enough real trouble in the world without going
about seeking for imaginary sorrows. So René
put the thing out of his mind.

The letters from Felix himself were always
bright and amusing. They came quite regularly;
written with obvious intent to cheer, but yet delightfully spontaneous. To René their sweet
gaiety was like a weekly ray of sunshine. He

read many of them aloud to Marguerite; it seemed to him that they could not fail to comfort her too.

At New Year came a beautiful engraving of the Fighting Gladiator, addressed to Marguerite. "I venture to send this to your sister," Felix wrote, "though I do not yet know her, except through you. It is such a large exception that I hope she will forgive my feeling as if she were an old friend."

Marguerite wrote a gracious letter of thanks, talked charmingly to René of his friend's kindness, and presently gave way to a fit of unreasoning irritability, ending in a wild outburst of tears, which her brother ascribed to the overstrung state of her nerves. The next morning she was in her sunniest mood, laughing at herself for "having been so cross"; and it did not occur to him to connect her momentary loss of balance with the New Year gift.

In March, René went to Paris for three weeks. The official records of the expedition were now ready for publication, and he was wanted to revise the maps. Also, Duprez had written, asking him to attend the annual dinner of the Geographical Society, and offering to introduce him to persons through whom he could obtain a post as soon as he should be free. The necessity of making a livelihood compelled him to accept the invitation; but he was so reluctant to leave Marguerite that she was forced to insist on his going. As always, her courage rose to meet the extra strain.

"And don't hurry back; I expect you to have a real holiday with your friend, and make love to all the pretty ladies, and enjoy yourself tremendously. Why, wouldn't anybody think you were going to the desert of Sahara, instead of Paris? You silly boy, I shall be all right. No, I won't have aunt sent for, I don't want her fussing about. Rosine will look after me splendidly; and, perhaps, when you come back, we shall have news for you. I believe, somehow, it's going to be successful this time."

René held his tongue. It had been "going to be successful" so many times that he was losing heart.

A disappointment awaited him in Paris; Felix had just left for London, to see the editor of a magazine to which he had undertaken to contribute a series of articles. He hoped to be back for the geographers' dinner, and wrote begging René to wait till then, if possible. But René was impatient to get back to Lyons; the thought of Marguerite, alone and suffering, made him utterly wretched; and, but for urgent business, he would have gone before the date of the banquet.

Being compelled to stay, he made use of the opportunity to see a good deal of Marchand; and, oddly enough, got to know him better in these

three weeks than in the four years which they had
spent together. Though they had liked each
other from the outset, the shyness of the younger
man and the black depression of the elder had
prevented any intimacy between them. Now,
for the first time, René found himself behind the
wall of cynicism which Marchand had erected as a
defence against his neighbours. The churlish
manners remained, but no longer formed a barrier.
Somehow Marchand was humanly approachable
now.

Ethnology had been, at the best, a stopgap,
something of scientific interest to still the clam-
ouring of the restless brain that must have work
to do. It had been better than drink; it had
even been the means of obtaining valuable side-
lights on the remnants of savagery still lingering
in civilized minds; but it was not psychiatry.
Now, though he would never touch private practice again, he had returned to his real work. He
was managing a big lunatic asylum, and tracing
out the preventable causes of certain forms of
mental disease. His analysis of the after-effects
of fear on the minds of children, though too technical to reach many parents directly, was likely
to prove an important addition to the knowledge
of thoughtful family doctors. "If I get one book
out," he said to René in his gruff, sudden way,
"I shall have done my job."

Felix reached Paris too late to see his friend before they met in the hall. As René entered, the first thing that caught his eyes was a laughing crowd of men surrounding and hiding a central figure. Guillaumet came up to him, nodding familiarly, and glanced with an acid smile towards the merry group.

"Our friend seems to be quite the lion of the evening. Not exactly good taste, that sort of thing, is it?"

The group had separated, and René could see the black head of Felix in the middle. He looked the Belgian coolly up and down.

"Backbiting the man that saved your life? No, perhaps it isn't quite in the best taste; but when one saves so many lives, there are bound to be a few second-rate ones among them."

He turned his back, leaving Guillaumet speechless, and walked through the hall, pausing here and there to exchange greetings with old fellow-students or comrades. A fresh burst of laughter from the listening crowd made his heart sink. Marchand's croaking was too absurd to bother about; of course it was nonsense; still, Felix was never funny like this unless something was wrong.

All through the interminable dinner he waited and watched. Felix was sitting at some distance from him, so they could exchange only a nod across the table; but the over-bright eyes and the incessant stream of stammering flippancies told him enough. After dinner followed speeches; dull, elaborate, solemn, facetious, complimentary. This was the first annual dinner since the return of the explorers, so there were many references to their work and adventures. Then Duprez spoke, and Marchand, bored and inscrutable, followed him with a few conventional phrases.

Felix rose amid smiles and applause. He was the show member of the expedition, and everyone was eager to hear him. A roar of laughter and hand-clapping followed his speech. To René the whole thing seemed hateful; this hard, metallic, scintillating creature was not Felix, was not even any disguise that Felix ought ever to wear.

The evening was nearly over before they had an opportunity to speak to each other; and then the first thing that Felix said was: "What about your sister?"

"Just the same. Bonnet is still very hopeful; I don't know that I am."

"And she?"

"She keeps up everybody's courage; she has done from the beginning."

"You go back to-morrow?"

"Yes; I was going to start early, but now you are here I shall take the evening coach instead;

that is, if you can spare me any time to-morrow.
I want to talk to you about two or three things."

Felix hesitated strangely.

"Very well. Will you come round to my rooms
in the morning? I'm not quite sure I can come
to you."

"Besides, I want to see the collection. I'll be
with you at midday. Look here . . ." He
broke off.

"Yes?"

"Is anything wrong?"

Felix lifted his eyebrows.

"With me? Nothing ever goes wrong with me
nowadays."

Nevertheless, René arrived next morning prepared to hear bad news.

"What was the matter with you last night?"
he asked, turning suddenly from the collection of
arrows, clubs, and blow-pipes that adorned the
wall.

"The matter?"

"Yes; you quite scared me, showing off like
that. Do you know, for a minute I thought you
were going to be ill again?"

"So did I," Felix answered softly.

"Felix! But you're not . . . ?"

"No, it's all right, I think. I got caught in the
storm in travelling, and was wet through for some
hours; and when I told Marchand, before you

came in, he made such a fuss that he frightened me. He has a notion that any bad chill might start the whole thing over again. I didn't mean you to know."

"Have you seen Leroux?"

"I've just had a note from him, saying Marchand went round to tell him late last night, and he's coming this morning. It's ridiculous, the way they fuss, both of them. There's absolutely nothing wrong; it would have started before now, if it were going to."

"Are you sure?"

Felix turned on him with fierce irritation.

"I'm sure that I'm a damned coward and that Marchand had better have held his tongue."

"Felix, I wish you had told me yesterday."

"Why? To have you insist on coming back with me, and spend a ch-cheerful night tramping the floor, before a journey, too? If I am a coward, that's no reason why you shouldn't get any sleep. There, that's Leroux at the door. I hope to goodness he won't be sympathetic, whatever's going to happen. It's funny doctors should be so emotional; one would think they saw enough to harden them — How are you, doctor? It was a sh-sh-shame of Marchand to bother you for nothing; I'm in robust health, I assure you. No, don't go away, René."

After a good deal of questioning and examining,

Leroux sat down and looked at the two friends with a triumphant smile.

"Not the smallest trace of any ill effects. A year ago such a chill would almost certainly have had disastrous consequences. Let me see; how long is it since the last bad attack? Three years?"

It was René who answered.

"Three and a half since the last very bad one; there have been slighter ones since then, but not since we left the Amazon."

"I think," said Leroux, "I may safely say, now, that the tendency has worn itself out."

Felix, still silent, took a cigarette and began to twist it in his fingers.

"Do you mean," René asked, "that he is really safe; that it will never come back?"

"Unless anything were to start it afresh. He will probably never be very strong; and mind" — he turned sharply to Felix — "don't risk any more wars or tropical exploring. Otherwise, short of anything like shipwreck, I think you're as safe as most of us now. Take reasonable care of yourself, and don't expose your constitution to any new shocks. On the whole, I think we may count it a cure."

Felix put the cigarette into his mouth and lighted it deliberately, with the air of a person who has been told something amusing.

"R-r-really? What a fondness for practical joking the Lord does seem to have! He's always springing surprises on one. This is rather a new variety, though; perhaps the other sort is getting a l-l-little monotonous. Oh, thank you very much; yes, it seems quite an occasion for congratulations, doesn't it? Why, of course; I know how busy you are. Don't let me keep you now. Good morning!"

As the door shut he turned on René with a gesture of savage impatience. He had begun to shake suddenly.

"Oh, confound you, René; get out! There, let me alone a minute. . . . Damn Leroux and his congratulations!"

He pulled himself together with a furious effort, and began to talk very fast.

"I say, René, do you remember old Marchand preaching to me in the Pastassa valley about its being good for the soul to make a fuss when things go wrong? N-n-nothing like bettering one's instructions. Here am I making all the fuss I know how because they go right. Seems a bit illogical, eh?"

René looked at him with a dawning smile. He had realized that the function of a friend at this moment was to keep talking for a few seconds without a stop.

"I don't often have the honour to understand

anything you do," he said; "but on a certain occasion I made the completest possible ass of myself because the thing I had been afraid of didn't happen. Oddly enough, it was not relief that upset me; it was sheer annoyance at having spent the day in screwing up for nothing."

He left the occasion unspecified; and Felix, who had already regained his self-command, glanced at him quickly and thought: "Something about the little sister. I wonder what it feels like to have anybody care for one as much as that."

René broke in on his thoughts: "By the way, don't you think you were rather unkind to poor Leroux just now?"

"To Leroux? What on earth do you mean?"

"Well, you simply frightened him away with blasphemies; and you know how conventional he is."

"I wanted to get rid of him."

"No doubt; all the same, I wish you wouldn't say those things to people who don't understand. It's all very well when one knows you; but it used to bother me at first."

"You! I dare say; but then you had a liking for me."

"And Leroux, according to Marchand, pretty nearly worships the ground you walk on. Hadn't you found it out? For so very clever a person you are curiously dense sometimes."

"But I scarcely know him! I only go to him as a patient."

"What has that to do with it? I don't suppose you know your landlady very intimately; but I'm told she wept bitterly when you went to London. And her son who cleans your boots treasures up the tip that you gave him at New Year, it seems, and won't spend it because it was yours. And why do you suppose I get better served than other folk at the Café Pregny? Only because the waiters idolize you, and Bertillon took upon himself to tell them I'm your friend."

"René, this is sheer nonsense. Not one of these persons has ever given me the smallest hint of such a thing."

"Of course not; they're all too much afraid of you. But you seem to have as many adorers as . . ."

Felix burst out laughing.

"'Oh God, your only jig-maker!' Quite a lot of people like me nowadays; but it's only because I play the fool and keep them laughing. If I were ever to be real for a minute, they'd all turn on me."

"All? Marchand, for instance?"

"Marchand's a good fellow when he isn't putting one under a microscope. Vivisectors seem to be quite a kindly folk when they're off duty. But lots of people are kind so long as you never trust them and never let them see that anything hurts."

"Well, Marchand has seen enough, in all conscience."

"Ah, don't! Dear me, I seem to be as jumpy as a cat this morning. . . . And it will never come back. Think of it — never! Yes, but he may be mistaken; what shall I do if he's mistaken, what shall I do! Oh, I should have to put an end to it. You know I couldn't go on . . . Look here, René, you've got to catch the afternoon coach. And there's a big rose-bush in a pot that you're to take to your sister. It's waiting at the diligence bureau."

"When did you get it?"

"I sent out for it this morning. It's a white rose; they hadn't got the velvet dark red sort you said she likes so much."

René carried the rose-bush into Marguerite's room in Lyons; and the girl, watching him with jealous eyes as he took off its wrappings, said to herself: "He never touches anyone else's flowers that way."

The bitterness of her resentment against her brother's unknown friend had become a constant torment to her. René's love was, just now, the only joy and consolation that her life contained. He was still, as he had been for twelve years, the centre of her world: and till last summer she had

believed herself to be still the centre of his. To
find, on his return home, that his orbit was no
longer circular, but elliptical, that his affections
revolved around two centres, had been a horrible
shock to her. Love, as she understood it, was a
limited possession, not to be acquired by one person except at a corresponding loss to another.
Formerly René had loved her alone; now his
love was divided between her and Felix; therefore
Felix, the happy, brilliant, and successful being
who already owned so much more than his fair
share of all desirable things, must have stolen from
her half of this, her solitary treasure. To realize
that the friendship had made of René a bigger
creature than he had been before, and that she
herself was richer in consequence of it, was utterly
beyond her.

There remained the fact that, but for Felix,
she would now have had no René at all. She
made herself wretched with self-reproach for her
ingratitude; and, remembering how immense
was the claim upon her goodwill which this
stranger had established, hated him only the
more.

Perhaps, if she had known of his former ill-
health, she might have felt more charitably towards him; but René had found it impossible to
speak at all of a subject connected in his mind with
things so private and so tragic. His instinct was

to shrink from renewing, in his own memory, the discoveries which he had made in the Pastassa valley; and, beyond the mere fact that Felix was "slightly lame," Marguerite had no idea that anything in his life had ever gone wrong. She took for granted that all was well with him; and hated him for that again, and hated the rose-bush because it came from him. But for the fear of distressing René, she would have had it thrown away. Out of consideration for his feelings she endured its presence in the room; and, looking at its fragile and costly gorgeousness, told herself that when one is rich and well and generally favoured of the gods, it is an easy form of philanthropy to enter a florist's shop in passing, and order expensive roses for an invalid.

This fear of hurting René had quite prevented her from being truthful with him in the matter of her feeling towards his friend. René, for his part, having no personal experience of jealousy, did not guess what was passing in his sister's mind. From his point of view, the beloved of our beloved, even though unknown, must be dear with a reflected glory of love. It would have seemed to him an inconceivable thing that anyone could love him without loving Felix for his sake; and this not because Felix had preserved his life, but because he had made that life so rich.

*   *   *   *   *   *

Summer came at last. Marguerite still persisted in her dogged hoping against hope; still, after eleven months of failure and disappointment, kept up her brother's courage. All the family entreated her in their letters to abandon the useless, cruel struggle; her father came to Lyons to persuade her. She shook her head and set her teeth, and answered: "I'll go on as long as Bonnet will."

The hardest thing of all was that René was again obliged to leave her, this time for more than two months. He was offered temporary work, excellently paid, in the north of France; and the expenses of the long treatment were so heavy that he did not dare to refuse. This time she consented to let Angélique replace him.

Coming back in the autumn, he found a change in her face that told him of good news. For the first time since the treatment began, there was a marked improvement in her condition. Another month made it clear that the obstinate malady was yielding at last. Gradually the treatment became less trying; and, as the local mischief disappeared, her general health and strength increased. "A few more months," Bonnet said; "and you will be quite cured."

"Still a few more months! Oh, I thought . . ."

She broke off, with a quiver of the under lip.

"Patience! I daren't let you use the leg for

U

some time yet; and then you will have to learn again how to walk."

"Dear," René said softly; "you have been patient so long; be patient just a little longer."

"A few more months," she repeated, and looked up at him. "Then, next year, we can really have the flat in Paris, after all!"

*   *   *   *   *   *

With Felix, too, all was going well. His health was now excellent; and his position as a journalist was assured in both Paris and London, where he had made many friends, and no more enemies than fall to the lot of most rapidly successful men. As time went on, many persons began to discover that his surface brilliancy concealed a surprising scrap-heap of miscellaneous information. Once, meeting at a dinner-party a very learned and eloquent French cardinal, he startled the company by entering into a discussion on Greek patristic literature, which ended in the prelate owning himself mistaken about the data on which his argument was based. "You have the better of me, M. Rivarez. I should have been more careful if I had known you keep St. John Chrysostom at your finger-ends."

"My finger-ends must apologize to your Eminence; they had forgotten that the G-g-golden Mouth is annexed by right of inheritance."

The cardinal smiled. "At least the golden mouth of the flatterer is yours, I fear."

"Where on earth did you pick up all that stuff, Rivarez?" someone asked when the cardinal had gone. Felix shrugged his shoulders.

"Oh, one just d-dips into things."

He had dipped into many things. Sometimes, if he happened to meet a man who interested him, he would drop the artificial flippancy which was his usual affectation in society. This happened on one occasion during his second winter in Paris, when he met in a fashionable house a little, care-worn, sedate Italian with wonderful black eyes.

"Signor Giuseppe —," murmured the busy hostess, introducing them hurriedly. Felix looked at him with interest, recognizing the name of a well-known political refugee, and at once began to talk graceful trifles in Italian. After a few sentences the refugee looked up, surprised.

"But . . . you are Italian!"

"Oh, no; I speak the language, that is all."

He deftly introduced one or two slips in grammar. Signor Giuseppe glanced at him sideways, and slid into small talk, shifting the conversation, a moment later, to Italy, then to Italian politics. When the hostess came up to them again an hour later, they were still talking. Two or three other persons had joined in the conversation, which was now carried on in French.

"Why, it's a real political debate," said the lady. "Confess, signore, you did not expect, when you came here this evening, to find so much interest in Italian affairs."

He looked up, smiling and grave.

"It is I that have been interested, madame. I should be glad if many of my countrymen had as clear an insight into the things that concern them most nearly as M. Rivarez has. I hope we shall meet again," he added, turning to Felix.

They exchanged cards, and a few days later Signor Giuseppe called and renewed the discussion. Felix returned the call, but after some delay. Signor Giuseppe, he thought, though undoubtedly one of the most remarkable of living men, appeared to have only one topic of conversation. Moreover, he was known in Paris as an incurable plotter, always buried in conspiracies and intrigues. To Felix, an impartial observer of men and manners, as a journalist who would make a career for himself must be, that sort of thing was interesting, in moderation; but he did not want too much of it. Certainly he did not want to be talked about in connection with a person so rich in enemies. He must discourage any attempt to force the acquaintance.

And just Italian politics . . . Any other subject in the world would have been less unwelcome.

Just Italian politics, that had driven him out, at nineteen, to wreck his life . . .

That door was shut and locked. What was he about, peeping through the chink now? He was a man of the world, a cosmopolitan, rapidly becoming a successful Parisian. His memories began from the day when he started, in a brand-new outfit, to cross the mountains with the explorers. Italian politics meant neither more nor less to him than any other matter of public interest; and if Signor Giuseppe could talk of nothing else, he was prepared to listen politely, and contribute the comments of the intelligent foreigner.

This time, however, the Italian made no reference to politics at all, but talked fluently and charmingly of other matters. After that they met again on several occasions, and exchanged a few casual phrases here and there, on a footing of amicable and courteous mutual indifference.

On the day of the geographers' dinner in April, Felix sat in the sunny window of his sitting-room, answering a letter from René. The room was sweet with violets and daffodils; outside, the river sparkled in spring sunshine. He himself was as gay as the weather. The good news of Marguerite cheered him, for her brother's sake, almost as if he had known and loved her personally. She was really cured at last, and gaining strength and vigour with every day. She had now mastered the difficulty of using her crutches, had been out driving with René, had walked twice round the garden. "Next month," René's letter went on, "we leave here for good. We shall go to Marteurelles for the summer, and in September we hope to take the flat in Paris. If I get the lectureship I am trying for, we shall be quite comfortable. Marguerite is looking forward to meeting you in the autumn. She will have done with the crutches by that time."

"A gentleman to see you, sir," said the landlady.

It was Signor Giuseppe. He had called on business, he said. Would M. Rivarez favour him with his attention to a question of some importance?

Felix put his letters aside, wondering for which the visitor was going to dun him; a subscription to party funds, or newspaper articles on Italian affairs.

The nature of the business, when he heard it, made him open his eyes in amazement. Preparations were being made for an armed insurrection in the Four Legations of the Northern Apennines; the "little private hells," which were autocratically ruled, ostensibly by cardinal-legates, in fact by their favourites and blackmailers and the lovers of their mistresses. The plan was to distribute arms and ammunition secretly among the discontented mountaineers; then, when the signal should be given from a small hill-town in the Legation of Bologna, and transmitted by bonfires along the ridge of the hills from province to province, armed men were to march upon the four cities, storm the palaces, seize the persons of the legates, and, holding them as hostages, dictate terms to Rome.

Sheer wonder kept Felix silent for some time.

"Pardon me," he said at last. "Such schemes are either very idle talk, or very deadly secrets. Why do you tell this to me, a foreigner, a complete outsider, almost a stranger to you?"

Signor Giuseppe smiled. "Personally a stranger; that is true. But an outsider . . . ?"

"Yes," Felix answered, looking at him steadily. "Understand me, please; an outsider."

"Does that mean that we are not to count upon you?"

"To count upon me?"

Signor Giuseppe leaned his elbows on the table and rested his chin on both hands.

"I need a man to help in organizing this. He must have had experience in dealing with rough people, and in meeting emergencies, and in getting men and animals and baggage up and down hills; and he must know how to make people obey him. Your South American training would be useful. It's nothing to me what your personal history is, or why you choose to pretend you are a foreigner.

No doubt you have your private reasons. I am not asking for your confidence; I am giving you mine. I know when I can trust a man. Will you come?"

Felix had listened in silence; but a smile hovered round the corners of his mouth.

"Signore," he said, when the Italian had finished speaking; "I too was young once."

Signor Giuseppe nodded. "That's just it; and you will be again."

"Oh, I think not," Felix murmured with lifted brows.

The other made no attempt to convince him, but turned to admire the view from the windows. For a few minutes the conversation flowed amiably round trifles; then Felix glanced at his watch.

"I shall have to beg you to excuse me now; I am to speak at a very dull anniversary banquet to-night, and it is time for me to go and dress. Well, I suppose we shall not meet again? Feeling as I do about your enterprise, it would be a mockery to wish your friends success; but I will wish them a safe return and a less bitter disappointment than I fear is in store for them and you."

"Thank you," Signor Giuseppe answered coolly; "and good-bye, since you will not join. For my part, I leave here to-morrow to make arrangements."

He took up his hat, and, dusting it with his

sleeve, added in a careless tone: "I shall sleep at my lodgings to-night."

Felix looked at him with half-shut eyes. "Yes? You will go to bed early, no doubt, and get a long night's rest before the journey. Good-bye."

At the banquet he acquitted himself creditably enough, talking easy and graceful nonsense for a few minutes, but without adding to his reputation for wit. "Yes, he's always a delightful after-dinner speaker," he overheard one journalist saying to another as they went downstairs; "but he's not really in form to-night. Now if you'd heard him at the dinner last year! That was a display of fireworks."

He passed them and went out into the street, smiling. He was not "in form" to-night; he would never be in form again. If those good folk could know what his "displays of fireworks" had meant. . . .

Yes, a year ago to-night he had been funny; so funny that when he sat down his audience had thumped the table, and shouted, with tears of merriment in their eyes; "Go on, go on!" And he had sat listening to the laughter and applause, and thinking: "It will come back; and there will be no way out but poison; no way out. . . ."

And now he was safe; "short of shipwreck," quite safe. That horror, like all the other trage-dies and miseries of his youth, was over and done with; and he would never again need to keep the fear-demon at bay by being funny. And never again would the pit swallow him up because any friend was false or any god a lie; he had done with gods as he had done with demons, and his feet were set upon a rock.

With friends he had not quite done. It would perhaps have been wiser; but a man must take into account the failings and weaknesses of his own nature, and he was so made that he could not live quite without love. He might allow himself one friend. And here, too, he was safe; no friendship would ever again mean enough to him to endanger his peace of mind, and René's affection was a refuge against utter loneliness. René was clean of soul and made no claims; he could trust René never to intrude, and never to betray . . . And, even if he were mistaken, it would not matter very much. Only one betrayal had really mattered; and that was so long ago that he had forgotten it.

Passing a bridge on his way home, he turned and crossed to the Ile St. Louis. There was no need to go in yet; he was not tired, and it was a fine night for a walk. He had always liked Paris better by night than by day; and now the stillness harmonized with the deep tranquillity of a mind that had cast off the curse of youth.

On the bridge between the two islands he paused

for a moment, watching placidly the reflection of street lamps in the quiet water, the rags of torn cloud hurrying across a slender moon. How windy and wild it was up there; how still here by the dreaming river, with lamps that burned un-flickering and shadows all asleep under the arches of the bridge. . . . Truly, the wind bloweth where it listeth; and with the wind, all drifting and unstable things are swept to their destruction. For him, within and around him was peace.

    *   *   *   *   *   *

"*. . . At the light of Thine arrows they went, and at the shining of Thy glittering spear. . . .*"

> Come out, come out, my people;
> Come out to war.
>
> I am the foam
> On the crest of a wave;
> As the wave breaks and passes
> The foam is gone.
> Come out, come out, my people;
> Come out to the high tide.
>
> I am the light
> On the wings of the stormwind;
> As the storm flies over
> The lightning is dead.
> Come out, come out, my people;
> Come out to the hurricane.

I am the flag
In the front of the battle;
As death rides out
With the trampling of armies
The flag is torn.
Come out, come out, my people;
Come out to the fight.

I am the voice
Of the wrath to come;
It is, and again it is not,
And silence has eaten it up.
Yet where it has been
Is dread in high places
And a burning
As with fire.

Come out, come out, my people.
Joy shall be yours, and sunshine,
And the wide sweet air.
And I, that shall see no daybreak,
I, that darkness devours,
That hell has cast up for a little
And sucks in again;
Even I go with you
Through the dark.

Come out, come out, my people;
Come out to war.

He travelled back from far distance, and struck with a crash against a wall of consciousness.

He was still leaning on the parapet of the bridge; but the river's face had changed. All the cloud-shadows were gone from the moon, and every ripple at the water's edge was flecked with silver. He looked up, and saw the shining sickle sharp in a clear expanse, the battered clouds cowering afar off, lost wreckage tossed aside in a forgotten corner of the sky.

Truly, the wind bloweth where it listeth; and with the wind, men and the careful schemes of men are swept to their destruction.

*   *   *   *   *   *

The lamp shone in Signor Giuseppe's window; and a sleepy woman pulled back the bolts of the street-door and held a candle to light the staircase. At the first gentle tap the Italian opened his door, with a welcoming hand outstretched, and no word to say.

On the table a plain supper was laid for two. Felix sat down in the rickety arm-chair by the stove, and Signor Giuseppe pushed the cigarettes towards him in silence. He took one and held it above the lamp-flame. His hand was quite steady.

"And now," the Italian began at last; "about ammunition."

CHAPTER VIII

FELIX rode down the steep hill-path slowly,
insecurely, the reins slipping through his fingers,
his head drooping over the horse's neck. He had
nearly fainted from weakness on first trying to
mount, but the goatherds would not shelter him
any longer. Most people would have given him
up to the soldiers, they reminded him, and claimed
the reward; they had let him lie in their hut for a
fortnight, out of charity, because he was ill, and
because they would not give a dog up to Mon-
signor Spinola's men. They had heard what
things were done in Bologna. But they had to
think of their own safety too; the search party
had been seen again yesterday. In these times
one might get shot for harbouring a fugitive. He
had paid them well, and they were very sorry for
him, but he must go.

The path was rough, and the horse plunged and
stumbled among the stones. But the rider,
swaying in his saddle, gave it no help; he was past
caring whether it fell and flung him down the
landslide or not. If it did, he would break his
back, and lie writhing for a few hours, and grow
still, and that would be the end. If not, the pur-

suers would find him, no doubt, before he could
reach the frontier. That would be a slower and
more wearisome end: blows and abuse, forced
marches into Bologna, prison, some hurried sem-
blance of a trial. But it would be the end, just
the same; and the manner of it mattered little.
Nothing mattered any more, nothing in all the
world.

He had done his best. It was no fault of his
that the scheme had failed; his part of the work
was good enough, but the mountaineers had not
answered the signal. After the fight and final
rout he had guided what were left of his men as
near to safety as he could, had given them precise
instructions, and left them for their own sake.
The search-party scouring the hills would have
scant mercy on anyone found in his company;
and even if he should not be recognized, the cut
across the cheek that a carabineer had given him
in the skirmish was evidence enough to get them
all shot at sight. He had gone off alone, on foot,
to take his chance of reaching Tuscany; had
turned and doubled, lied and acted, fooled the very
soldiers who held his personal description, stolen
away with one of their horses while they slept,
and nearly gained the frontier. And then — oh,
it was not his doing, it was the fever from the fresh
wound. He had opened the shut door, and called
out the spectre of the past. He had gone mad in

one moment, and, because his enemies failed to
destroy him, had destroyed himself.

He had turned the horse's head eastward, and
ridden, ridden all day long; ridden in driving rain,
in bitter wind, in hunger, in burning thirst. At
dusk he had reached some wretched hamlet, and
in the wine-shop there had learned that he was
too late.

"Brisighella? It's a long way from here.
And if you got there you wouldn't find the bishop;
we saw his carriage pass this morning. He's gone
into Bologna, to the legate, to ask mercy for the
prisoners, they say. What prisoners? Haven't
you heard about the riots down Savigno way?"

While he stood, dazed and stupid, staring at a
world that had grown empty, the wine-shop keeper
had come up to him with greedy eyes, lit by the
hope of reward.

"You look as if you ought to know something
about Savigno. Who gave you that cut across
the face?"

At that, the instinct of the hunted creature had
waked again; and he had lied and cajoled once
more, and somehow had twisted himself out of the
net and taken refuge in the bleak and wind-swept
hills. There he and the horse had crouched together on the stones of the mountain-side, starving,
too weary to go further; and all night long a piti-
less sky had pelted them with rain that was like

ice. At dawn, unable to mount, he had led
the horse to the nearest goatherd's hut, and had
fallen, face downwards, in the mud before the
doorway.

Of the days that had followed he dared not
think. Sometimes, in the hideous nights, it had
seemed to him that he was back in the half-caste
circus, and that all the intervening years were a
dream. Sometimes the delirium of unbearable
pain would show him a mocking image of the
face that he had flung away his chance of safety
to see, and had not seen. Then, when the grey
light of dawn shone on the filthy hut, on the sullen,
sleepy mountaineers, the face would fade out and
leave him to meet the horrors of another day.

How long was it now since the fight? He had
lost all count of time; but they had spoken of a
fortnight. All his men must be either taken or
in safety by now. There was nothing more to do
for them, nothing more to do, or think, at all;
only a monstrous nightmare of being alive, that
ought to have left off long ago, and still went on
by some mistake.

The horse started and laid back its ears, sidling
away from a heap of ragged clothing huddled behind a rock. Felix barely lifted his head to look.
The next instant the heap sprang into life with a
choking cry, threw itself across the path, and clung
sobbing round the horse's neck.

x

"Ah, the Gadfly . . . the Gadfly! Blessed saints, I'm saved . . . saved . . . saved!"

He sat upright, and reined in the horse. The mere sound of the nickname which his men had given him waked the dulled brain into swift activity. Immediately he was again an officer on duty, responsible for the safety of his subordinate.

"Hold up, man!" he said sharply. "Let me look at you. Ah, Andrea! Where are the others?"

"The carabineers caught us up. . . . My brother was killed as we ran . . . Tommasino got away, but Carlì was taken . . . I saw . . . Ah, the brutes! Ah, poor Carlì!"

The boy broke into uncontrolled lamentation; but soon went on, sobbing as he talked, breathless yet voluble. His broad mountain speech was difficult to follow.

"I jumped into a stone-quarry . . . I got down to the road . . . an old woman gave me a lift in her cart. May the saints reward her! I was afraid on the road . . . I got back into the hills, and lost my way . . . I've been wandering . . . wandering . . . I'm nearly starved to death. The search-party went by again yesterday."

Felix sat thinking intently, his forehead knotted in a frown.

"Give me that handkerchief you've got on your neck," he said. "What do you say? Yes, I've

been ill; never mind that now. Fold it flat, so.
I want it round my head, as if I had toothache.
Wait, I can draw my hair forward. Is the cut
quite hidden now? Are you sure? Now, pull
my left boot off; there's money inside. That's
right. Go down to the stream there; keep away
from the village, the landlord of the wine-shop
would give you up. Wait for me among the trees,
and mind no one sees you. I'm going to the house
over there to buy food. Yes, of course, there's a
chance they may send for the carabineers; I must
risk it. If I don't come before nightfall, go on
alone; it will mean that I'm taken. Here's
some money, in case of that."

Two hours later he rejoined Andrea by the
torrent, bringing with him black bread, goat's
milk, and hard cheese. They hid among the
bushes till dusk, then crept round outside the village, and, following the plan which Felix had
made out from the directions given him by the
goatherds, found the smuggler's path leading to
the frontier, and reached Tuscan territory the next
day. At the first small town Felix engaged a
rough carriage to take him to Florence, where
the fugitive leaders had agreed to meet; and
parted from Andrea, leaving with him the horse, a
little money for immediate needs, and a letter of
introduction to sympathizers on the Tuscan side
of the frontier, who would find him employment.

The lad kissed his hands at parting, and stood weeping bitterly as the carriage drove away.

The drive was an endless nightmare; but it was no use to rest in these dirty little taverns on the way; better reach Florence at once, and get it over. Then, if need be, one could lie down and die. But at Florence the escaped insurgents came crowding round; Felix was the last to arrive, and everyone had given him up as killed or taken. Again it was he who must be strong for the others, must brace them against disappointment and the ruin of their hopes, as he had braced Andrea against starvation and physical terror. They were all broken-hearted at the failure of the insurrection, at the ferocities of the court-martial in Bologna; as for him, he did not care a jot for that, or anything else in earth or heaven. So for four days he laughed and jested, worked and thought; roused this young man from suicidal brooding, suggested to that one ways to earn a livelihood in exile; and at night, alone in his bed, went on planning, and scheming, and inventing witty phrases, because he dared not stop.

The cut on the cheek was healing unevenly; so one of the Florentine sympathizers, a surgeon named Riccardo, opened it again and sewed it up to prevent unnecessary disfigurement. Felix submitted to this small operation almost without wincing; and wondered, dimly, why it did not hurt more. Was he losing all sensibility, and would he end as an idiot, placid and grinning?

Then the exiles dispersed; some to France, some to England, some to various parts of Tuscany. Felix, on his way to Paris, travelled as far as Marseilles with companions, cheering and upholding them all the time; then, after seeing them off by diligence, turned back, still smiling, to the hotel. He had made an excuse to stay behind for a day or two; he had nothing to do in Marseilles, but he must be alone, he must be alone. There was no more need to think about anything; he would just go into the smoking-room and read a newspaper.

He woke up in bed, with an unpleasant smell of brandy in his nostrils and strange men leaning over him, one holding his wrist. He pulled it away.

"What are you doing?" he asked fretfully.

"It's all right now," a voice answered. "You fainted in the smoking-room. Drink this, and don't move."

He obeyed, and shut his eyes again. "I wonder if I'm going to die?" he thought. "It doesn't matter at all, but it seems rather absurd. I wish I weren't so cold."

He lay still for nearly a week, tended by a sister of mercy and the servants. Having plenty of money, he was well cared for, though the hotel people cheated him grossly, tempted by his utter indifference.

Most of the time he lay quietly lethargic, not asleep, not suffering, careless of all things. There was no return of the inflammation; nothing but a dangerously feeble pulse and long fainting-fits. For the benefit of the doctor who had been called in he made up a tale of Algerian adventure to explain the sabre-cut; but he was too weary to choose his lies discreetly, and the Frenchman only looked at him askance and answered:

"Well, it's no business of mine. But it's my duty to warn you that if you play any more tricks with your constitution you'll wake up one morning and find yourself dead."

"That would be annoying," Felix murmured, and laughed softly to himself.

In a few days his vitality returned, bringing with it a wild panic of fear. "Short of shipwreck," Leroux had said. Yes, but this was shipwreck. If the horror could come back once, might it not come again? As soon as he could travel, he rushed through to Paris with frenzied haste, not even stopping to ask, at Lyons, whether René and Marguerite had really left. He must get back, and learn his fate.

It was August, and Leroux was out of town; but he found Marchand, who took few holidays, at work on the new book. At the sight of his face the old man rose with a long indrawn breath, and stood looking at him.

"Yes," he said at last. "Well, sit down, my son, and tell me how it happened."

Felix began in a low voice, faltering and stammering. Somehow, he could not lie, with Marchand looking at him like that; and for the truth he had no words.

He had been abroad, had been . . . fighting. Yes, that was a sabre-cut. He had been exposed to the weather, to great fatigue and strain; had been all night on a mountain in a storm, wet through and starving. . . .

The voice quivered, and stopped.

"Yes," said Marchand again. "And then you had one of the old attacks. Was it a bad one? As bad as the one on the Pastassa? How long did it last?"

He dropped his head on both arms.

"I don't know if it wasn't worse. I can't tell; the conditions were so hideous. . . . And I was off my head. Ah, don't make me talk about it, Marchand; I shall go mad if it happens again."

Marchand stood beside him, silent, with a hand on his shoulder.

"We'll have a consultation," he said. "Leroux comes back to-morrow, and I'll get old Lemprière. We will see; perhaps something can be done."

The consultation was held in Marchand's house. When Leroux and the professor had gone, Felix came up to Marchand. He was quite self-possessed now.

"Tell me the truth. They mean kindly; but, you see, I've brought the thing on myself, and I knew what the risk was. I'd rather hear the worst at once. What are they hiding from me? Is it utter shipwreck?"

Marchand turned white, but answered without hesitation, looking him in the eyes.

"Yes, just about that. If you want to go on living, you can probably do it for a long time yet; but you'll always be liable to this sort of thing, more and more liable; and one day it will kill you. Not the pleasantest death, either. Meanwhile, there isn't much left, now, that anyone can do for you. Opium helps a little for the moment, as you know; but when you find you're beginning to depend on it, shoot yourself at once."

He nodded gravely.

"I fought that out long ago. Don't be afraid; I shan't take to drugs and I shan't shoot myself. How long will it give me?"

"I can't tell you. Some years, very likely, if you take care. But it will be a precarious life. If you have any work to do, you had better begin it soon."

"I have begun. That's how it happened."

Marchand's voice dropped to a whisper. "May I know? What was it?"

"That happened? I wonder if you remember the Jivaro devils; the Gurupirá that speaks with a human voice? It came to me and spoke about Italy, and I followed it into a bog. There, you know, you meet the Ypupiara, the monster with feet reversed; and you think you're running away, and all the time . . . Well, that's all."

Both were silent awhile.

"I'm half Italian, you see. Those were all lies I told you about the Argentine; you guessed that, of course. The other half of me is English; but only the Italian piece matters now. Some day, if I have any luck, I may get killed."

He paused again, and went on with averted eyes: "Do you remember my telling you, after we passed Madeira, that I was going to cultivate my garden? I did mean to; but you knew better, it seems. I've quite done with gardens now."

Marchand looked at him, long and mournfully.

"But not with Cunégonde; eh? Your life won't be an enviable one, but I wouldn't mind changing places. She'd have no use for me. When a man burns his work and drowns his brain for a personal trouble, goddesses let him alone; and devils too. He's not worth devouring."

"The better for you," Felix answered very softly; and went out.

Marchand stared after him, then pushed his work aside. It was big work, and he knew it; bigger even than that first love, whose outraged corpse he had burned years ago. Because he had lived to get it done, there would be fewer children driven mad by fear. Yet he would have burned this also, to clear his past of Guillaumet and the Discoverer of Secrets. But for them, perhaps, Felix might have . . .

He put a hand over his eyes for a moment. "You can't have it both ways," he thought. Instead of his saving his patient, his patient had been forced to save him.

Well, well; at whatever cost, he was saved, and must get on with his work.

In the street Felix found himself panting for breath. He controlled it with an effort, went into the nearest café and drank black coffee to brace his nerves; then walked on along the quay.

"Why, Felix!"

He started violently.

"Oh, is that you? I didn't . . . see."

He scarcely realized who was there till he found René walking along the quay beside him. They walked without speaking for a little while, and Felix was conscious of only one dim thought: "Oh, well, it might be worse; at least he isn't going to talk." He had not noticed at all how old and haggard his friend was looking.

"Have you had a letter from me?" René asked at last. "One written in May."

"Yes; didn't you get my answer? May? No, April, wasn't it?"

"Ah, then there's one waiting at your bankers. They told me you had gone away and left no address."

"I went abroad in May. I got back three days ago; I haven't sent to the bankers yet."

He relapsed into silence; then remembered that one must take some interest in a friend's joys. Fate had been kind here; it was only he that was shut out from hope. He began cheerfully: "And how is your sister getting on? Has she discarded the crutches yet?"

René took a long time to answer.

"It was about her I wrote to you. You remember she had been out in a carriage?"

"Yes, and even walking a little."

"Well, one day we were driving, and she wanted to call at a shop to choose a present for me. She had never been inside a shop. As I was helping her down, a dray, in charge of a tipsy man, dashed round the corner into our carriage. We were knocked down, and before I could reach her the wheel passed over her spine. No, she's not going to die, and it hasn't brought back the local mischief; she's quite well and strong now. But it's the end of everything, just the same. She'll never stand again."

Felix walked on. He saw the clear-cut lines of the quay, the glittering and broken surface of the river, the towers of the cathedral dark against a windy sky, and the first yellow leaves that came running towards him as with feet along a sunlit pavement.

Then the old, familiar, dreadful thing happened; the street faded out, and fear took hold on him and showed him visions. This time he saw a perpendicular wall, circular and smooth, green with slime, oozing with a damp that was like sweat. He was looking at the inside of a well. A slanting ray of sunlight came in from above; otherwise it was dark. Then he saw that the green wall was alive with creatures swarming up it, clinging to its slimy coat, to the spaces between the bricks, to one another. Very small they were, and lean, and flabby; bluish white, with the skin of sickly plants grown in the dark; and they moved their limbs with frenzied effort, slipping, falling, struggling up again and always up. A few, only a very few, had reached the sunlight at the top; there the wall was dry and safe, and they scrambled up hurriedly. One raised a bloodless claw to grasp the edge, and hoisted itself up higher, till its head peered over, in bright sunshine. Just beside it was another, clinging to its arm. Then a great hand came down and flicked them off, and sent them headlong to the bottom; and then a lid was put on to the well-head, and there was darkness and a faint, far-off splashing of water. . . .

The sunny quay was there again, and the towers of the cathedral dark against a windy sky, and the yellow leaves came running towards him as with feet. He looked round.

"I'm sorry; my head got muddled. Didn't you speak to me just now?"

"I was wondering whether you could help me over the worst of this. We took her home last week; then I came on here about my new post. I want to get to work as soon as the holidays are over; but I have to go back home now. I don't . . . I don't quite know how we're all going to face each other. Oh, we shall get used to it in time. But just at first . . . Will you come down with me? I think we should get through it better if we were not quite alone together. I know it's a lot to ask."

"Of course I'll come if it will help you. When do you start?"

"Next Wednesday, unless that's too soon for you."

"No, I'll be ready. But are you sure your sister will want to have a stranger about at such a time? We have never met, remember."

René hesitated, then turned to him.

"Look here, I'm not sure about anything. I don't even know how she'll receive you at first.

She's not quite herself just now. We're all a bit shaken, I suppose. My brother Henri told me the other day the accident wouldn't have happened if he'd been there. He's the kindest fellow, too. Oh, well, I may as well own up; it's just that I'm scared. I'm an idiot, I know. I got some poison away from her in Lyons. She's promised me not to try again, but I can't help her. You see, the very sight of me reminds her. She'll go melancholy mad if she doesn't have something to take her mind off it. Come and try what you can do, anyhow."

"Very well; we'll start on Wednesday."

"Thank you," René said; and added: "I must run off now. I have an appointment."

"Are you free this evening? Then I'll expect you to dinner. I can put you up for the night if you don't mind chaos; my things aren't unpacked yet. They were stored while I was away."

As he turned to shake hands, talking lightly, the scarred cheek caught Rene's eyes for the first time.

"Why, what on earth have you done to your face? It's been cut right across!"

Felix laughed.

"Yes, I've come to the end of what our kind friend Guillaumet calls my 'effeminate good looks,' haven't I?"

"Damn Guillaumet! How did it happen?"

"Damn Guillaumet by all means. It happened
the way dear pussy-cats get pieces bitten out of
their little ears; I've been fighting."

"Fighting!"

"Oh, well, it's a long story; we'll keep it for the
château.   I've had quite an am-m-musing series of
adventures since I saw you last."

René was looking at him critically.

"They don't seem to have agreed with you."

"No? All the more reason why I should try
country air. Think what a lot of good a holiday
in Burgundy will do me; you couldn't have hit
on a better notion."

Two or three times during the journey it occurred to René in a dim way that he was being
entertained, that Felix was making conversation
for his benefit. The idea worried him a little;
but he soon reassured himself. This even cheer-
fulness had nothing in common with the showy
and artificial gaiety which had frightened him
so at the geographers' dinner last year. One
need never be really anxious about Felix unless
he was being funny. He looked wretchedly thin
and worn; but the cut on the cheek must have
pulled him down, and probably he needed a holiday.

Yes, but . . . fighting?

René stole a glance at the unspoiled profile that
was turned towards him. He had long realized

that he knew very little about Felix; but he was not troubled with curiosity. A man does not help his friend by knowing the private sorrows that he cannot heal; and, for the rest, the king can do no wrong.

Before they arrived, however, Felix himself approached the subject. He said nothing of his personal misfortunes, and nothing of Signor Giuseppe; but explained, with grave impartiality, the main aims and outlines of the attempt in the Apennines, merely adding: "I was one of the organizers."

René listened without comment. "And then?"

"Then, when it failed, I escaped and came to Paris. I shall go back to Italy when I see a chance to do anything."

"You have quite made up your mind about that? Then, I suppose, some day . . ."

René paused.

"Some day I shall get caught, and the consequences won't be pleasant; that is clear. But you see, René, this thing happens to be my particular bit of work in life. Meanwhile, here I am, prep-p-paring to invade an ultra-conservative country-house, and confront your pious aunt and your aristocratic family with a fresh cut that convicts me of atheistical and blood-thirsty sansculottism. What are you going to tell them?"

René winced perceptibly; but after a moment's thought, answered in a tranquil voice:

"I think it will be better to say nothing about it, for the present, at any rate. My father and sister never ask indiscreet questions, and the others will think you have been duelling, which from their point of view is not a solecism, though it may be a sin. I think the family relations would become almost impossibly strained if my aunt and brother were to learn the truth just now, when they are so overwrought. You see, they would think it such an appalling crime."

"And you?"

Felix was looking at him with a half smile, shadowy and subtle. He met it without flinching.

"I? What I think about you and your affairs? But that question is already answered; I told you years ago, on the Pastassa."

*　　*　　*　　*　　*　　*

Henri, Angélique, and Blanche received the stranger politely, but with a certain frigidity. At any other moment they would have been glad to welcome the man to whom they owed René's life; but it seemed to them tactless on his part to accept an invitation to a house of mourning.

René, by giving such an invitation, had outraged beyond all patience their sense of propriety; it was scarcely decent. "I'm sure I don't wish

Y

to be inhospitable," said Angélique to her brother-in-law. "But dear René shows a strange want of consideration for everyone's feelings. How can we force ourselves to entertain a guest at a time of such affliction?"

"Don't you think," he replied, "that René, too, may have some feelings to be considered? If his friend's presence is a comfort to him, he need not consider anyone else just now, except Marguerite herself."

Angélique sniffed indignantly.

"There's not much doubt how she feels about it, poor darling. She wouldn't say anything, because it's René's doing; but when I told her he was bringing a visitor, she went quite white and bit her lip. It's nothing less than heartless of René."

"Heartless is scarcely the term I should apply to René," was all the answer she could get from the marquis.

His own welcome to the travellers was in his most charming manner. The guest responded with equal graciousness; to René, as he watched them, their polished amenities seemed like the clashing of blue steel against blue steel. "I wonder why father hates him so," he thought; then he saw his father's eyes dwelling for an instant on the disfigured cheek, and added mentally: "And I wonder what he is thinking about that?"

Presently they went up to Marguerite's room. It was gay with flowers, and the sunlight shone in at the open window; but the girl herself made a sombre splash in the brightness. To-day her black gown had no ornament to welcome René, and her hair was swept out of sight and coiled at the back of her neck. When she shook hands with the guest, her face wore a hospitable smile, but the eyes remained sullen, tragic, unapproachable. She entertained him with small talk, uttered in a hard, thin, cheerful voice.

"I am so glad to meet you at last; we have been always just going to meet for a very long time, haven't we? Do you know, I really began to wonder whether you had any existence at all, outside of René's imagination."

"I haven't," he answered promptly. "This form of me certainly hasn't, anyhow. There would have been no such p-p-person in the world if he hadn't dreamed about me."

"That's a slander," René protested. "I don't have nightmares. He's responsible for himself, Pâquerette."

But Marguerite was not listening; she was looking at the guest from under dropped lashes.

"Do you . . . ?" she began softly, and broke off. He filled in the unfinished question, answering her look with a smile.

"Do I hate him for it? Only sometimes."

Marguerite leaned her head back and looked at him silently; first with swift attention, then with a slow, grave wonder. He did not fit her mental image of him; that image of an intolerably fortunate and successful person, which she had hated in secret for so long. When he first entered the room she had noticed his limp; now her gaze wandered to the mutilated left hand, the scarred cheek. Suddenly she saw his eyes dilate and the nostrils whiten and quiver. The next instant she realized that René was asking her some question, and answered at random: "I don't know, dear."

Felix turned his head away. Everything had gone red before his eyes. "You Beast," he thought; "You infernal Beast, to hurt a little helpless thing like that! Couldn't You have been satisfied with me?"

Then he remembered that he was an atheist; and then that plenty of other folk in the world also get more hurt than seems quite reasonable. Andrea's voice sounded lamentably in his ears: "Ah, the brutes; ah, poor Carlì!"

He turned back, smiling.

"I was l-l-looking at the decorations of your wall. I didn't know René had brought home so many pretty things. You have quite a museum."

"Nothing like your collection of weapons, surely?"

"My collection is gone; I have no curios now."

"Why, Felix," said René, in amazement; "you haven't given up collecting?"

"Yes; I sold the things before going abroad in the spring. Ah, there's the feather head-dress. Did René ever tell you about the old chief who gave it to us?"

"Wasn't that the man who wanted a charm to kill his brother? Yes; I have often sympathized with him; haven't I, René? Brothers are the natural recipients of all one's evil tempers. I've heard about the day you wore the head-dress, too. You must have been an imposing sight. I don't wonder the natives were impressed."

"It would have looked much better on René; I'm not tall enough for such magnificence."

"Ah, but he's too fair."

"The colour of the skin doesn't show. These things are worn with war-paint; red and black and yellow stripes and rings."

"You did paint your face, didn't you? I suppose they think it a compliment for a white man to imitate their ways?"

"Yes; and then it's so useful when you're g-g-green with funk and daren't show it. I wonder if that's how the custom grew up."

Marguerite flashed a look at him.

"Wouldn't it be convenient if we could smear

on all our respectable lies from the outside, instead of having to live them?"

"Such as p-p-pretending to be brave when we're not?"

"Yes, it only makes us worse cowards; and pretending to feel charitable to people when we hate them makes us more unjust."

"Dear Pâquerette," her brother put in; "I don't think that particular sin need weigh upon your conscience. Hypocritical amiability was a fault of yours when you were quite a small child; but you soon outgrew it. Nowadays, when you detest people, the poor things generally find it out."

"Do they?" she asked; and looked, not at him, but at Felix, who answered demurely:

"Oh, I should think they would manage to find it out, unless they're very stupid indeed."

They both laughed as their eyes met.

"Do you know," René said afterwards to Felix; "that's the first time I've heard her laugh naturally since the accident."

A few days later, returning with Henri from fishing, he heard in the garden the sound of her merry laughter. It seemed to him, as he approached the group under the walnut trees, that he had never realized before what an easy matter it would be to cut one's throat, if doing so would help Felix out of any trouble.

"What's the joke?" he asked. Felix did not turn round, but Marguerite answered, laughing again:

"We were talking about Blanche being afraid of cows; and then we began wondering which kind of South American animal you had all found most terrifying. Aunt guessed a jaguar, and Blanche a snake, and I a cockroach. So when M. Rivarez came out we asked him which he had minded most, and he said, 'An orange-throated humming-bird.' Why, René, you jump like . . . Are you afraid of humming-birds too?"

"I was once," he murmured; "desperately. But I've quite got over it."

Felix looked up.

"Have you? Quite? Then perhaps I shall, some day."

The next time the two friends went for a walk together, he came back to the subject.

"René, is it true you have quite got over it? Or did you say so just to be kind?"

René shook his head.

"My dear Felix, declarations of love are not things that will bear repeating. Do you still want to be assured that I can get on without explanations of whatever you may do that I don't happen to understand?"

"Does that mean that you never ask yourself 'Why'?"

"Why you followed me? I have a notion about it; but if it's a mistaken one I'm quite indifferent. You must have had some good reason, or you wouldn't have done it."

Felix persisted, with lowered eyes. "What notion?"

"If it interests you . . . I have sometimes thought you saw I was running a foolish risk, and . . . Well, we'd none of us given you cause to feel particularly free with us, had we? Perhaps you were . . . shy, or doubtful about how I should take a warning; I might have been any sort of cad for all you could tell. What puzzles me about the thing is not your share in it, but my own. I can't understand why I told them all a perfectly unnecessary lie. It was just one of those idiotic impulses . . . Unless I was trying, in a blundering way, to prevent anybody asking how you came to be there."

He stopped speaking and turned round. Felix was standing still, looking at the turf.

"And afterwards?"

"Afterwards I felt like a cur, of course, when you backed me up in the lie. Naturally, you hadn't any choice. For some time I was always expecting you to speak to me about it; but you never did. I suppose you saw I was a little ashamed of the whole business, and didn't want to make me feel awkward."

"Oh, René, René, you were born young!"

"A polite way of implying that I was born an ass?"

"Let us say: a cherub. Did it never occur to you that anybody but yourself could have anything to be ashamed of?"

"Look here," René broke in quickly; "if there's anything you . . . would rather have had different, I don't want to know about it."

"Don't you? I'm afraid you'll have to know, now we have got so far."

"All right," said René, lying flat down on the grass, and tilting his straw hat over his eyes. "Let's be comfortable, anyway. Yes, I'm listening."

Felix sat down beside him, and began pulling up little tufts of grass. Presently he threw them aside and sat still, looking straight before him.

"At that time," he began, "only two things about human beings interested me at all: Could I make use of them? and, Need I be afraid of them? I was afraid of you."

René sat up.

"There, you needn't go on; that's been well rubbed in."

He heard a little catch in the breathing of the figure beside him.

"Is that . . . one of the things I talked about?"

"Yes. You ticked us off on your fingers. Then

you began about me. I suppose I must have driven you pretty near to suicide; but I think you paid some of it off that night."

Felix looked away again.

"There are worse things than suicide. Anyway, I was afraid you would advise Duprez to turn me adrift at the first mission-station. I knew what that means. I managed to get round the others by doing their work, and fooling them in various ways, but I didn't even try to fool you or Marchand. Only, you see, it was different with Marchand. He's not troubled with ethical principles; and then I knew, if it came to the point, he'd understand, and you, perhaps, wouldn't. It just makes all the difference. So I followed you to get you quite alone. I was going to tell you some of the things that had happened to me . . . No, we won't talk about that. . . . I daren't think of them, even now. But the idea was to tell you . . . as much as I could; and appeal to your mercy. And then, if you threatened to get me turned out as an impostor, or if you . . . laughed . . ."

"Laughed!"

"Ah, I had been so long among people that laughed. Well, then, I was going to have an accident with my gun, and sink you in the river, and get back to camp. I knew I could twist Duprez round my finger if you were out of the way.

"I don't suppose I should ever have done it; one doesn't, when it comes to the point. Probably I should have shot myself instead. But the intention was there, clear enough. When a man's fighting in his last ditch, he thinks he'll do anything.

"Then I saw the jaguar. It's a l-l-little discon-c-certing to set out to commit murder, and f-find you've got to save your man instead of killing him. I lost my head for a moment . . . otherwise I might have fired a few seconds earlier. It's just a chance I wasn't too late. As it was, I let you get that scratch on the arm."

He began pulling up the grass-tufts again.

"Well," he said at last, with a little grating sound in his voice; "there's the end of a not very pretty confession. Are you going to t-t-treasure it up against me?"

"What else am I likely to do but treasure up the first bit of voluntary personal confidence you have ever given me? As for sinking me in the river — if I'd been capable of behaving that way, why shouldn't you? There, let us go home to lunch, and forget all about jaguars and the still more unpleasant beasts that laugh. Marguerite's right; a cockroach is worse than a jaguar, any day."

"But c-cockroaches don't laugh."

"Oh, I'm not Marguerite! One accurate person is enough in a family. Besides, I'm inclined to believe they did laugh, at Guayaquil, when they swarmed all over us in the night, and heard us swearing."

"Take care," said Felix. "If you think that sort of thing about them they'll turn into gods."

At that René glanced at him in a troubled way; but said nothing. He already knew that atheism, with Felix, was an imperfect refuge against some incurable malady of the soul; some horrible, persistent curse, that had once been religion and that would not die.

*   *   *   *   *   *

In September, René left his friend at Marteurelles, and returned to Paris, to engage and furnish the new flat for Marguerite and himself. The girl had conquered her nervous dread of travelling, and had consented to spend her winters in Paris and her summers at the château. Henri and his wife protested earnestly against this arrangement when René's back was turned, though they did not venture to say much in his presence.

"It is condemning René to perpetual bachelordom," said Henri to his father. "Now that he has got such an excellent post he could find plenty of girls of good family and with good dowries; but, of course, if he has an invalid sister living with him, he can't marry."

"It's quite time for René to settle down,"

Blanche added with some asperity. She did not like Marguerite, and was inclined to think that too much fuss was made about her. The marquis looked at his daughter-in-law, then at his son, gravely, observantly.

"Curious how the boy has deteriorated since he married that underbred person," he thought; but aloud he said only:

"Perhaps that is René's way of settling down. Quite good work has been done in the world by bachelors."

"I am sure," said Angélique, with an indignant glance at the younger woman, "René could have no dearer companion than our poor darling. And dowries are not everything, Blanche."

But when the married couple had left the room, she sighed heavily.

"Not that I don't feel anxious about it for the dear child's own sake. Paris is a dreadful place for a girl to live in with only a brother. The Latin quarter, too! They say the blasphemies that are talked among the students there are horrible. And Marguerite has no spiritual humility to protect her."

"Perhaps physical affliction will prove as effectual a safeguard," said the marquis, drily. "She is not likely to see anyone in Paris except the guests invited to the flat; and I should think René quite capable of dealing with any student who forgot his manners in the presence of his hostess."

Angélique threw out her hands.

"Oh, Étienne, if it were only students, and manners! Can't you see?"

She was on the verge of tears.

"It is terrible! She is utterly changed since that man came into the house. Oh, I wish René had never brought him here! I knew it would lead to no good; I knew!"

"My dear Angélique, are you suggesting that Marguerite has fallen in love with M. Rivarez?"

"You're the only one in the house that hasn't found it out. Why, her colour changes when she hears his footstep. You must have seen how different she is."

"I have noticed that she seems much brighter and happier of late. Surely, even if you are right in supposing that to be the cause, one can only welcome anything that makes her life less wretched."

"Étienne! Less wretched for the moment. And afterwards? And when he marries? He is sure to marry some time; a successful man like that. And anyhow, what has Marguerite to do with love? And the man is an atheist; Blanche showed me a paper with an article of his. It was nothing less than blasphemous mocking at holy things. And yesterday I came in, and he was sitting by the couch reading Molière aloud to her, and she was laughing!"

The marquis shrugged his shoulders and went back to his work. The mental attitude of anyone who could love Marguerite and yet be distressed at seeing her laugh, was incomprehensible to him. Jealous as he was of Felix, he could not find it in his heart to grudge the girl one poor little ray of happiness.

In October he took her to Paris, where René was now ready to receive her, and stayed a few days at the flat before returning to Marteurelles. Felix, who had travelled with them, lodged near, and usually came in after dinner to read Spanish with Marguerite. Covertly watching her face when the door-bell rang, her father told himself that Angélique had guessed right.

"Come back to us in June, my darling," he said, as he kissed her at parting. "And let me think of you as not too unhappy."

She looked up; he had never seen her eyes so softly radiant and kind.

"But you must think of me as happy, father. There are many kinds of joy in the world, and being able to walk is only one of them. There isn't anybody living that I would change places with, in spite of everything. Besides, there will be such a lot to do; I shan't have time to mope."

Her programme of work for the winter was in-

deed an arduous one. Besides the housekeeping,
for which she insisted on making herself solely
responsible, she was learning Spanish and mathe-
matics, fitting herself to help René with the
preparation of his lectures, and reading English
prose and old French verse with the same ruthless and meticulous thoroughness that she had
formerly brought to bear upon her father's manuscripts. English poetry she had utterly refused
to touch. Felix, while at Marteurelles, had
offered to give her some lessons in literature.
One day he brought to the flat a parcel of English
books.

"Oh," she cried out in a dismal tone, "I believe
it's verse! You're not going to make me wade
through all that, are you? I hate English poetry."

"How much have you read?"

"Oh, such a lot! Aunt Nelly sent me a huge
book of selections, and Aunt Angélique worried
me into going right through it. I never read such
dreary stuff in my life. There was Dryden, and
Mrs. Hemans, and Rogers, and 'The Lady of the
Lake,' and 'Paradise Lost' . . ."

"Now, Pâquerette," her brother interrupted;
"be accurate, it's your speciality. It was 'Paradise Regained.'"

"It doesn't matter. I've skimmed a translation
of 'Paradise Lost.' It's just the same kind of
stuff."

"And Shakespeare?"

"No; I've read what Voltaire says about him, and that's enough. Besides, we haven't finished Calderon yet. English poetry can wait for the present. I'd rather have Locke and the theory of simple ideas!"

Felix was beginning to discover, as her father had discovered long ago, that to teach Marguerite was to brave a continuous fire of cross-examination. Her greed for knowledge was insatiable.

"I shall have to furbish up my rhetoric," he said one evening, when René came in and found teacher and pupil together. "Mlle. Marguerite has just convicted me of disgraceful ignorance. She has been quoting Aristotle at me, and I'm grovelling in the dust because I couldn't place the quotation."

"I warned you that she is a layer of traps," said René, stooping to kiss his sister. "You just do it out of malice, don't you, sweet?"

She put both hands on his shoulders, and looked at his face.

"If I do, that's no reason for you to have such tired eyes. What has happened?"

"Nothing." He sat down and rubbed a hand through his hair. "I've just met Leroux," he added, turning to Felix. "He stopped me in the street to ask if you were back yet."

z

"I saw him in August."

"Yes; he told me he had seen you."

"Ah! Did he tell you . . .?"

"Not intentionally. He supposed I should know, as you had been staying with us. He didn't tell me any details, of course."

Marguerite looked from one to the other. "Then there is some trouble. A secret?"

"Oh, not a secret at all," Felix answered lightly; "but nothing to bother you about. This very tender-hearted brother of yours is upset because a man has been t-t-telling him my health isn't satisfactory. It's entirely my own fault; I smashed it up in the Apennines."

"Is it the old thing?" René asked after a moment.

"Yes; it has come back. I'd just seen Leroux that morning when we met on the quay. I didn't want to bother you."

"And it's quite hopeless?"

"So they tell me. But I'm not going to die just yet, and I shall get p-p-plenty of time between the attacks. There has been only one, so far. It might be worse. You will see, Mlle. Marguerite will have opportunities enough to f-find me out in all sorts of things . . . including mistakes in Sp-p-panish."

He glanced at René as he uttered the last words; but the challenge passed unnoticed.

"Well," René said heavily; "I'll go and change for dinner."

He went out of the room. Marguerite looked at Felix with miserable eyes.

"You too . . ."

At the broken whisper he turned to her with a smile that was like sunlight.

"Ah, mademoiselle, the world is so democratic! You can't get even the condemned cell to yourself."

She put out a little passionate hand and clasped his. He touched her hair softly with the finger-tips of the other hand.

"Poor child," he said; "poor child!"

CHAPTER IX

RENÉ and Marguerite gave their first dinner-party on New Year's day. Except the hostess, who presided from her couch, starry-eyed, with a green wreath in her hair and a white gown, chosen by Felix and designed by René, only men were present.

"I don't want ever to have any women here," she told Marchand, the first guest to arrive. "I hate women; I've never known one yet that was not inquisitive and mean."

"How many have you known all together?" he asked, smiling at her with deep-set eyes.

"Not very many, I confess; but I haven't known many men, for that matter, and yet I can count up several that wouldn't do things . . . oh, petty things that the nicest women will do. Come, you know I'm right, doctor; you only shake your head for the sake of disagreeing. You're the most contradictious person I've ever come across."

She and Marchand had already struck up a friendship. It expressed itself chiefly in ferocious argument, which both enjoyed enormously. Except the perfections of René, they had as yet found no subject on which they could not triumphantly disagree.

"I was merely envying your good luck," he retorted. "I have known a few folk of both sexes that wouldn't steal or murder without a strong temptation; and that's as much as one can fairly ask of human nature. If you begin cavilling at the tiny things, we might as well all hang ourselves at once."

"But it's the tiny things that matter! I could forgive a man committing murder or highway robbery if he were hard pressed, or even taking to drink, rather than gossiping and . . ."

"Ah, be merciful, mademoiselle!" broke in a voice behind her. "Leave me s-s-some remnant of self-complacency. I am the most inveterate of gossips; but I don't usually go as far as murder; unless, as Marchand so charitably puts it, under strong tempt-t-tation."

Felix had come up with his noiseless tread. She held out a hand to him, laughing.

"Listeners hear no good of themselves, it seems."

He stooped over the hand, murmuring New Year wishes and compliments. By the time he moved out of her light, Marchand's face had quite regained its normal expression.

"Another present!" she cried, taking up the parcel which Felix had laid beside her. "But you promised not to bring me any more!"

"All promises are broken at New Year," he replied carelessly; and stood watching her with a black look as she untied the parcel.

Who would have thought her capable of such brutality? To twit an old man, her own guest, with the ugliest skeleton in his private cupboard. . . . And René! What right had he to tell her Marchand's secrets?

His face cleared suddenly. Ah, what a fool he had been to think such a thing! Of course, no one had told her; why, this was just the proof of it. If she had known, she could not possibly have referred to the subject. She had stumbled against the sore place in sheer ignorance. He might have known René would hold his tongue. One could always trust René.

Marguerite's rapturous outcry interrupted his thoughts.

"Oh, how lovely! And how did you come to choose just sweet marjoram? Did René tell you it's my pet flower? Look, doctor!"

It was a white shawl, very fine and soft, embroidered round the edges with sprays of sweet marjoram. As the girl shook out the gleaming folds, a card slipped from between them. She picked it up and looked at the lines written on it; then read them again, with a puzzled face.

"English, is it? What queer spelling; I suppose it's old? No, let me see if I can make it out

myself. '*With margerain . . .*' Is that marjoram?"

He bent over her shoulder, explaining the
words; ashamed that he had harboured so unjust
a thought against her.

> "*With margerain gentle,*
> *The flow're of goodliehead,*
> *Embroider'd the mantle*
> *Is of your maidenhead.*"

She looked up with pink cheeks.

"What darling words! Where did you get
them?"

"It's only some of the English poetry that you
despise. You'll find it in one of those rejected
books."

She held up clasped hands.

"I capitulate! I'm as meek as the burghers of
Calais, and I'll begin on the biggest book to-morrow. Yes, you may well look sympathetic, doctor. If you knew the size of it!"

"That's the first time I've ever heard Marchand
accused of looking sympathetic," said René,
coming in with Bertillon. "Why, Felix, I thought
the shawl was to have daisies for a border?"

"I changed my mind," he answered. "I don't
like daisies."

The brother and sister cried out together in
amazement. "Don't like daisies! Why . . ."

He laughed.

"Is that heresy? I like them well enough, but they disconcert me. Their eyes are so horribly wide and clear; they set me wondering how many secrets they've found out."

"Oh, but they hold their tongues," said Marchand.

The next day René found Marguerite struggling with Chaucer.

"I think the English is too archaic for you," he said. "Suppose we try Shakespeare. We might choose a play and take parts."

"But he stammers."

"Never when he's reading. I didn't know what English poems can sound like till I heard him."

When Felix called she proposed Shakespeare. "If I've got to have English poetry, I want to hear you read it; René assures me that your elocution would redeem anything. Is it true that you inflicted Milton on him at Manaos, and actually made him like it? I'm a docile pupil, but I warn you that I won't read Milton; that's flat."

"I read 'Samson' to him when he was laid up with a touch of fever. I hope he liked it; but, at any rate, I certainly love it too much to waste it on a frivolous young lady who couldn't appreciate it. Henry VI is what you shall have, all three parts; you deserve it for speaking that way of Milton."

"Oh, look here," René protested; "this is cruelty to animals! Let us have Richard III; anyhow, we shan't go to sleep over that."

"No; I won't have a pupil of mine taught to call folk ugly names."

"For fear she should use them against you if you ever set her down to Milton?"

"Yes; 'bottled spider,' for instance. Appropriate? Oh, I dare say; but even a p-p-poisonous bunch-backed t-toad has its feelings. No, it shall be Henry V, English lesson and all. You shall be Princess Katherine, mademoiselle; you're quite as prejudiced as she is. And René shall be Fluellen."

René looked up, laughing.

"'So long as your majesty is an honest man'? . . . And even if your majesty were not. Don't look so mournful, Pâquerette; Henry V is quite endurable reading."

"I don't believe it," she answered sulkily.

Both she and Felix were in a mood of riotous gaiety; during supper they teased one another incessantly, and when the table was cleared and the books were brought out, they seemed unable to settle to their reading. Throughout the prologue and the opening conversation of the two bishops they behaved like naughty children, encouraging each other in irresponsible absurdities. For the first time she displayed in his pres-

ence her gift of mimicry, putting into the part
of the Bishop of Canterbury a reminiscence of
Father Joseph, so irresistibly comic that René
burst out laughing at the words:

"*God and his angels guard your sacred throne.*"

The discourse on the Salic law afforded her an
opportunity for mock heroics. Her mastery of
English was remarkable in a girl who had never
been out of France; the slight foreign accent only
increased the bombastic effect of her peroration.

"*O noble English . . .*"

She put down her book in the middle of the line.
"I don't mind foraging in blood of French nobility; one's used to that, nowadays; but I wish
the old gentleman weren't so prosy. Is all Shakespeare like this?"

"Not quite all. Suppose we skip a page or
two."

Pistol and Nym restored her good humour;
but she made a doleful grimace at the re-entry of
the king.

"Oh, dear, more long speeches!"

A moment later she had forgotten to gibe.
Felix was reading the king's speech to Lord Scrope
of Masham.

"*But oh,*
"*What shall I say to thee . . .*"

The sudden deepening of his voice made her look up, and she saw the colour die out of his face as he read.

" Thou that didst bear the key of all my counsels,
That knewest the very bottom of my soul . . ."

"Was it a woman?" flashed through her mind, as it had flashed through René's long ago.

She glanced round at her brother. He was listening with parted lips, motionless, absorbed in the splendour of the lines, in the rise and fall of the wonderful voice; he had not seen the reader's eyes.

" Oh, how hast thou with jealousy infected
The sweetness of affiance.   Shew men dutiful,
Why, so didst thou ; or seem they grave and learned,
Why, so didst thou.   Come they of noble family ?
Why, so didst thou.   Seem they religious ?
Why, so didst thou . . ."

Fear caught at the girl's heart as she listened. No, it was not a woman. There was a burnt mark across his life; but it was no woman's mark. She was quite sure of that now.

The voice sank, heavy and cold; all the passion had gone out of it.

" And thus thy fall hath left a kind of blot,
To mark the full-fraught man and best endued
With some suspicion."

"Suspicion . . . suspicion . . ." She repeated the word to herself, shivering. It seemed to her that there was a ghost in the room.

"Why, Pâquerette," said René, "you've missed your cue. You're Exeter."

She stumbled hastily into her part.

"'*I arrest thee of high treason* . . .'"

Felix recovered his merry humour at Mrs. Quickly's first words; but Marguerite's gaiety was dead for the evening. She remained anxious and timid, watching him covertly from under her lashes.

"What a creature of moods she is!" he thought. "It's lucky dear old René has such steady nerves to supply the balance."

Very soon English poetry took possession of Marguerite's affections. Felix spent two evenings a week in the flat, and much of the time was devoted to reading aloud. If René was in, the readings were often dramatic, all three taking part; when he was out, the lyric poets were usually chosen. In time the girl became familiar with many of the finest English poems, from Border ballads and Elizabethan plays to Wordsworth and Coleridge. Even Felix never taught her to share his passion for Milton; but Shelley took her imagination by storm.

"I want you to read me this," she said one

evening when Felix was alone with her. "I've gone over it till I know it by heart, and I can't get away from it; and yet I don't know what it's about."

It was: *"Come, be happy."*

"I don't care for that thing," he said quickly. "Let us have another."

She looked up, surprised; such ungraciousness was not like him. Then she understood, and made haste to say: "Certainly, if you prefer it."

"Some of the songs?"

"No, read the first act of 'Prometheus Unbound.' I want great poetry to-day."

From the first tremendous lines he forgot her existence; his voice swept round her and dragged her with him down the foaming cataracts of the verse. What she had hitherto calmly admired as fine poetry, now shook her with the dread of avenging thunderbolts.

"Ay, do Thy worst. Thou art omnipotent . . ."

"Do you know," she said, after he had put down the book; "the thing that terrifies me most in the whole scene is that the furies are 'hollow underneath.' One can scarcely face such an appalling thought. I don't know how Shelley dared to write that; it makes me want to creep into a hole and hide."

He turned, with eyes dilated and shining.

"Ah, that's just the only consolation. Don't you see what he means? They're not real, and they know it, and that's what makes them so angry."

"You're real enough," she said, looking straight at him. "Why are you angry?"

He drew back with a startled movement, and sat watching her. Then he smiled, and his eyes grew dangerous.

"How do you know I'm not hollow underneath? And as for being angry, my dear girl, I'm not c-c-capable of it. You couldn't make me angry if you t-t-tried."

"Hasn't God tried?"

His eyes narrowed.

"I'll tell you a s-s-secret. He's like the furies; He isn't real, and He knows it."

"Oh," she whispered; "that's worse than the curse."

For a long time after that evening he would read her nothing but comedies and gay or martial ballads. René begged him once for Wordsworth's "Ode on the Intimations of Immortality," but he read it so mechanically that Marguerite yawned in the middle and declared it impossible to listen respectfully to a poet who could begin a sonnet with: "Jones."

Felix looked at her with a mischievous twinkle,

and, throwing the volume aside, began to declaim
in lugubrious accents:

> *"Peter was dull — he was at first*
> *Dull — O, so dull, so very dull!* . . ."

"But you see," said René gently; "I don't find
Wordsworth dull."

Marguerite laughed till tears ran down her
cheeks.

"Oh, René, you lamb! You angelic lamb!"

He smiled, well pleased to see her laugh, though
he had not the faintest notion what she found so
funny.

"I beg your pardon, René," said Felix, suddenly ceasing to laugh. "The rebuke was deserved."

He took up the book again and read the ode
magnificently. Even Marguerite was quite solemn
before he finished.

"And now," he said, shutting the book; "don't
you think I ought to have a reward, René? Well,
then, sing me: 'Compagnons de la Marjolaine.'
I have to go to London to-morrow, and I know
it's going to be a rough crossing. I want something cheerful to console me."

"Shall you be away long?" Marguerite asked.
He shrugged his shoulders.

"I don't suppose so, but one never knows."

He was given to sudden journeys. He chose to

keep up a fiction that they were connected with his newspaper work; and both René and Marguerite pretended to believe him. But they were always wretchedly anxious in his absence. Once, in the spring, he had disappeared for three weeks, leaving a message that he was "called away"; and afterwards they had found that he had been in Paris all the while, laid up with an attack of illness. Marguerite said nothing at the time, but spoke to him about it some months later.

"Don't you think that was a cruel trick to play? Why couldn't you let us know the truth instead of leaving us to find it out?"

"But I d-didn't want you to find it out; and you need not have if Bertillon hadn't been a fool. There's no use in letting René know those things; he takes them so absurdly to heart."

"Don't you suppose we . . . he takes it to heart when you vanish without an address and leave him to wonder whether you've gone to Italy?"

"Italy!"

"Did you think I didn't know?"

He faced round. "Did René tell you?"

"René? No; did you ask him to?"

It had not occurred to her that he could suppose René would speak of the subject unless expressly requested to do so.

"Who told you?" he persisted.

"Why, you did! Anyway, you told me you had 'smashed up' your health in the Apennines, and you came from there with a fresh cut on your cheek, just after there had been riots. And I know you're an anti-clerical, and . . . oh, I do wish you could realize that I'm grown-up!"

She sighed impatiently; the memory of his "Poor child!" still rankled. Then she looked at him, and began to wish he would speak.

"You would make a fortune as a detective," he said; and took up Shakespeare.

This time he really went to England, and for a month letters came from him twice a week. They were addressed to both brother and sister, and formed a cheerful diary of sightseeing, society, politics, meditations, and weather in London. It was December, and the fogs had begun.

"I am begrimed inside and out," he wrote. "The stuff they give you to breathe here is a mixture of lentil soup and charcoal, and the pavement is made of churned grease. There isn't a scrap of me that is clean. (This refers to my body and my clothes; it's too dark to see whether I've got a soul or not, and I've left the last rags of my intellect strewn on the floor of the Strangers' Gallery at Westminster.) I took sanctuary in the British Museum to-day, and tried to find a refuge under the mighty head and arm of Ozymandias, King of Kings. I don't know what his other name is,

2 A

but this will do for a makeshift. He comes from
Karnak. He wears a granite crown that doesn't
give him a headache, and a granite smile, eternally
unchanged; and he doesn't mind the dirt one bit.
You don't need to if you're big enough and hard
enough. It's all very well for him; he knows it
will rub off in time. Anybody could be philo-
sophic at his age. Perhaps in twenty centuries
or so I shan't grumble at trifles. But, as I pointed
out to him, my days are short, and I'm neither a
dynastic god nor a chunk of rock, but just a man,
and lame at that. How can I be expected to keep
my footing in the mud or my head above the fog?
He wasn't a bit sympathetic. That's the worst
of these stone-hearted immortals; they're always
so superior."

In Christmas week they heard nothing; then,
after ten days of silence, came a parcel addressed
to Marguerite. It contained a necklet of rainbow-
tinted shells, caught together by tiny gold chains,
and a long letter, which began, without any form
of address: "Thousand and One Nights: The
Tale of the Tipsy Cabman and the Lame Foreigner."

A few days later René walked into his friend's
London lodgings. Felix, very wan and haggard,
was lying on the sofa. He jumped up with a cry
of amazement.

"René."

"Lie down," said René, coolly.   "Why on earth didn't you let me know before?"

Felix stared for a moment, then allowed himself to be helped back to the sofa.   He was still not quite fit to stand.

"Who told you I'd been ill?" he asked resentfully.

"Marguerite."

"But who told her?"

"I don't know, I haven't seen her for a week. I've been lecturing at Amiens, and she wrote, telling me you were ill, and begging me to come over at once and look after you.   Of course, I thought you must have written to her."

"I suppose it's that fool Bertillon again," said Felix.   "He's been attending a review here. What an ass it is! I particularly asked him to hold his tongue.   You d-don't mean to say you came over on purpose? Oh, it's absurd! I'm quite well again now, only a bit shaken."

They went back to Paris together, as soon as Felix was able to travel.   René insisted on escorting the tired convalescent to his lodgings and making him get to bed before going home himself.

"Was it Bertillon who told you?" he asked Marguerite in the evening.

"I haven't seen him.   Surely he's in England?"

"Then who told you? Felix was rather worried about it."

She unlocked a drawer in the table by her couch, and handed him a letter.

"Doesn't that tell one enough?"

"'Thousand and One Nights: The Tale . . .' Did Felix send this to you? It's not like his hand. Oh, I see; that's how you knew."

"There's more evidence than the writing; read it, and you'll see."

The shaky lines, scrawled unevenly up and down the page, were not very easy to decipher. The thing was a rambling account, evidently intended to be humorous, of an unsuccessful attempt to reach a Christmas party with the help of a drunken cabman who objected to foreigners, and a horse that refused to budge unless encouraged by "Rule Britannia." There were several very bad puns; here and there words were repeated or missed out. In the middle of describing a collision with a low-comedy dustman, the story broke off with: "That's all I can remember; but I solemnly declare it was the cabman that was drunk, not I."

"Yes, of course you're right," said René. "It's not like Felix to make such feeble jokes."

"And do you think it's like him to make any sort of joke about carriage accidents and drunken drivers, just to me, if he'd not been too ill to know what he was doing? Mind, René, you must never let him know how I found out: it would upset him. He must think somebody told me."

Felix came to see her the next day, and found her alone, decked for his benefit in the new necklet and last year's white silk shawl. He was in one of his most charming moods, quietly cheerful and brotherly; but her heart contracted at the sight of his face. She had never seen the lines of pain so deep about his mouth, or such a tragic shadow in his eyes. At first she scarcely dared to speak to him, let she should burst out crying; then she gathered up her courage, and, with trembling lips, began to talk of trifles. Neither he nor she referred to his illness or to the story of the tipsy cabman.

"And how goes English poetry?" he asked presently.

"Ever since you went away I've been completely buried in the Shakespeare sonnets. Why did you never tell me anything about them?"

"I wasn't quite sure you would like them."

"I'm not quite sure I do. In fact, at first I was quite sure I didn't; but then I began reading them over and over again. They puzzle me so; I don't know what to make of them."

"They're very difficult."

"Oh, it's not the language; I've had no difficulty with that. It's the inside of the man's head. There's always a feeling about them of

something looking over one's shoulder. I wish
you would read some of them aloud to me.
There's the book, on the table."

He took it up. "Which do you want? It's
so long since I read them, I have nearly forgotten
what they are about."

"Any after the first twenty. I know them
pretty well now; it's just to hear."

He fluttered the leaves for a moment, glancing
from sonnet to sonnet; then began at:

"Full many a glorious morning . . ."

"Please go on," she said when he stopped. He
went on for a little while, skipping one sonnet and
reading another; and the girl, watching him as he
read, saw that he had slipped away into a world
that was very far from her. The sound of his
voice on certain lines caught her breath. It
was as if she had heard a cry out of deep places
where lost things wander in the dark.

" But what's so blessed-fair that fears no blot ?
Thou may'st be false and yet I know it not."

His eyes darkened horribly at the words; but
he read straight on through the next sonnet and
the next again, dropping to the stern cadence with
a menacing throb. She lay still, crushing her
hands against one another under the shawl.

"Lilies that fester . . ."

Oh, what had happened to him? What awful thing had happened to make him look like that?

After a moment of silence he turned the page and began at random in another place:

> " *Alas, 'tis true I have gone here and there,*
> *And made myself a motley to the view . . .*"

His voice died out. It had not shaken at all; simply there was no sound left in it. He rose and crossed to the window, pulled the curtain aside and stood for an instant, looking into the street.

"I thought I heard someone calling," he said, coming back. "Let me see, where were we? Ah, yes, the 110th sonnet. I don't think it's an interesting one. Altogether, do you know, these sonnets don't seem to me v-v-very satisfactory reading; they're so . . . what is the word? Not exactly over-elaborate . . ."

"No," she answered under her breath. "Just naked."

He shot a swift glance at her.

"Airless, anyway. It's rather like being a cheese-mite in a sandwich-tin, and seeing the lid come down on you. Suppose we read something breezy."

She shook her head. "No, I'm rather tired for taking in any more to-day. Do you mind seeing whether René has come in yet? I know he wants to talk to you. Yes, you can leave the book here; thanks."

When he had gone into the other room she took up the volume again, and went over and over three or four of the sonnets. Tears gathered slowly and fell on to the book.

"Oh, if he wouldn't lie about it — if he only wouldn't lie about it . . ."

*   *   *   *   *   *

Felix remained so thin and fragile-looking during most of the year, that his friends were in a state of constant anxiety about him. In the summer he travelled a good deal; but, though he persisted in assuring them that he was holiday-making and enjoying himself, when he came to Marteurelles in October all the family united in begging him to take a quiet holiday, as Leroux had advised, in sea or mountain air.

"It's getting late for Switzerland," he said. "Also I should be bored to death, alone and with nothing to do. Look here, René, if you come with me I'll go to Antibes, or somewhere in the Estérel district. You need a holiday too, and you have another month before you need go back to Paris. We'll come round here on our way home and fetch your sister."

René had been hard at work all the summer, and gladly consented. They started at once, leaving Marguerite at the château. From Antibes either one or the other wrote to her almost daily, that she might share, as far as possible, in their enjoyment. René's letters were mostly descriptive; those of Felix were often a miscellaneous stream of gay and tender nonsense; it seemed to her that the ice-wall of his distrustful timidity was slowly melting. Already he had begun to credit her and René with some measure of genuine affection for him; perhaps, she told herself, before they should be old and grey, he would learn to realize how much they loved him.

"My dear Marguerite,

"You signed yourself 'Marguerite' to me the other day, so I venture to use the name without prefix. Indeed, I really have to remind myself sometimes that we are not brother and sister. There's some muddle, as usual, on the part of the authorities who conduct human relations. How can you be René's sister and not mine? It's just their ridiculous red tape.

"Autumn is growing shaky in its old age, and forgetting its identity; it has been mistaking itself for summer. Your side of the hills it is quite capable of mistaking itself for winter, so be sure you keep warm. Here the roses are still blooming in the gardens, and everything is a riotous blaze of sunshine and delight. I have done nothing since we came but dawdle and talk and eat and sleep; and am growing so fat and well in consequence that you will scarcely know me. As for René, he blossoms with the roses, and is a joy to see.

"To-day we are picnicking, like English tourists, at the high cross-roads to see the view. René's way of seeing it is to lie flat on his back with his head in a lavender-bush and a hat over his nose. When he wakes, he will say he has been listening to skylarks. I am sitting on a stone at the highest point of the cross-roads, and the only cloud on my happiness is the cloud of dust left by an old woman who has just gone by with a donkey-cart full of onions. (Yes, I know they ought to have been nectar and ambrosia, or grapes and peaches at the very least, to fit in with such a heavenly day; but I'm a veracious person, and they were just onions.) However, the dust is settling; and again I have all France behind me and all Italy before me, the Mediterranean on my right and the Alps on my left, and a hollow sapphire above my head; and all five so close and clear, so sweetly familiar in their gracious mood, that I could stretch out a hand and pick any one of them to send you. But even if the post-office didn't complain that they were unsuitable for transit (red tape again — this plague of bureaucrats!) — their humour would be sure to change on the way, and they would reach you gigantic, and threatening, and terrible. So I send instead this sprig of wild rosemary; that's for remembrance.

"All the same, I am annoyed with the old woman. She and her donkey came by just in the middle of the fairy story I was telling myself, and spoiled it all. Do you ever tell yourself fairy stories, or are you too grown-up? This was like a Benozzo Gozzoli fresco; the one with the hilly landscape and the little king riding along on his little horse, very neat and spruce, as a self-respecting king should be, with a beautiful spiky crown, all made of real gold-leaf. That's what I like about the old painters; they were never stingy with their gold-leaf. They didn't cheat one with yellow paint and lighting effects, like the clever modern folk; a king was a king to them, and if he needed gold for his crown, they just cut it to the right shape and stuck it on properly. But my kings were grander even than Benozzo Gozzoli's; they would have turned up their royal noses at crowns of mere gold-leaf, and their robes were starred with gems, and they were riding towards Italy.

"There, René is awake at last, and collecting rosemary sticks to make a fire; so I must help him, or the kings, and the onions, and the old woman in her donkey-cart will be halfway to Italy before the kettle boils."

Marguerite read and re-read this till she could

have repeated it by heart. Every word that came from Felix was precious; but this fanciful gay mood of his seemed to her so unattainable and so lovely, that the alien charm of it softened even the bitterness of his casual admission of having to remind himself that she was not his sister.

"I wish I could see crowned kings in jewelled clothes, if I happen to look at a dusty road," she said to him wistfully, when he came to Marteu-relles with René on the way home. "I should have seen nothing but the old woman and the onions."

"You needn't grumble," he answered lightly. "Onions and old women have their good points."

After they returned to Paris she read part of the fairy-tale letter to René. He rejoiced her by vehemently denying that he had been asleep.

"I did lie with my head in a lavender-bush, but it's true that I was listening to skylarks, so why shouldn't I say so? By the way, you haven't seen the water-colour sketch of that view."

"Yours?"

"Yes; I did a set of six for Felix. They're at his rooms, but I'll borrow them to show you before I go to Amiens."

"Is it this week you go?"

"Saturday. I shall be back in a few days; I've only two lectures to give there."

On Friday he came home late, with a portfolio.

"Felix was out," he told Marguerite in the morning, "but the sketches were put ready for me; I
had written that you wanted to see them. Oddly
enough he had forgotten the one taken from the
cross-roads; but I found it on his desk."

As she opened the portfolio she noticed pencilled
words on the back of a sheet.

"He has written something here," she said.
"Isn't this the view from the cross-roads? Perhaps that's why he put it aside; there may be
something private written on it."

"Oh, surely not," said René. "Isn't it verse?"

"I think so."

"Then I know what it is. He wants to have
these framed and hung over his bed, and some
verses carved to run beneath them. He has
probably totted them down. I don't know what
he finally chose; one notion was to have a passage from Lycidas. This is too rough to frame,
I think; but you can see what the view was like.
Those blue hills far off are in Italy. Well, this
won't do; it's time for me to start. Why, of
course I'll write every day. Do I ever miss?"

When he had gone she took up the sketch of
the cross-roads and tried to picture the glittering
procession of kings. Presently she remembered
the lines on the back, and turned to see what
quotation Felix had chosen.

THE CROSS-ROADS

In the dust I sat by the wayside,
In the dust of the cross-roads three;
A road runs down from the mountains
And a road runs up from the sea,
And a road runs on to Italy.

And the kings of the earth came riding
Up to the cross-roads three;
They were shod with steel and with splendour,
They were crowned with jewels of iron,
Iron and misery.

And the kings of the earth took counsel
There by the cross-roads three,
Where a road runs down from the mountains
And a road runs up from the sea,
And a road runs on to Italy.

With gold were they clad, and with foulness;
Their gem-starred robes were gay
With the gleam of carrion rotting,
And the pestilence that destroyeth
Clung about their way.

To the right and the left they turned them
As beasts that cower and flee,
For a wind blows down from the mountains
And a wind blows up from the sea;
But no wind blows out of Italy.

In the dust I sit by the wayside,
In the dust of the cross-roads three;
But the kings of the earth are riding,
Riding to Italy.

Felix came in unexpectedly in the afternoon.

"Did René bring you the water-colours?" he asked. "Ah, yes, there they are. Doesn't he handle his distance delightfully? If one could cure him of his excess of modesty he'd do better work than many exhibitors; everything he does is always unaffected and spontaneous."

"Yes," she answered under her breath, without looking up. He turned with tender solicitude.

"You are pale; does your head ache? Perhaps I'd better go away."

"No, stay, please; I'm quite well."

He began looking over the sketches.

"By the way," he said carelessly, "there's one that I put aside to frame, and I can't find it; I wonder if he took it. No, it doesn't seem to be here."

She unlocked the drawer in her table.

"It's here."

He started slightly as she handed it to him with the pencilled writing uppermost.

"Have you read it?"

"Yes, by accident. René thought it was some quotation you had chosen for the frame. He hasn't read it. I had nearly finished before I realized that it's private. I'm very sorry."

She spoke in a low, unsteady voice, still keeping her lashes down. He recovered his self-possession at once.

"Oh, you needn't mind about that; it's of no consequence. I shouldn't have willingly shown anybody that sort of r-r-rubbish, of course, but once it has happened . . . It's just the other aspect of our little Benozzo Gozzoli fresco. Did it ever oc-c-cur to you that most fairy tales have two faces? The whole art of living is to look at the pretty one and not b-b-bother over . . . But, Marguerite! Why . . ."

She burst into convulsive weeping.

"Ah, you are cruel, you are cruel! I've no right to ask for the truth, but don't tell me fairy tales!"

He stared at her in dismay. She was sobbing uncontrollably.

"Benozzo Gozzoli! And I shut my eyes and tried to see them . . . and joked to you about it . . . and this was underneath all the while! Ah, how could you do it!"

He sat down beside her and stroked her head with a caressing touch.

"Child, you wouldn't have me inflict my ugly fancies on you? We should keep those for ourselves; it's the pleasant kind that belongs to our friends. Don't cry, dear; it makes me unhappy to have grieved you. I wouldn't have sent you the silly letter if I'd known. After all, what is there to be so upset about? Just that you've found out I write bad verses? At least I have the grace not to publish them."

She threw back her head.

"What have I done that you should treat me this way? When have I ever pried into your secrets, or forced love on you, or . . . Why must you go out of your way to lie to me, and humour me, and make up fairy tales, as if I were a child that has hurt itself and wants to be comforted? Do you manage René like that? Oh, it's hopeless! I can't make you believe — you'll never believe I care."

She controlled herself with a passionate effort.

"It's foolish of me to be angry; you can't help it. It's a disease in you!"

"What is, dear?" he asked humbly. "S-s-scribbling dismal v-verses? It's just a bad habit, and I only do it on holidays. Why should you mind so much?"

She turned and looked at him.

"No; suspecting people, and fooling them, and never believing that they really love you. Will you go on all your life wearing fancy dress? Will you never trust anyone again because one man has betrayed you?"

2 B

He rose hastily and stooped over the sketches, pulling them about with restless fingers. His back was towards her.

"D-d-do you know," he said presently, in a light, artificial tone, "this convers-s-sation seems to me v-v-very like the English game of cross questions and c-c-crooked answers. I'm sorry to be so dense, but I haven't the f-faintest notion what you mean."

"No, I thought you hadn't," she answered bitterly. "You wouldn't treat me as if I were six years old if you did."

Then she flung out a hand and caught his.

"Oh, that's nothing! What does it matter how you treat me; it's how you treat yourself that matters. Dearest, I know . . ."

Her voice broke again in a sob. He had not moved and his face was still turned away from her. She laid her cheek against the hand she held.

"I know you trusted a man . . . and he deceived you. I know it ruined all your youth . . . and all your belief in God . . . Oh, my dear, my dear . . ."

She started back with a scream. He was laughing.

"Don't!" she cried. "Don't! Ah, I'd rather you'd kill me than that!"

He went on laughing, very softly. She had fallen face downwards on the cushions: when she took her fingers out of her ears he was still laughing.

The sound left off at last, and there was silence. Then came a stealthy movement, a rustle of torn paper; and then the door was gently shut.

She lay as she had fallen. The noise of the outer door closing struck a blaze of white fire before her eyes. She raised her head and looked round.

She was alone, and the sketch with the verses lay beside her torn across.

* * * * * *

René came back from Amiens to find a change in Marguerite which he could not understand. She assured him that she was perfectly well; but her expression belied her. Also, she had not written a line to him during his absence. This had never happened before; and he came to the conclusion that she must have been ill or have had a bad fright while he was away, and must be concealing it from him out of mistaken considerateness. If anything were wrong, Felix would be sure to know; he had better go round to him in the evening and find out.

The windows were brightly lighted, and three men in evening dress went up the stairs before him. The landlady eyed his travelling suit in surprise.

"M. Rivarez is giving a reception."

"Oh, I didn't know," said René, rather puzzled. "I won't come in, then; just ask him to come out here for a minute, please. I want to speak to him."

Felix came out smiling, with eyes alight. For the first time it flashed across René's mind that Guillaumet had been right in saying he bore some resemblance to the panthers of the Amazonian forests.

"Why, this is a del-l-lightful surprise. I thought you were in Amiens."

"I got back to-day. I just wanted to see you for a minute, about . . ."

"But come in."

"No, you have guests."

"Wh-what does that matter? You shall be a guest too."

"Oh, I can't; I'm not dressed."

"Nonsense! You're always perfectly dressed, the most comp-p-letely dressed person I know. Come in, please; there's a man here I want to introduce to you."

René followed him into the crowded room.

"Such a f-fortunate thing, baron; my friend M. Martel has turned up unexp-pectedly. My little good-bye party would have been incomplete without him. M. Martel, Baron Rosenberg."

A sleek, oily thing, smelling of scent and be-dizened with orders and jewellery, hoisted itself

up from the sofa with an ingratiating smile. The
touch of its fingers made René long to run away
and wash.

"The M. Martel who took part in the South
American expedition?"

"Yes," said Felix. "M. Martel and I are old
comrades. We have been through all s-s-sorts of
adventures together, and grown q-q-quite confidential."

"Delighted to meet you," said the baron. "I
have a peculiar sympathy with explorers; a life
of intrepid adventure has always been my own
unrealized ambition."

René murmured something inaudible; and,
turning in dazed wonder to ask humbly what all
this could mean, saw that Felix was watching him
with half-shut eyes. It seemed to him that they
were lit from behind with a green flame.

"You will miss M. Rivarez, won't you?" said
the baron. "I tell him we shall keep him in
Vienna when we get him there."

"Vienna?"

He repeated the word mechanically. Points of
light were dancing before him.

"M. Martel has j-just returned from Amiens,"
said Felix, smoothly. "He hasn't been told the
news yet. I'm leaving Paris, and going to V-v-v-
vienna for this winter. Afterwards I don't know
where I shall settle. I start to-morrow evening.

Pardon me, baron; I see some more guests have arrived."

René stood looking after him as he moved away. The rancid stream of the baron's voice trickled on.

"What a charming personality. So original, too; who else would decide a step like that, and make all arrangements and give a farewell reception, all within a week?"

"Martel, I want you a minute."

He wheeled round. "Marchand! Marchand . . . what has . . ."

"Wait. Come over here."

He felt himself being guided across the room.

"Sit down. Don't try to speak; just drink this."

He swallowed the brandy and sat up.

"I went a little giddy; I hope no one noticed?"

"No, I stood in front of you. Martel, do you know the meaning of all this?"

"I know nothing; I've only just heard."

"We can't talk now. Wait till all these fools are gone. Be careful, he's looking at us."

Left alone, René turned his back on the crowd and looked out of the window.

"Don't you remember me, M. Martel."

It was a talkative, excitable little Neapolitan named Galli, whom he had met at a dinner-party.

"Aren't you very sorry to lose M. Rivarez? Paris won't seem the same place without him, will it?"

"I suppose it won't," René murmured.

The little man rattled on with a cheerful gleam of white teeth: "He seems very popular here. I scarcely know him; we met in Florence two years ago, after the Savigno affair. Isn't your sister disappointed at his going?"

"My sister?"

"He told me just now that you and she are his best friends. Does she live in Paris?"

"Yes," René answered, holding on to the window-sill behind him. He felt as if he were being pricked to death with small needles.

If only all these people would go! Whatever frightful thing had happened, it would be endurable when he knew; anything would be endurable but this.

He got rid of Galli somehow; but the baron fastened on to him again, persistent as a horse-leech.

"M. Rivarez has just told me of your marvellous escape from a jaguar. I never heard a more thrilling story. Extraordinary, wasn't it, his coming up just in time! How very witty he is! Sometimes one can scarcely make out whether he is joking or not. He assured me that a jaguar isn't half so terrifying at close quarters as a cockroach; and, really, you would have thought he meant it. Another absurdity that he said in a perfectly serious way was that he had been intending to shoot you, and was quite disconcerted at having to save your life instead. Some little rivalry, eh? I wonder whether there was a lady in the case? *Cherchez la* . . . Sir, this is an insult — I am speaking to you!"

But René was gone. He was running down the stairs, and the landlady was calling after him: "M. Martel! M. Martel, you've forgotten your hat!"

*   *   *   *   *   *

Felix stood by the door, a smiling automaton, taking leave of his guests, and answering again and again in the same words to the same phrases of conventional regret and goodwill. He was very pale now, and the brilliant eyes were dim as with fatigue.

Marchand was the last to go. He had waited till the end, hoping for an opportunity to consult René before speaking to Felix. When the crowd thinned he had noticed, with a shock of amazement, that René was no longer there.

Everyone was gone, now. Felix was still standing by the door, evidently expecting him to say good-bye. He came up with the lop-sided, slouching gait that seemed to shove obstacles out of the way, and put both hands on his shoulders.

"Now, my son, what's the meaning of this?"

Felix smiled into his eyes.

"Ask Martel."

"I have asked him, and he knows no more than I do."

"No?" said Felix, with lifted brows. "How quaint!"

"Do you want any help?" was Marchand's next question.

"Not a bit, thanks. I must learn to manage for myself s-s-s-sometime, mustn't I? One can't always depend on one's friends."

Marchand's hands fell slowly from his shoulders. There was a moment's silence.

"So you're going to throw your friends over, are you?"

"My dear doctor!" Felix spread out his arms in protest towards the table laden with coffee-cups. "Haven't I j-j-just been entertaining seventy of them?"

Again they were silent. Marchand walked into the passage and took up his hat. He was trembling a little when Felix helped him on with his overcoat.

"Well, I suppose this is the end," he said. "God knows I don't blame you. Good-bye."

He went downstairs. "I did that," he thought; and as he went the wings of the Discoverer of Secrets brushed against his cheek.

Not till the street-door had shut did it occur to Felix that Marchand supposed he was going to commit suicide. Well, it wasn't such a bad guess.

As far as personal life was concerned, that was about what he had done; and the only thing that he had to go on living for was not Marchand's affair. Anyhow, he had got through the evening, and by to-morrow night he would be out of Paris.

Still smiling, he called up the landlady and helped her to pile the crockery on trays and put the room in order. When she had finished carrying away the litter and arranging the furniture, she paused at the door to offer help with his packing.

"No, thank you," he answered. "It's too late for packing to-night; we'll do it in the morning. You must be tired out."

"It is late, sir, that's true; but I'd work all night for you. I'm sorry to lose you; a more considerate lodger . . ."

Her apron went up to her eyes. Felix yawned.

"I'm really very sleepy, Mme. Rambaud. I'm sure it's bedtime for both of us. Good-night."

He locked the door and leaned against it, laughing weakly. First René, then Marchand, and now Mme. Rambaud! Her grief, at any rate, was doubtless sincere; he had paid her regularly.

Well, well, he must get to work. The packing could wait, but not the clearing out of plague-spots.

He went round the rooms, collecting everything that spoke of René or Marguerite. Water-

colours, needlework, framed drawings: whatever
they had made or chosen or ornamented for him
was broken or torn with a quiet and concentrated
fury, and the wreckage piled on the floor in a heap.
Then came letters out of the desk; the rare ones,
mostly from Lyons, in which René had haltingly
tried to express what he was too shy to say aloud,
and the timid little note signed "Marguerite."
Here was one from Marchand, written two years
ago, purely professional; elaborate directions,
from the brain-specialist's point of view, for the
avoidance of unnecessary suffering. He had felt
at the time that he did not quite understand it,
and had put it aside for further consideration.
Now he read it through again.

". . . Since you have made up your mind to
go on, it is well for you to understand just what
mental dangers threaten a man in your case. I
do not anticipate for you anything of the nature
of an ordinary nervous breakdown, nor do I think
you in the least likely — though even the bravest
of us is never quite safe — to fail in courage and
take refuge in drugs. But physical pain is an
insidious enemy, and we cannot come to the end
of the traps that it can lay for our imaginations.
Above all, avoid falling in love with your own inevitable isolation; and do not use the conquered
torments of your body as stones to build a walled
castle for your mind."

For a while he hesitated, seeing quite clearly that here was a very solemn warning from a very wise man. Then he remembered the Discoverer of Secrets. Ah, there is safety in walled castles; no moths can enter them. He tore the sheet across and threw it on to the heap. Better be done with everything at once. If René could betray . . .

Another paroxysm of icy rage swept over him. He would never have wanted to insult even a traitor; he would have gone quietly, without a word, without a look of reproach, as he had gone from Marguerite last week; just slipped out of their lives and passed on his way. But René had come here — ah, that was impudent — had come here to poison his sight with the false face that he had thought so honest. Perhaps he had come to brazen it out, to demand an explanation. "Why have you cut her? She tells me you . . ."

He laughed again at the fancied words. Oh, yes, she would have told enough. Doubtless he had been well discussed between them. After you have repeated to a girl what your friend said when he was delirious, and she has listened — perhaps pumped you out of curiosity — there seems little scope left for reticence.

Well, if René wanted an explanation, Baron Rosenberg had furnished him with an adequate one. He had chosen to admit a third person into the private sanctuary of his friend's confidence; why not the whole street?

He made up the fire, and, sitting down beside the stove, fed it from the heap. It took a long time to burn everything. As René's signature shrivelled and disappeared, he flung an arm across his mouth to choke back a cry. Oh, it was he that was burning.

Yes, he had scorched his finger, trying to pull the letter out of the stove; and it had fallen back; and was gone in flame. Everything was gone in flame. There were a lot of ashes left, and he was left. He would be alone now, till he died.

Well, ashes are better than treachery. And it was not the first time that he had made a clearance of infected loves. Far back in a dim vista of the past he could see himself, a laughing boy with a hammer, smashing a crucifix. He had thought this purifying process would not have needed to be done twice in one lifetime; but, apparently, one gathers things round one as warm garments against the cold. Then they fester, and eat into the flesh, and have to be burned out. Luckily it takes a long while for that to happen, and his life would be short.

Anyway, he was making a quite unreasonable fuss over a minor matter; he had been hurt before, and worse than this. Still, though René had never held the supreme place, he had managed cleverly enough. Among the ways of betraying, his was worthy of admiration; it was so beautifully simple. You take advantage of your man's physical suffering; nurse him as a devoted friend, listen to what he says in delirium, gain possession of the most private of his sorrows; and gossip.

Curious, in what a variety of ways one can be betrayed. It is so unnecessary, too; a man can manage to wreck himself completely enough, even without betrayals. There had been no taint of treachery, for instance, in the ruthlessness of Signor Giuseppe; it had been a mere sacrifice of a stranger to urgent political necessity. The soul of Italy was kept alive by these successive revolts. Even though each one ended only in reprisals, the blood that drowned it washed away the poison of stagnation. When the Savigno attempt failed, the great man had calmly denied all connection with it. Why not? That also was political necessity, and thereby justified.

Yes, Signor Giuseppe might sleep in peace; he had been honest, and no avenging ghost need haunt his conscience. He had given fair warning at the outset: "It's nothing to me what your personal history is." He had neither asked nor offered love; work had to be done, and the cost to the doer was no concern of his. It was done, and he had gone his way; like the Gurupirá, but

not like Judas. The betrayal of love is reserved
for the beloved.

Sitting by the open stove, staring into the faint
glow of the dying embers, Felix reviewed in memory the long line of persons who had successfully
deceived him. He must have been born singularly credulous, for they made quite an imposing
procession. There was the mother who had
nursed him and lied to him, the adored angel
mother who had died in his arms with a kiss and
a lie on her lips; the priest who had betrayed his
secret, told in the confessional; the young men
who had called him comrade, and had been so
quick to believe him guilty of vileness at the first
slanderous word; the girl who had been the chosen
companion of his youth, till he turned to her for
help in mortal agony, and then had struck him on
the cheek. And there had been the friend: saint,
and father, and liar. . . .

He jumped up and stretched his arms. If ever
a man was making an ass of himself, he was;
sitting here getting "pins and needles" and catching cold, with the night half gone and a long journey before him. All those memories belonged to
the life before last; they were as grey and flimsy
as the ashes. What he had to do now was to get
to bed.

He went into the other room, and began to un-
dress. Something came over his shoulder; some-

thing fetid, flashing white eye-balls, glistening with white teeth.

"Have all your fine friends betrayed you? Try trusting me, for a change."

It was the negro fruit-seller. He sprang back screaming, striking with both hands at the foul black face. It squashed, and deliquesced on the floor, a putrid lump.

He stood gasping and sweating, shaken with long shivers. Oh, it was cold, it was cold; he must get back to the fire, or he should die of cold. He stepped cautiously over the rug, avoiding the spot where he had seen the thing fall. But it had rotted quite away; no trace was left of it now. In the sitting-room he knelt by the stove, arranging logs and fanning the reluctant fire. As he stooped to blow up the embers, a musky smell of stale scent blew back at him.

Ah, the women, the painted women — the shameless mulatto girls! They came about him, clinging, fondling; their arms round his neck, their reeking hair against his lips.

"Why will you hate us so? We never betrayed you. We laughed when you fainted in the circus; what does laughing matter? Come, kiss and be friends."

It was no use to wrench their arms away, they came back and always back. The mincing voices coaxed and wheedled, tittered and squealed.

"Trust me, I won't betray you." "No, don't trust her, trust me."

Now the voices rose together in a shriek of derisive laughter, cackling negro laughter, yelling laughter — oh, if they laughed like that he would go mad, he would go mad. . . .

"Jaime! Jaime, keep the women off me — only the women!"

He lay prone on the floor, clasping the feet of the drunken half-caste whose slave he had been.

"Jaime, I'll never run away again! I'll clown for you till I die — only keep the women off . . ."

"So you've found out there's worse than old Jaime? I may have kicked you about a bit, but I never listened to your secrets when you were light-headed; it was nothing to me what you said."

"Help!" he moaned, and struggled up again. "Oh, help!"

"Carino, come to me for help."

Ah, not that voice, not that! Better the black men, the painted women; he had never loved them.

"You lied to me — you lied to me! Rather the window — rather the pavement than your love."

The cold night air blew in; the lifted curtain whirled and swayed, and fell about him like a shroud. From the outer blackness the Crucified stretched mocking hands.

2 c

"Come to Me. The spectres are upon you; spring, and have no fear. If you fall, you fall into My arms."

"Lies, lies!" he cried. "All lies!"

He flung the window to in the vision's face; and all the world crashed down and vanished in a roar.

*   *   *   *   *   *

He woke on the floor beside the window. The torn curtain was tangled round him, and there was a bruise on his cheek where he had struck it in falling. Holding by the sill, he dragged himself up, and looked out.

The dawn . . . the dawn . . . It had come, and there was respite. Just for a few short hours there was respite even in hell.

FROM THE UNPUBLISHED VERSES OF
FELIX RIVAREZ

I

BEHOLD, my God, I am a little thing,
My life is little, compassed round by death;
I am too weak to fight Thee, or to fling
Back in Thy Face Thy mocking curse of breath.
My God, my God, I am a little thing,
Broken and wingless, naked and alone;
But hadst Thou been the slave and I the King,
Would I have done to Thee what Thou hast done?
Behold, my God, I am a little thing.

II

Out of a land of drifting, wounded things
I come, to beat against a human breast,
That human love may heal my broken wings
And human understanding give me rest.

Ah, they are dear and warm, the souls of men;
And yet they hunt me back to my cold land.
I call to them, and wait, and call again . . .
They listen, but they cannot understand.

EPILOGUE

RENÉ was spending a summer holiday at Marteurelles. Marguerite had been there since the
last summer, learning Egyptology and acting as
secretary to her father. She seemed to have
grown tired of Paris, and René was thinking of
giving up the flat and going into lodgings. It was
a useless expense to keep the place on if she was
not coming back.

"Will you come to church with me?" asked his
aunt, opening the door of the room where he was
sitting with Henri and Blanche. "It's a lovely
morning for a walk."

He rose at once. It was a matter of indifference to him, now, with whom he went to church.

They walked down the avenue, he pulling lime-
blossoms to smell, and Angélique holding her
prayerbook stiffly in both hands. Her face wore
an expression of important gravity.

"I want to have a little talk with you," she
began presently. "Don't you think it's time you
settled down? You're getting on, and if you're
ever going to marry you ought to do it soon."

"I'm thirty-five. But I don't see why that makes it necessary for me to marry. I'm quite contented as I am."

"Yes, dear, you have a cheerful disposition. But it's very lonely for you in Paris now Marguerite isn't there. It makes my heart ache to think of you always alone."

"I'm not always alone, aunt; I know plenty of very nice people. Besides, there isn't anybody I want to marry."

"Dear, couldn't you think of Jeanne Duplessis? She's a good pious girl, and very sweet-tempered; I've known her since she was in pinafores. And she'll have an excellent dowry, though I know you're too unworldly to think of that. You're right, a Christian spirit is more important than riches; all the same, it's a very nice property; so near, too. She isn't a beauty, of course, but she's good-looking enough; and it would be such a happiness to us all to have you settled."

She stopped, out of breath.

"But you see, aunt," said René, smiling; "however nice Mlle. Duplessis and her property may be, I don't happen to want them. Come, you've got one married man in the family; why shouldn't I be a bachelor, for variety?"

The old maid's chin began to quiver.

"Henri and Blanche are childless. I did want a baby to love. Marguerite's grown-up, and cold;

sometimes, lately, she seems to me older than I am."

René had left off smiling. "I'm sorry, aunt," he said, and drew her arm through his. The gentle voice gave her courage.

"René, what is it that has come to her? It's not the accident; she got over that. Last year, when she came home, I knew something had happened; she has just withered. What ails her?"

He was silent.

"It's that man's doing!" she cried out. "There are never any letters or presents from him now. I always knew it would end so; what else could you expect from an atheist? He has trifled with her — with a cripple — and forsaken . . ."

"Be quiet!" René interrupted sternly. He released her arm and stood still, looking her in the face with eyes that were unknown to her.

"If you say a word against Felix to me, I'll never speak to you again. Understand that. Now let us come on, or we shall be late for church."

She walked beside him, scared into silence.

When they returned, René was met by a message that he was wanted in the study. He went up at once, and found his father waiting for him with pale cheeks and anxious eyes.

"René, there's bad news."

The marquis paused for an instant, putting up a hand to his lips, to stop their trembling.

"Colonel Duprez has sent me a cutting from an English newspaper . . . for you. He didn't know where to find you. . . . It's . . . Oh, I can't tell you, boy; you'd better read it."

René took the cutting from his hand and read it through. He remained quite motionless for a long time. At last he rose and walked to the door.

"René," his father gasped; and he stood still without looking round.

"Yes?"

"What about Marguerite?"

"I'll tell her myself," he said; and added: "Presently."

Half an hour later there was a tap at the locked door of his room.

"René, can I speak to you?"

It was his father's voice, hurried and low. He opened the door at once.

"Did you take the newspaper cutting?"

"No, I left it on your table."

"Then Blanche has taken it. I left the room for a few minutes, and when I came back it was gone. René, I'm frightened. She's a prying woman that loves to tell news. She has just gone into Marguerite's room."

René dashed past him and down the stairs. He opened his sister's door softly, without knocking. Blanche was standing by the couch, and the newspaper cutting was in Marguerite's hand.

"Atrocities in a Papal fortress. Horrible treatment of a political prisoner.

"In the House of Commons, yesterday, Mr. P. A. Taylor asked the Under Secretary for Foreign Affairs whether it is true that . . ."

René snatched the paper out of her hand.

"No, no! Don't read it!"

"Give it back to me!" she cried hoarsely. He turned to Blanche, and his eyes were black with anger.

"Go out of the room. At once, please; Marguerite and I want to be alone."

He locked the door behind her and came back.

"Pâquerette . . ."

"Give it to me!" she shrieked again.

"Pâquerette, he's dead."

The appalling voice cried out a third time: "Give it to me!" He dropped on his knees beside her.

"Don't read it! Why must you know the details? It's all over; they don't matter any more."

"Not a bit," she answered, after a pause; "so there's no need for you to hide them from me. It isn't worth while to make a mystery of their precise nature, is it?"

Her tone was ice. For a moment he was back in the Pastassa valley, hearing another voice that asked: "What did it matter which particular thing they might do?"

He gave her the paper. Then he went and stood by the table, staring at a bowl of roses without seeing them. The silence seemed a wingless monster, dragging interminable coils along the floor.

"René," she said at last.

He came back, and, kneeling down, took her in his arms and laid his cheek against hers. Horror seized him by the throat as he felt her edge herself gently out of his embrace.

"Pâquerette!" he whispered, catching her wrists with unsteady hands. "Pâquerette, what has come between us? It's as if I'd lost you as well as him. I can't understand. . . . We're living in a nightmare, or going mad. . . . I lost him before he died, and I've never known why. Am I to lose you, too, before you die?"

She looked at him, and he shrank away.

"No, I am dead. I died two years ago next November. I'm sorry for you, René, but we're both dead. He's a corpse and I'm an Egyptologist. It's much the same. Nothing that's less than three thousand years old interests me at all."

He rose, and stood looking down at her.

"Could you explain to me, dear? It's a bit hard to love only two persons in the world, and

have them both . . . die, like this, and not to
know why. Is it . . ." His breath stopped.
"Was it anything that Felix did?"

It was some consolation to hear a human note
in her voice again, even though it was only a
note of bitterness.

"It was no fault of his. He was right to break
off."

"Did you think I was blaming him? Whatever
he did is right, to me, because he did it. I've
never known why he cut me; I never shall know,
now; but it makes no difference."

"I know why he cut me," she said under her
breath.

Her face was gray when she looked up.

"I disgusted him with love that he didn't want.
Is that explanation enough? Why he cut you
I don't know, unless he thought it was best to
break off with the whole family at once. Now I
would rather be alone."

He went out in silence. Angélique met him on
the stairs.

"My dear, what has happened? Blanche is
crying and scolding in the salon, telling Henri you
insulted her. Ah, René, René, don't look at me
like that — it breaks my heart! Oh, indeed, I do
beg your pardon if I forgot myself this morning.
I know how fond of your friend you are, and I
wouldn't hurt your feelings for the world. But

I've been so upset lately. Blanche isn't much of
a niece to me, or much of a daughter to your dear
father, for that matter ; and I'm half afraid to
speak to Marguerite, nowadays. If only you
could have liked Jeanne!"

He turned, with a little laugh.

"Don't cry, aunt; I like Jeanne well enough.
Oh, you can arrange it if you want to; one must
marry somebody, I suppose."

*   *   *   *   *   *

Jeanne made a good wife, according to her
lights, and bore her husband fine children; so
Angélique, at least, was happy; and, so far as anyone could tell, he, too, seemed content.

Marguerite also settled down and appeared quite
satisfied with her Egyptology. As Blanche said,
if a woman is a hopeless cripple, it is a merciful
dispensation of Providence to make her a dried-up
blue stocking as well. Egyptology is one of the
few things at which a bedridden person can work
without inconvenience. By the time the marquis
died, his daughter was fully competent to edit his
manuscripts, which kept her occupied for the rest
of her rather short life. At forty it was ended by
the after-effects of a chill; and Jeanne, Henri,
Angélique, and Rosine mourned sincerely for her
loss.

To René their grief seemed only one more

puzzle in a totally incomprehensible world. His mourning was over long ago. It had ended with a certain conversation, a few years before her death.

He had come to Marteurelles for his annual visit, and in the morning found a decent-looking peasant woman sobbing inconsolably in the lime-avenue. A few kindly questions brought out a pitiful story. Her young daughter, a housemaid at the château, whom he remembered as a quiet and modest girl, had "got into trouble," and the lover had deserted her. Terrified at the wrath of her strict and pious father, and at the inquisitorial cross-examinations of Blanche, she had flung herself, with her unborn child, into the stew-pond. The curé refused her Christian burial, and the mother had come to beg that the chaplain whom Blanche had engaged when she inherited money might say a few prayers over the coffin in the private chapel of the château. But Blanche refused to permit such laxity; now that she was lady of the manor she held herself responsible for the morality of the villagers.

"And my brother?" René asked.

"He says these things are women's matters, and he can't interfere."

"Why don't you go to Mlle. Marguerite, then?"

The woman began to sob more bitterly.

"I did; and she won't help me."

"I think there must be some mistake," said René. "I'll speak to my sister."

He found her in the garden, correcting proof-sheets.

"Lisette's mother has been talking to me," he said. "Can't we persuade Blanche to let the poor thing have the chapel?"

"My dear René," Marguerite answered in her level voice, "you can scarcely expect me to have any opinion one way or the other. I'm not devout, as you know. It's for you religious people to decide what are the right uses for a chapel."

"That isn't my point. It's Blanche being so hard."

"Oh, as to that, Lisette has made her bed, and must lie on it."

"Marguerite!" he cried out. At this moment the old pet name would not come to his lips. "Marguerite! But she's dead!"

"Well, what of it? You are still a bit of a sentimentalist. People aren't let off from the consequences of their actions, just because they happen to be dead."

She looked up at him for the first time. The line of her mouth was hard and thin.

"I'm dead, too; I told you that once before. It hasn't helped me. Why should it help Lisette? There's an iron law for women, a law of modesty;

and if they break it they must pay the penalty. But it's all one to me; if you want the chapel for Lisette, you'd better talk to Henri."

"I see," he said, after a long pause. "Well, I'll take the dogs for a run."

She returned to her proof-reading, and he walked away, calling to the dogs.

"God! How hard women are!" he said to himself as he went. "And that's my little Pâquerette. . . . Ah, well, well, my children are boys."

*   *   *   *   *

René lived to be old and successful. As a professor he was respected by his colleagues and popular with his students, and in private life was an admirable husband and a model father; but neither in the university nor at home was he intimate with anyone. Even his children never knew much about him.

His only attempt at confidential speech was a failure. Perhaps he had been silent too long. The occasion was the departure of his soldier son Maurice for the front, in the spring of 1870. When the family farewells, and tears, and blessings were over, and the orderly had started with the luggage, father and son went into Avallon on foot. They had taken many country walks together, and this might be the last.

René remained silent still the hazel-copse shut

out all possibility of looking back any more at the big rambling house that had been part of Jeanne's dowry. Then he turned to his boy with a smile. "Well, there's one thing; if you should fail to distinguish yourself, it won't be for want of enough good advice at parting."

Maurice laughed, rather shakily. The dear old papa! One could always trust him not to be emotional at the wrong moment.

"Indeed it won't. I wouldn't mind if it were only mamma and grandpapa Duplessis; but when it comes to all the relatives, one gets too much of it. When I went to Marteurelles to say good-bye, Uncle Henri and Aunt Blanche went about twenty times through every temptation that can assail a young man at the front; and then I had to go up to poor old great-aunt's room and hear it all over once more."

"Yes," said René; "Aunt Angélique was always good at improving the occasion."

He frowned at the hedge for a little while before he spoke again.

"I'm not, as you know. All the same, there's one thing I should like to say, if it won't seem to you an intrusion."

"Papa! How could it?" cried Maurice. "There's nothing in the world you mightn't say to me. But can't I guess what it is? 'Don't back other men's bills'? Papa, indeed that was a lesson to me last year — all the more because you were such a dear, and just paid up and never said a word about it."

He was growing rather red and inaudible; and he slipped a hand through his father's arm as they walked. "You seem to have a gift for not saying anything," he went on. "General Bertillon told me the other day he had made an ass of himself once, when he was my age, and was ready to blow his brains out; and you just set him a job to do in a hurry, and never reminded him of the thing again. He said he'd been grateful to you all his life, and he'd do his best for your son. And . . . and, papa . . . I'll do my best, too. . . ."

René patted the hand. "That's all right; you'll find your own level. But I wasn't thinking of that. . . ."

He looked at the hedge again; it was not easy to speak.

"It's just this: War brings a man into contact with all sorts of folk. If you should ever come across anyone who seems to you . . . different from yourself and all the rest of us — one of the rare spirits that go through the world like stars, radiating light — try to remember that it's a great privilege to know such persons, but a dangerous thing to love them too much."

"I don't think I quite understand," said Maurice. He was a good-tempered, healthy boy, likely to make an excellent officer, and not at all likely to wreck his happiness by caring too passionately for anything.

René passed a hand through his grizzled hair, sighing. "No, it's difficult to explain. You see, the little personal joys, and sorrows, and affections, that are everything to us ordinary mortals, are not big enough to fill the lives of such folk; and if we set our hearts on their friendship, and think we possess it, the chances are that we're only boring them all the time. . . ."

He pulled himself up quickly, lest he might be guilty of even one instant's disloyalty to the tragic shadow whose eyes still haunted him.

"Don't think I mean they would wilfully deceive us. It's small people who do that; the really big people always want to be kind. But that's just it; they put up with us, out of compassion, or because they're grateful for any service we may have been lucky enough to do them. Then, when we wear their patience right out, and it breaks down suddenly — that's bound to happen at last, because, after all, they're only human — then it's a bit late for us to start life again."

"But . . ." said Maurice.